THE
CODE BREAKERS
SERIES

JACKI DELECKI

AWARD-WINNING AUTHOR

ISBN 978-0-9899391-4-0
Published by Doe Bay Publishing, Seattle, Washington.

Cover Design and Interior format by The Killion Group
http://thekilliongroupinc.com

To the two people who never stopped believing in this book. My love and deep gratitude to my husband, and to my dear friend, Cynthia Garlough.

ENGLISH CHARACTERS

Cordelier Richard Beaumont, Earl of Rathbourne

Lady Gwyneth Beaumont

Lady Euphemia Beaumont

Lady Henrietta Ormond Harcourt

Michael Ormond Harcourt, Earl of Kendal

Edward Ormond Harcourt

Lord Charles Sayers Harcourt

Lord Cedric Ramston

Lord Marcus Blenseim, Duke of Wycliffe

Viscount Henry James Ashworth

Lord Charles Brinsley

FRENCH CHARACTERS

Comte Lucien De Valmont

Gaston Le Chiffre, Code Master

Mademoiselle Isabelle de Villiers

Charles Maurice Talleyrand

Joseph Fouché

Giscard Orly

PROLOGUE

1802, Paris

Lord Michael Ormond Harcourt crept along the darkened passageway. He had earned his reputation as a brilliant code breaker, but never before had he ventured into the realm of housebreaker. Henrietta was going to be furious not to be part of tonight's exciting intrigue.

He strained to listen for the sounds of the house in the wee hours of the morning. He heard nothing but his heartbeat pounding in his ears. Reassured he was the only one about, he allowed himself to release the breath he had been holding since he sneaked into Gaston Le Chiffre's house. He moved down the narrow corridor to his French colleague's office.

He had only been in Paris a fortnight when he developed suspicions about Gaston—a series of sensations, hushed silences when he walked into a room, the papers on his desk seeming to have been moved, and the persistent feeling he was being followed.

The final impetus to search Gaston's office came yesterday with the arrival of an anonymous note: "Something's afoot."

He gingerly opened the office door, inspecting the darkened corners before he entered. The dying fire cast shadows on the book-lined walls. A log shifted. The small crash startled him, causing his heart to thump against his chest.

He closed the door and moved to the center of the room, lit a taper, and placed it in the holder on the desk, then shuffled through the neat stacks of papers. He opened drawers, searching the contents.

He ran his hand across the smooth mahogany surface of the desk then passed his fingers along the rough underside. There he found a slightly recessed area in the far corner. His fingers returned to the uneven surface. Applying pressure, there was a sudden give, followed by a compartment popping open on the top of the desk.

The secret compartment contained a leather book. He scanned the room before he removed the worn volume. He had never seen a code quite like this one: French scrawl preceded by endless rows of numbers. This French puzzle was better than a wrapped Christmas present. He stuffed the incredible find into his waistband. He would crack the code in the safety of his room, then return the book to its hiding place, all before Gaston awoke.

He blew out the taper and left the office. He backtracked through Gaston's garden. Carefully closing the garden gate, he entered the alley. The mixture of fog and smoke from the city's coal fires blanketed the city. He could see no more than a few feet ahead. The cloying darkness muffled the distant voices, the clatter of carriage wheels, and horses' hooves.

Approaching the street, he slowed his pace. Hanging lanterns illuminated the walkway where he emerged from the unlit alley.

He turned and walked toward his house. In the thick fog, the sound of his footsteps resonated, booming with each step.

The hairs on his neck prickled when he heard another set of footsteps shuffling behind him. With only a few yards to reach home, he ran, never pausing to look back.

With his right hand, he reached into his greatcoat for his pistol; with his left, he lunged for the doorknob.

The report of a pistol echoed down the street. An intense heat penetrated his awareness. He stumbled forward.

The door opened from the inside. The lights around Denby, his manservant, gave him an angelic halo.

"Close the door, man."

"My lord, what is it?"

"I've been shot." The room grew dimmer. "Get this book to Hen."

CHAPTER ONE

1802, London

"Help! Hen! Help!"

Abandoning all manner of propriety, Lady Henrietta Harcourt broke into a dead run. With her muslin dress bunched in her hand, she ran toward Edward's alarmed plea. Following the sound of her younger brother's panicked voice and the insistent barking of Gus, she darted along the rocky path to the edge of the Serpentine.

Edward bobbed in the dark water of the lake with his dog circling and barking. Tremors of terror spread through her body, making it hard to breathe, hard to think. How could things have gone so terribly wrong in the few minutes those two had rushed ahead of her?

The hysterical youth flailed his arms in the air.

"Edward!" Her voice thundered over the still water.

"My leg...tangled," he sputtered, coughed, swallowing water in his distress. His fear pierced straight through her. Blood rushed and thundered in her chest.

"Edward, I'm coming... I'll have you out in a trice."

She tore off her bonnet and pelisse and plunged into the frigid spring water. She walked knee deep in the icy water toward her brother, trying hard to project calm as shock spread through her body. "Edward, I'm almost there."

The dog whined but had stopped barking.

"Hold on to Gus if you are tired."

The boy and his dog were ten feet from the shore, but the water deepened quickly. She couldn't touch the bottom after a few feet. Her dress floated around her, weighing her down. Kicking hard against her skirt, she fought to get closer to her brother.

"Edward, which foot is tangled? Can you move it at all?"

He squealed in a high-pitched voice, "I'm stuck."

Her brother's panic was palpable. She couldn't breathe, as if the glacial water were blocks of ice compressing her chest.

"Edward, give your leg a great pull. Heave as hard as you can."

Her brother remained paralyzed. His face pale, a faint blue outline surrounding his lips.

She moved closer and stretched across the water, reaching for his arm.

"Edward, you can do this. I'll hold your arm. Pull, now."

He nodded with a whisper, "All right."

She held firm to his arm. Edward jerked his leg once, twice. "I got it, Hen...I got it." He was free.

"Good work, Edward. Now let's get out of this blasted cold water."

Edward started to laugh, either giddy from his close encounter or her blasphemy.

"Do you want to hold on to Gus? Or can you get back on your own?"

"I'm fine now. Come on, Gus." The boy and dog paddled across the water as if nothing unusual had occurred.

Relieved to see her brother making his way to dry ground, she started toward the shore. The effort of saving Edward and the freezing spring water had taken its toll. Her leaden arms and legs flailed in futile strokes, her movements uncoordinated. The weight of her dress dragged her down into the black water. She kicked and kicked harder. She tried to tread water but her arms wouldn't move. The feelings of relief over Edward's rescue turned swiftly to a need to survive.

She searched the shore for someone other than Edward to help her. No one was about on the wet, cold day.

"Henrietta, come on. I'm freezing and Gus is all wet," Edward shouted.

She considered the idea of Edward pulling her out of the water but, even from a distance, she could see him shaking from the cold. She couldn't risk his life. She suppressed the alarm darting in and out of her frozen brain.

Fighting against the ponderous dress, she struggled not to sink. Her movements became frenzied, clumsy and ineffective. Her chest ached and her breaths became short. She gulped, trying not to swallow the water when she went under for the second time. She heard a muffled shout but couldn't answer.

An overwhelming lethargy seeped into her, pulling her into a safe cocoon of heat. She drifted into the warm sensation. The enveloping heat was heavenly. Heavenly? Was she drowning?

She struggled against the hot steel vise closing around her. She couldn't allow herself to drown. What would happen to Uncle Charles and Edward?

Freeing her arms, she began to punch, fighting for her life. With one wild swing, her hand thudded against a hard wall.

Strong arms lifted her from the cold. "Henrietta, stop or we'll both be under water."

She looked up into the intense blue eyes of Lord Rathbourne—the man she detested. The man who made a mockery of all women's sensibilities.

He pushed her wet hair away from her eyes then pulled her closer to his chest. He caressed her back as he moved effortlessly to the shore. "You're safe. We're going to get you and your brother home and out of these wet clothes."

"Edward? Where's Edward?" She shifted her weight in his muscular arms.

"Hen, I'm here. Lord Rathbourne's friend gave me his coat. I'm going to ride on his horse."

She couldn't comprehend what Edward had said. It was as if her brain had frozen with the rest of her body. She couldn't stop her teeth from chattering or her body from shaking.

"My coat, Ash. We've got to get her home." Lord Rathbourne directed the man who stood with Edward.

Lord Rathbourne's companion retrieved the coat that had been thrown to the ground. Though aware of the motion around her, she couldn't focus. Edward was safe, and they were on their way home.

Warm hands rubbed her arms and legs, and then she was wrapped, bundled, and held securely on Lord Rathbourne's horse.

She nestled into the heat of London's most notorious rake.

With her hands planted on her generous hips and her feet apart, the housekeeper stood at the top of the Kendal house's steps. Mrs. Brompton's shrill voice shattered Henrietta's torpor. "What's happened, Lady Henrietta?"

Lord Rathbourne answered before Henrietta could frame a response. "Both Harcourts have taken a plunge in the Serpentine. We must get them out of their wet clothes and into a hot bath."

"Lady Henrietta, how...how?" She heard the distress in Mrs. Brompton's question.

"Direct me to Lady Henrietta's room. She needs to be out of these wet clothes immediately."

There was a flurry of activity around her, but Henrietta couldn't summon any energy to respond.

The housekeeper and her husband snapped into action. Mrs. Brompton directed Lord Rathbourne into Henrietta's bedroom.

Henrietta didn't want to be put down, cold and alone again. She must be in shock. She wanted to stay in the arms of a man who had more mistresses than cravats.

His voice, like his body, was warm, mesmerizing. "Can you stand or should I put you on the bed?"

The idea of her bed and the heat of Lord Rathbourne stirred something deep and primitive. The coldness of her skin collided with the warmth pumping through her veins. "I can stand."

He moved her closer to the fire that Mrs. Brompton stirred. With his arms wrapped around her tightly, he slid her down his hard body and placed her feet on the ground.

Excruciating sensations engulfed her. She was unsteady and swayed toward him.

"Maybe it is better if you lie down." His voice sounded strained, rough.

She shook with chills as white heat raced through her body and into her face. "I'm fine. Thank you."

His look was tender but held something she couldn't comprehend, something she would reflect upon when she wasn't so cold.

Mrs. Brompton stepped forward. "I'll help Lady Henrietta." Mrs. Brompton placed her arm around Henrietta's shoulder. "Thank you, my lord. I must get Lady Henrietta out of these wet clothes."

He walked toward the door then turned, as if reluctant to leave. "Make sure your man has called a doctor."

Mrs. Brompton nodded at his words.

Finding it difficult to speak, Henrietta whispered in a small voice, "Thank you."

"I leave you in good hands. I'll return."

Lord Rathbourne bowed and quietly closed the door.

The housekeeper helped Henrietta remove the soaked garments then wrapped a towel around her body and tucked another over her dripping hair.

"How could you've gotten yourself into such a McGregor? I promised your mother I'd take good care of all three of you." Mrs. Brompton's voice choked. "What if something happened to you or Master Edward and with Master Michael in France, what would I do?" A large sigh moved her generous bosom.

"Oh, Bromie, it wasn't a McGregor. We just got too close to the water."

The housekeeper continued to dry Henrietta with a soft towel. "Terrible woman, she was, that Nanny McGregor. Used to frighten you both, she was wicked cruel to Master Michael. The Scottish are a brutal race."

She and her older brother had named their childhood pranks after their nasty nanny. The code name was a warning for possible dire consequences for their mischief.

"I'm glad the old earl saw fit to dismiss the woman after she whipped Master Michael that awful day." Mrs. Brompton's familiar mutterings and the warmth of the fire had stopped Henrietta's shaking.

Mrs. Brompton pointed at the housemaid who carried hot water into the room. "Polly, if you're finished filling the bath, bring up hot tea and a bottle of brandy."

"I'm going to need a nip myself. You and Edward almost drowning..."

"Bromie, there was no danger of us drowning. Lord Rathbourne overreacted but was kind enough to bring me home." She felt guilty for the lie but the arrogant lord's ego could sustain the blow. "Edward and I'll be right as rain once we warm up." With that pithy reassurance, she sunk into the hot bath. "Oh, I thought I would never be warm again." A sigh of pleasure escaped her lips when she sank deeper into the tub. She closed her eyes and let the warmth of the hot water seep into her body.

Blue eyes, she hadn't realized he had blue eyes, like quicksilver, changing colors rapidly with his mood. The cold must have gone to her brain. She and Edward had almost drowned and she was musing over the eyes of a cad with arguably the worst reputation in London. She sank deeper into the tub and placed the sponge over her eyes, shutting out all visions of the seductive lord.

Cordelier Richard Beaumont, Earl of Rathbourne, crossed his legs at his ankles and savored the aroma from the delicate snifter, a delightful combination of comfort and cognac. The warm room of the club and the aged brandy were easing the chill from his plunge into the frigid Serpentine earlier in the day. His childhood friend and war compatriot sat across the dark mahogany table, poised, waiting to pounce.

Cord sighed dramatically. "Spit it out."

"Lady Henrietta." Viscount Henry James Ashworth chortled. "The look on your face today was worth the ruin of my new coat."

"My God, she was drowning. What look did you expect to see on my face?" His stomach clenched with the memory of how close Henrietta had come to dying. "It was damn lucky we were riding by."

Ash raised his eyebrows, his eyes light with humor. "Her distress was evident as was..."

Like Ash, he had registered every wet, soft, delectable part of Henrietta during the rescue. How could he not appreciate those thinly disguised generous curves? His face heated with the unsuitable thoughts.

"Your face is turning red. I never thought I'd see the day," Ash needled.

"I felt depraved to be noticing...while the lady was distressed. Hell, I can't believe I'm admitting that to you."

"What are friends for? And as a good friend I should remind you it was the same lady who four years ago found you loathsome, if my memory serves me right."

Cord took a large gulp of the brandy. "As you damn well know, your memory is excellent."

She had looked at him with a mixture of disregard and disrespect when he had asked her dance at Chillington's ball—no other woman had ever looked at him in such a way. Spirited and confident, Henrietta acted neither grateful nor thrilled for the opportunity to dance with him. She clearly believed him to be a reprobate. The most uncomfortable part of the memory was that he knew her to be absolutely correct.

"Cord, don't be so hard on yourself. You were in a rough patch after Gray died. You're not that man any longer."

"You and I might agree that I've improved, but convincing the lady will be the challenge. My new position as Head of Abchurch is going to be a problem. Both her brother and uncle work for me."

"It is ill-timed that your position is a secret and can't be revealed to Lady Henrietta."

"It's not exactly a position discussed in social circles."

"But the responsibility of the post would recommend you to the lady."

"She isn't going to believe I'm capable of guarding her loved ones. You saw how protective she was of the young cub."

"An irresponsible rake making decisions for her

family." Ash shook his head. "You did manage to rescue her, so you better start pursuing her while she remains grateful."

"I took flowers over this afternoon. Mrs. Brompton informed me that Henrietta was indisposed, but I will call again. At least the housekeeper likes me."

Ash's eyes danced with merriment. "An auspicious beginning. Tomorrow will be the perfect opportunity to demonstrate your new worthiness."

"Why tomorrow?" Cord asked.

"The Wentworth Ball, a respectable event to approach the lady." Ash didn't hide his grin. Cord was surprised that Ash wasn't rubbing his hands together in glee. His friend was definitely looking forward to the entertainment of watching him squirm. "Do the polite thing. Invite her to dance. Escort her to dinner."

Cord didn't want to do the polite thing, he didn't want to wait. Courting took time and patience, and he was short on both when it came to Henrietta. He hadn't forgotten her for four long years during his tenure on the Continent for his country and King. Her frank green eyes and her unwillingness to be impressed by him or his title had captivated him.

Twirling a walking stick, Comte Lucien De Valmont strolled confidently toward them. De Valmont was currently being scrutinized by the office for possible covert connections to Talleyrand, the foreign minister of France.

"God, I think he means to talk with us," Ash said.

"Have you dried out from your rescue of the luscious Lady Henrietta, Rathbourne?" De Valmont stood over the table, one hand placed jauntily on his hip, the other leaning on a heavily carved ivory walking stick.

Cord maintained his nonchalant gaze, but his jaw and body tightened, ready to spring into action.

De Valmont postured, unaware of the danger. "Was it the lady's charms, so flagrantly displayed, that made you play the role of the gallant?"

Cord was going to put his fist right through the carefully arranged foppish French face.

Ash stood. "The evening grows tiresome. Shall we depart?"

Cord ignored Ash's burning stare. He could floor the French bastard with one punch right between his shifty eyes. He stood ready to decimate De Valmont, his hands twitching at his side.

De Valmont stepped back, his smile fading.

He moved close to De Valmont, close enough to watch the French man's pupils dilate in apprehension, close enough for the Frenchman to hear the menacing tone in his voice without attracting the attention of his fellow club members. "If I hear one word of today's accident or a mention of the lady's name, I will find you and grind you into the ground."

With a swift kick, Cord knocked De Valmont's stick to the ground. A deafening sound resounded off the oak floors in the quiet room. A footman rushed over to pick up the gentleman's stick.

Ash caught up with Cord in the hallway. He patted Cord on the back. "Well done. That was the finest undercover work I've seen in a long time." Ash's laugh echoed off the high ceilings in the entrance way.

"I'm glad I made your evening entertaining."

"And I'm glad you showed some measure of restraint. God, man, I thought you were going to kill him."

"He's lucky I didn't call him out right there." The thought of De Valmont alluding to Henrietta's body, vividly exposed by her soaked gown, infuriated him. The blood continued to rush through his body. "I still might have to challenge him."

"I can't believe how quickly word has spread about the rescue," Ash said.

"It is interesting that De Valmont already knew."

"And felt the need to comment to you. I'd say he was testing the waters?" Ash chuckled. "No pun intended."

A companionable silence lengthened between the two friends.

Cord's reaction stunned him. What had happened to the cool detachment which made him legendary in espionage circles? "I acted like an idiot."

"De Valmont has a great deal of interest in Lady Henrietta. Is he a jealous suitor?"

A primitive possessiveness surged through Cord's body. "He better not consider approaching Henrietta."

"I think the lady might have something to say about it," Ash said.

"I won't give the lady a choice."

Ash snorted. "If he isn't a suitor, why the interest in Lady Henrietta?"

"I believe De Valmont was looking for a reaction from me. And he got it."

"But why seek you out?"

"He couldn't have known of my interest in the lady. And he wouldn't insult a lady he was planning to pursue. Either he wanted to challenge me or has an interest in the Harcourt family. Either way, De Valmont bears closer scrutiny."

"Someone in his house?" Ash asked.

"Yes, I think Talley would be perfect for the job. I want to know De Valmont's whereabouts."

"And Lady Henrietta's whereabouts?" Ash chuckled.

CHAPTER TWO

Gus pounced as Henrietta rose from her knees, the task of weeding the flower beds complete. Henrietta teetered but the impact of the four-stone Labrador couldn't be stopped. She fell backward on her heels, giving Gus the perfect position to lick her face. His wet kiss landed squarely on her lips and was followed by a full frontal assault. Her shrieks encouraged Gus to intensify his slobbery affection.

"Gus, you kiss better than the gentlemen of the ton." She stood, brushing the paw marks from her pale yellow muslin dress.

"You never told me that you kissed a lot of men." Edward came down the steps. Her younger brother never appeared to be listening, but it was like him to hear her slightly risqué comment.

"I was joking, and a gentleman would never ask a lady whom she has been kissing."

"Why were Michael and his friends laughing about Lady Hawksley's lips?" Edward asked.

Henrietta was going to wring their older brother's neck for being indiscreet about the voracious widow in front of Edward. "I'll let Michael explain what he and his friends were discussing."

"I knew you weren't going to tell me anything. Michael is in France and isn't going to be home for at least four or five years."

With his round baby cheeks and the golden Harcourt hair, Edward looked like a cherub in a Raphael painting. Leaning over, she tousled his hair. "I'm sure Michael will be home before you're twelve years old and will answer all your questions."

She had definite plans for educating Edward on the relationship between women and men, to shatter the male balderdash that women needed to be protected and thus excluded from the workings of the real world. With Michael's departure to France for intelligence work, the management of the entire household fell on her shoulders.

Edward chased Gus over the grass and behind a tree. The dog came then waited for Edward to give chase again. The boy and dog ran circles around the giant oak.

Watching their enthusiastic play, she felt a deep longing for something she couldn't identify. When Edward and Gus came to a halt near her, she hugged her younger brother. "I'll tell you about kissing. It's delightful when you're kissing someone you care about, like your younger brother or your dog."

"Hen, I'm not talking about that kind of kissing." Edward, appearing to have no interest in the conversation, drew away and threw a stick to Gus.

"Kissing between women and men is exactly like kissing between families, a sign of mutual affection between people who care about and respect each other." She shook her gardening gloves, carefully choosing her words. "Women want to know men respect them for their minds, their wit, who they really are, before they share their affection."

Why was she thinking of a man whose kisses wouldn't be the least respectful?

"May I go to the park now?"

"You may go to Hyde Park. But, Edward Michael Ormond Harcourt, you aren't to go near the Serpentine."

"I never meant to scare you." Edward hung his head and kicked at the grass.

"I know you didn't plan what happened but it will take a while to forget our dunking." And the man who rescued her, the man who pressed her to his chest and held her tenderly in his arms. "Please walk Gus on a lead. Remember what happened last time he was off."

"It wasn't Gus's fault. The lady had no control of her horse."

"Edward, promise me you'll keep Gus on his lead near the horse trails."

"Yes, Hen." Leading Gus out of the garden, Edward called to his tutor, Mr. Marlow.

"And be back for teatime," she reminded him. The Harcourt men had no sense of time. They could forget to eat and sleep when they focused on solving a knotty problem. They relied on her to maintain their expected routines.

A breathless, frantic Mrs. Brompton hailed her from the steps. "A letter...a letter from France."

The stout woman continued talking during her descent of the brick steps. "I hope this is a letter from Lord Michael. I can't believe he would forget to write just because he's having a jolly time there in Paris."

Mrs. Brompton was unaware of Michael's work for the Abchurch office, delving clandestinely into French code breaking. Under the guise of visiting French relatives, Michael, a renowned linguist, was to develop a scholarly relationship with Gaston Le Chiffre, France's secret code master.

Henrietta tore open the blue envelope. The letter, marked with the stamp of the Paris Ormonds, was from her cousin Genevieve, not from Michael. Scanning the letter quickly, she spotted a postscript in Michael's hand at the bottom of the page. *I'm in a* McGregor, *sending a package.*

Henrietta's heart thudded against her chest. She reread Michael's scrawl. How could Michael be in a

McGregor? He was no longer a ten-year-old doing silly pranks or a young buck at Oxford causing mayhem. He was in France on a covert mission, doing dangerous work.

"The letter is from my cousin Genevieve, an update on her darling children and their escapades. Michael added a postscript that he is too busy to write but will soon."

Mrs. Brompton chortled. "He's up to his old tricks, getting into trouble. I've got to check on Cook. Tell Uncle Charles fresh crumpets with strawberry jam for teatime."

"Uncle Charles will be delighted."

Michael's position was vital in uncovering how the French were changing their codes in anticipation of Napoleon's next aggressive attack on Europe. If the French were to suspect Michael—her stomach churned with the possible danger, twisting into knots. Her plants had lost their allure. She didn't linger in the gardens.

Entering the house, Henrietta walked down the passageway to the library. Sunlight gave the book-covered walls in the expansive room a new patina. Particles suspended in the air sparkled like fairy dust. Uncle Charles was bent over a heavy tome at his desk. His glasses, propped on the top of his head, pushed his white hair into clumps.

"Henrietta, hieroglyphics are the key. Egypt holds the secrets for this new code from Abchurch. Didn't I just break one using the ancient symbols?" he asked.

"It has been several months since we've broken a code with hieroglyphics."

She had hoped Uncle Charles would not return to his obsession with Egypt. Increasingly, there seemed to be no rhyme or reason to the flow of his thoughts. There were days when he was brilliant and other days when he slipped into one of his previous sixty-five years. He had been a man with great focus.

"Perhaps you should rest before teatime? You've been working a long time. Cook has promised hot crumpets with strawberry jam."

"It might be a good idea for a little lie-down. I'll get back to this code straight away after tea."

Her uncle attempted to push himself up from his seat, but he faltered and fell back into the chair.

Henrietta placed her hand under his elbow and helped him to stand. His waist coat bulged with his collection, an odd assortment of scraps of paper mixed with melting wax and a penknife. His best notes scattered like his thoughts in a holy disorder.

Uncle Charles looked up quizzically. "I do appreciate the help with these old bones. I was remembering when Stephen and I were both courting you. I always thought you would marry me."

"Uncle Charles, it is I, Henrietta."

Her uncle searched her face, his eyes blank, lost.

"Therese and Stephen are both gone," she said.

He studied her face as if it held the clues to unlock the newest code. "Was I wandering?"

"Just a little bit, you were remembering *Maman*."

The same bright Harcourt smile as her brothers' softened his wizened face.

"It has been two years since *Maman* died. I miss her, too."

Tears pooled in her uncle's eyes. "You're like Therese, the same lilt in your voice, your hair, the color of wheat fields."

Brompton stood at the door waiting to enter.

"Here is Brompton to help you, Uncle Charles. At teatime, you will need to tell me about your first dance with *Maman*."

Uncle Charles grasped her hand and nodded then shuffled out of the library.

Henrietta returned to her desk, lowered herself into

her chair and opened the gold locket she always wore
around her neck. She gazed at the portrait of her
loving mother, smiling back at her. Melancholy filled
the empty spaces around her heart. She missed her
mother and her guidance on how to take care of all the
Harcourt men.

Her mother would've supported Henrietta's
decision to protect Uncle Charles by taking over his
code breaking workload. She didn't know how long she
would be able to keep up the deception from the
Abchurch men. The possibility of discovering that their
codes weren't deciphered by the legendary Charles
Harcourt but by his niece was highly entertaining to
her and Michael.

She missed her older brother and wished she
could've gone with him to France. If she weren't a
woman, she would've been the right choice for the
assignment: brilliant linguistic ability, impeccable
French connections, and a seeker of adventure.

The ever-growing uneasiness about Michael's safety
expanded and spread through her body like her
mother's wasting disease. No matter how she analyzed
and reanalyzed his message, the deduction was the
same: her brother's insatiable curiosity had gotten him
into a mess. He'd pursued a lark with an unexpectedly
dangerous outcome. Except this time the result
wouldn't be a beating by his nanny. A spasm of anxiety
twisted her gut.

She wished there was someone to talk with,
someone who understood Michael, someone to share
her worries about her impetuous brother.

She had been tempted to speak with Uncle Charles
since he had seemed to be in one of his lucid periods
earlier in the morning. But by teatime, he had
reverted to his obsession with hieroglyphics.

Lord Ramston, the Head of the Abchurch offices and
a long-standing family friend was the only person who
could address her concerns. As a gentle bred lady, she

was not supposed to know about Lord Ramston's position with the office. She was doing high-level espionage work but wasn't allowed to enter the office. She took a slow, deep breath, trying to release her frustration. She was not going to wait another month to find out about Michael. Tomorrow afternoon she would speak with Sir Ramston at Abchurch, the sacrosanct center of code deciphering.

CHAPTER THREE

Henrietta hurried down the crowded streets of Mayfair. She tried to mince her steps and walk as a lady, but after her disastrous morning of the fireplaces smoking up the library, she was late for her friend Amelia's final gown fitting. She longed to be in Paris solving secret codes with her brother, not solving household problems.

Henrietta broke her brisk stride at the sound of a man's groan from the alley to her left. A loud thwack followed. She peered down the darkened alley, trying to track the noise.

An older lady, dressed in a bright coquelicot dress and a green bonnet, was attacking a man, whacking him over the head with an umbrella. By her dress, the older woman was a lady, although her choice in colors was abominable. The lady didn't appear threatened or intimidated. She raised her knee quickly and delivered a blow to the man's nether region, bringing him down to his knees. The brutish looking man moaned in pain. The woman hit him on his back one last time then turned and marched away.

The unusual lady turned the corner at the far end of the alley. The man started to rise from his knees. A sneer crossed his face. Henrietta hurried on to the modiste.

When she stepped into the shop of Madame De Puis,

the cloying scent of cloves and roses overwhelmed her. Everything in the shop was done in billowing white with accents of gold on the chairs, frames, and vases holding bouquets of heavily-scented, scarlet roses. Swatches of cool white silk hung on the walls and on the entrances to the changing rooms.

Amelia, her slender, winsome friend, stood with her back to Henrietta. At tonight's Wentworth Ball, Amelia would wear a ball gown she had designed and Madame De Puis had constructed.

"Amelia, I'm sorry for my tardy arrival, but I must tell you about the incredible thing I just witnessed."

Her friend turned with a big grin and brought her finger to her lips. "Shhh...listen"

Bursting to tell Amelia about the lady's assault, Henrietta found it difficult to stand still. A voice from the dressing room was barely audible. Henrietta strained to listen. Amelia's violet eyes were bright with mischief.

"It certainly leaves little to the imagination." The woman behind the curtain spoke with a French accent.

Henrietta didn't recognize the voice, although she knew many of the French émigrés. Madame de Puis' response was muffled.

"I want his focus right here, with the promise of what is to follow." Her laugh was husky and deep.

Amelia blushed at hearing the lady's sentiments expressed in a public manner.

Henrietta didn't blush. She was trying to suppress a giggle. Both she and Amelia leaned toward the dressing room, waiting for the lady's next comment, assuming she was a lady.

Madame De Puis emerged. Shock registered on the modiste's face. "Lady Henrietta, Miss Amelia. You're early...for your appointment. Please, ladies. Let me take you to a dressing room." Madame de Puis pushed firmly against their backs, trying to prevent them from seeing or hearing the daring lady.

Neither of them budged. Henrietta dropped her reticule. Amelia bent slowly to retrieve it.

"Who made this fabulous reticule?" Amelia asked in an innocent voice.

Henrietta snickered. Amelia had made the reticule.

Madame de Puis, aware of their stall tactics, gave one more discrete push. "Mademoiselles, please, let us adjourn to the dressing room."

A stunning woman with dramatic black hair and catlike eyes threw the curtains back. The woman's dark eyes raked over Henrietta, missing no detail of her simple, countrified dress. With the household problems, she had no time to change into one of her nicer gowns.

"Bonjour, Mademoiselles." The woman pitched her silky voice low. She spiced "Mademoiselles" with a sardonic twist.

Henrietta didn't recognize this woman, but by her revealing décolletage, Henrietta recognized they should never be introduced to her. "I'm Lady Henrietta Harcourt, and this is my friend, Miss Amelia Bonnington."

"Harcourt?" The woman paused. "Lady Henrietta Harcourt?" Her vivid eyes rescanned Henrietta from her unadorned bonnet to her Nankeen half boots. The woman's full crimson lips turned down in a moue of distaste. "What a beauty, with a country complexion and an air of innocence."

Henrietta was stunned into silence. Why would this woman direct unseemly comments toward her?

Amelia said, "Madame De Puis, please introduce us to your client, since we haven't had the pleasure."

"I'm Isabelle de Villier and the pleasure is all mine." The woman's deep-throated laugh vibrated down into her bared chest, causing the pale skin and abundant décolletage to tremble. Her practiced laugh drew their eyes to her chest. "Neither of you requires the services of Madame de Puis. Your charms will attract men young and old. Men are always drawn to virtue and the pursuit of despoiling it."

There was a gasp from the voluble modiste. "Mademoiselle de Villier, please. Your dress will be delivered this afternoon."

"You'll make the changes, as we discussed." The voluptuous woman sent one last penetrating stare toward Henrietta and then departed.

Henrietta looked at Amelia and burst out laughing. "Why do I feel as if I were a mouse, just mauled by a vicious cat?"

"You were Hen. I got the feeling she knew of you," Amelia said.

"It did seem that she knew the Harcourt name."

"She probably knows Michael." The playfulness went out of Amelia's voice.

Amelia feigned indifference to Michael's rakish activities, hoping that he would notice that she was no longer the childhood playmate of his sister. So far her attempts had failed.

"Why would she feel the need for such spite?" Henrietta asked.

A young woman swept into the shop. "Ladies, Madame de Puis, good morning." Beneath a simple bonnet, the woman's face was flushed.

"Lady Beaumont. You're early for your appointment." The modiste's French accent got heavier with the strain of another early arrival.

Amelia raised her eyebrows toward Henrietta. "Lady Beaumont, are you related to Lord Rathbourne?"

"Yes, I'm his younger sister, Gwyneth." Her face warmed, as did her voice, with the mention of her brother.

Amelia moved closer to the vibrant woman. "I'm Miss Amelia Bonnington. This is my dear friend, Lady Henrietta Harcourt."

All three curtsied. Lord Rathbourne and his sister

shared the same raven black hair and high angular cheekbones, but their eyes were distinct. Lady Gwyneth's eyes were shaped like almonds and the color of warm chocolate, while his were cobalt blue, like a frosty winter sky.

"I don't believe we've had the privilege of seeing you in society?" Amelia inquired innocently.

"My aunt and I just arrived in London. We've come a day earlier than planned." Lady Gwyneth beamed at the modiste. "Madame de Puis was kind enough to see me today for a fitting." The young woman's speech was as unaffected as her manner.

Madame de Puis curtsied to her prestigious customer. "It's an honor to serve you, mademoiselle. Does your aunt join you?"

"My aunt had a prior engagement, but she should've arrived by now." A notch formed between the eyebrows of the expressive woman's face. "I'm not sure what has delayed Aunt Euphemia."

Madame de Puis said, "Don't worry, mademoiselle, your aunt will arrive. May I serve you tea?"

"No thank you, madame. I shall wait for my aunt."

Like a good terrier, Amelia stayed on the scent of Lord Rathbourne. "Your brother must be thrilled that you've come to London."

Lady Gwyneth's eyes rounded in excitement. "You know my brother?"

"No, I've not had that pleasure." Amelia's eyes brightened with mischief. "Henrietta knows your brother."

"I've a slight acquaintance with him." Henrietta could feel the heat moving to her face when she remembered the feel of his muscular arms holding her tightly against his chest, the intimacy of his hands on her back. His captivating touch was branded into her brain. "Just a mild acquaintance."

Amelia responded with an unladylike snort.

"It is fabulous to meet friends of my brother on my

first outing in London. He isn't expecting us until tomorrow. We'd hoped to surprise him, but his work keeps him away from the house," Lady Gwyneth said.

"I'm sure he'll be pleased to have you join him. Will the rest of your family come as well?" Henrietta asked.

"I've only my brother and Aunt Euphemia. My parents are deceased."

Amelia patted the young woman on the arm. "How wonderful to have your brother to escort you for the season's activities."

"He's going to be bored, attending all the balls and soirees, but he has promised to attend any affair I choose. He's the best brother."

The modiste directed Amelia to a changing room. "Miss Amelia, please, we must get to your final fitting if I'm to finish your gown for tonight's ball."

"Is there a ball tonight, Lady Henrietta?" Lady Gwyneth asked.

"Tonight is the Wentworth Ball."

Henrietta and Lady Gwyneth proceeded to sit on tiny gilded chairs, padded with fluffy down pillows.

"You must see Amelia's dress. She designed it herself. She has a wonderful sense for the dramatic," Henrietta said.

"I wish I were going to the ball tonight." With a heavy sigh, the young woman sat back against the tiny chair.

Henrietta smiled, remembering her own excitement for her first ball. "Your first ball. How very thrilling, Lady Gwyneth."

The young woman's face spread in a wide grin. "Please, you must call me Gwyneth." Her eyes, after closer inspection, were more the color of ginger snaps than chocolate, Henrietta decided.

"And I'm Henrietta."

"Tell me about when you met my brother. Was it before his travels to the Continent?"

"I met your brother in my first season. I believe we

might have shared a dance." His sister would be
ignorant of his wild reputation.

"You met him during his wild oats days–which is
how my aunt refers to those years. Neither my aunt
nor Cord will give me any details. Please tell me what
was he like? Dashing?"

Gwyneth was as animated and volatile as Edward,
rushing into feelings and conversations without any
sense of propriety. Lord Rathbourne would be appalled
if he heard his sister's comments.

Amelia stepped out of the changing room, wrapped
in a diaphanous slip of a dress. The gossamer creation
of violet silk tissue was draped across one of her
shoulders. The cool purple fabric shot with silver
enhanced Amelia's red hair and pale white skin. Fitted
at the bust line, the dress floated to the floor in a heap
of luxurious color, like the fields of lavender in
Provence.

"Do you like it?" Amelia turned full circle, allowing
her skirts to billow around her ankles.

"You're   stunning.   You've   outdone   yourself."
Henrietta jumped up from her chair to hug her friend.
"I'm jealous of all your talent."

"Your talent serves a greater purpose." Amelia's
voice warmed to their familiar dispute.

"Your   talent   graces   the   world   with   beauty,"
Henrietta replied.

"Now you've stirred my interests. I see Amelia's
talents, but what are yours, Henrietta?" Gwyneth
asked.

"Henrietta tries to keep it a secret, but she is
devoted to linguistics. The entire Harcourt family is
gifted, but she outshines them all," Amelia said.

"Gwyneth isn't interested in my talents. Amelia,
turn around again. The fabric seems to have been
made by fairies."

Gwyneth stood and walked around Amelia. "The
dress is wonderful and you look magnificent." She

whispered, "I should have you design my ball gowns but I don't think Aunt Euphemia would allow it."

All three chuckled, aware that demure and white was de rigueur for a debutante.

Madame De Puis pulled Amelia aside to discuss minor alterations to the gown.

Henrietta and Gwyneth sat back down. "Do you know what your family has planned for your first appearance in society?"

"Besides my introduction to the men of the ton?" Gwyneth's perfect porcelain skin flushed with pink when she spoke of meeting men. She was going to have quite an effect on the gentlemen.

"Not yet. My aunt and I'll need to discuss my brother's schedule with him. He's very busy with his work. Of course, I must have fittings and get my wardrobe ready." She breathed another heavy sigh.

"Next week, Lady Chadwick is holding a soiree in support of the French émigrés, a few ladies who are concerned about the living conditions of the émigrés. A debutante is allowed to attend soirees before her presentation."

"Henrietta, are you starting on one of your causes?" Although in the changing room, Amelia heard the conversation and spoke through the gauzy curtain. "Which is it? Ancient Egypt, French émigrés? Beware, Gwyneth, next she'll have you attending a dreadful talk on Greek civilization or..."

"I'd love to attend a soiree, and I'm sure both my aunt and Cord are sympathetic to the plight of the émigrés. Cord works tirelessly for many causes. My aunt and I worry he works too hard," Gwyneth said.

This didn't sound like the man Henrietta knew. Gwyneth leaned forward speaking in a hushed voice. "My aunt and I've come to town to find a wife for Cord. Of course, he doesn't know. He believes he's going to find a husband for me. My aunt and I both agree that I'm too young to settle down. I'm here for experience."

Henrietta bit the sides of her cheeks, trying hard not to laugh. Amelia chortled behind the curtain. The experience Gwyneth spoke of was meeting respectable gentlemen and exchanging innocent kisses.

Gwyneth's face had gone from pink to a bright red. "I don't mean that kind of experience."

"We didn't mean to embarrass you. When you get to know Amelia and me better, you'll learn that we love to tease," Henrietta said.

Amelia hastily arrived from the changing area, adjusting her pelisse. "Do you have a specific lady in mind for your brother?"

Henrietta hoped Gwyneth didn't see Amelia's raised eyebrows.

"No, we've just come to town." Gwyneth paused, turning toward Henrietta. "But I'm sure it won't be difficult to find a pleasing lady."

Madame de Puis returned to the sitting area. "Lady Beaumont, shall we wait for your aunt before beginning your fitting?"

"We can begin. I'm not sure what is delaying my aunt." Gwyneth stood. "It has been a delight to meet both of you. I'll plan to bring my brother and aunt to Lady Chadwick's soiree."

Gwyneth curtsied as did Henrietta and Amelia. The young woman walked toward the change room then turned and winked at Amelia. Henrietta didn't miss the conspiratorial sign.

CHAPTER FOUR

On the short walk back to Kendal House, Henrietta considered what retributions she was going to exact on her brother for Isabelle Villiers' spite.

Issabelle Villier—a stage name for sure. The woman had been offensive when she discovered Henrietta's name was Harcourt. She was likely another of Michael's McGregors. Why would Michael be attracted to a woman of that stamp? Henrietta considered Isabelle's generous chest and snorted aloud as only a lady could.

The moment Henrietta climbed the steps, the front door of Kendal House swung open and Mrs. Brompton bounded out, tendrils of gray hair hanging out of her tight chignon. "I'm glad you're home. Lord Charles..." The housekeeper sobbed, unable to continue.

Henrietta had never seen Mrs. Brompton this distraught. Her heart hammered against her chest, racing in spurts. "Is he ill?"

"I've lost him. He's nowhere to be found. It was such a fine morning that I served his tea in the garden. And now..." The woman gave another wrenching sob.

Henrietta took Mrs. Brompton's arm. "Let's go inside."

"I left him for no more than a few minutes. He was sitting in the sunshine, reading out of one of his big books. I got distracted by Mary asking about the fireplaces, and when I went back to check on him, he was gone." The housekeeper's voice boomed in the marble entrance.

"Have you searched the entire house? You've checked the library, his room?"

"We've looked throughout the house and the garden. You know how distracted he can get when he has a code on his mind." As Mrs. Brompton became more desperate, each word became louder. By the end, the housekeeper was nearly shouting.

"We'll find him, Bromie. He can't have gone far." Wishing she could believe her own reassurances, Henrietta put her hand on her chest, trying to alleviate the crushing sensation of panic.

"Brompton and Thomas are searching the streets. I've sent Mr. Marlow to the park," Mrs. Brompton said.

Henrietta quelled the urge to run through the house.

"I was waiting for you before I sent Polly to ask the neighbors. I didn't know if you would want them informed." The implications of alerting their neighbors to her uncle's mental condition were left unspoken.

"Polly is capable. Instruct her not to give any unnecessary details. Its teatime and Uncle Charles loses his sense of time when discussing history or linguistics," Henrietta said.

"I just don't know where he would go. All he thinks about is his books," Mrs. Brompton said.

Henrietta couldn't believe that Uncle Charles might be lost. He got confused, but he always knew Kendal House and all its inhabitants.

"I believe I know where Uncle Charles might have ventured," Henrietta said.

"You know where he went?"

"I'm hoping he went to his book lovers' club, The Set of Odd Volumes. It used to be one of his favorite haunts."

The thought of her brilliant uncle, incapable of

crossing the street to go to his club was too painful to contemplate. "You've done a great job, Bromie. Uncle Charles will return hungry and ready for tea. I suggest you start preparing."

Mrs. Brompton's thick hand blotted the beads of perspiration on her forehead. "It would be just like him to get it into his head that he needed a book and get up and leave the garden. I better see Cook gets the crumpets in the oven. Everyone will be hungry after this morning's adventures." The stout woman moved toward the kitchen.

Henrietta walked toward the front door then turned. "Everyone should continue the search until I get back."

She walked at a furious pace, cutting through the park. Silently, she prayed she'd find Uncle Charles, uninjured at his club. Her hands twisted the sides of her gown. She swallowed hard against the fear that had risen into her throat and chest.

Ahead on the path, Edward and Gus ran toward her. With Edward's easy lope, his blond curls lifting in the wind, he looked like a younger version of Michael. She couldn't allow Edward to see her distress.

"Henrietta, Uncle Charles is missing." Edward shouted loud, enough that all of Mayfair would know their business. Edward's face was taut, his lips downturned as if he might cry with any provocation. She wanted to hold him tight and spare him this pain.

"Uncle Charles left the house and we can't find him," he said.

"I know. I'm sure he decided to go to his club. I'm walking there now." She struggled not to betray the tumultuous emotions fluttering in her stomach.

"Should Gus and I come?"

"You should search on the other side of the park, in case I miss Uncle Charles on this side."

"Gus and I can do that, Hen. Where else should we look?"

"Bromie is in a tizzy, and it would be a great help if you could keep her busy. Ask her to make tea. I'll bring Uncle Charles home."

"Gus can help with his amazing nose."

"You and Gus are helping a lot if you look for Uncle Charles on the other side of the park. And then, can you pretend you're hungry for Mrs. Brompton's sake?"

The boy flashed the famous dimple-creasing Harcourt smile. "Gus and I can pretend." The boy patted his plump partner. "If you don't come back after tea, should I meet you at the club?"

The panic had returned to her chest. She didn't want to consider the next step, should Uncle Charles not be found. "Why don't you wait until I get back? If we need to change our strategy, I'll want us all together."

Her brother searched her face, his green eyes wide.

"I'm sure Uncle Charles is fine and reading some obscure tome on ancient Egyptians." She tried to sound confident.

"He is probably looking for something on embalming. He loves mummies."

"You're probably right. You and Gus head that way. I'll go this way," she said.

The pair turned back toward Kendal house. She waited for them to disappear before she renewed her frantic pace.

In Uncle Charles' present condition, he might not fare well with his friends. The club was made up of a motley group of eccentrics who might not notice the dramatic change in her uncle. Unlike other men's clubs, The Odd Set of Volumes required neither a title nor aristocratic connections. The requirements were a curious mind and a passion for all books. Her uncle retained both, and hopefully, would still fit in.

She burst into the old brick building, home to the collection of odd books and the odd set of men who read them. A familiar musty scent assaulted her nose.

Oblivious to the stares, she scanned the large room teeming with men and their books. No sign of her uncle. Flutters somersaulted in her stomach.

The clerk began to move from behind his desk.

She dodged the older man and skirted down the opposite aisle of tables. She nodded to the shocked gentlemen who looked up from their tomes to find a woman racing through their club. She headed to the rear of the library, where the oldest books were shelved.

Turning a corner made up of tall shelves, she heard her uncle's rambling speech. Relief surged through her whole being down to her toes. Her white-haired uncle, his waist coat teeming with his collection, chatted amiably.

"Uncle Charles." The high pitch and intensity of her voice reverberated in the narrow shelves of books.

Her uncle greeted her as if they had just parted company. "Henrietta, I'm glad you've come. I've been having the most interesting conversation with this gentleman. He shares an interest in Egypt, especially hieroglyphics. I was beginning to tell him how I've applied the principals in my work."

"Uncle, I'm sure the gentleman must return to his own work."

An impeccably dressed gentleman in all grey, with a complicated cravat turned toward her. "Mademoiselle, I'm interested in everything from ancient Egypt, especially hieroglyphics."

Henrietta failed to recognize the gentleman who leaned on an ivory walking stick. His nonchalance belied the tension in the set of his shoulders and jaw. The perfect lines and planes of his face clashed with his round, sensual lips. His thick blond hair was combed back, as if the wind had blown it into disarray. The locks curled around his ears and one curl fell on his forehead.

"Comte Lucien De Valmont, at your service." He

bowed.

Henrietta curtsied. Their eyes locked when each straightened. His piercing gaze didn't match his formal manner.

"Your uncle was just beginning to explain the modern applications of hieroglyphics," he said.

She felt breathless, as if the room had lost all its air. Had Uncle Charles revealed anything critical about his code breaking?

She forced herself to keep smiling. "Yes, my uncle is knowledgeable about many facets of Egyptian life. Did you also discuss your fascination with mummies, Uncle Charles?" Shifting to her uncle's other obsession usually did the trick.

"I've little knowledge of mummies. My interest has always been in hieroglyphics." The comte turned toward her uncle, his face and smile immobile. "Lord Harcourt, as a linguist, your interest must be in ancient Egypt's language?"

The hairs on the back of her neck lifted with the comte's interest in her uncle. As a renowned linguist, her uncle was often sought after to share ideas. But there was something disquieting about Lord De Valmont's curiosity.

"Language can never be isolated in the study of a culture. My uncle is fascinated with all aspects of Egypt, including the architecture. Don't you find the pyramids fascinating, my lord?"

"I'm biased by my own heritage. I find the architecture of France magnificent. Is there any more grand than the Louis XVI style?" he asked

"I've never had the opportunity to travel to France," she said.

He leaned on his stick, closing the distance between them. "But I understood your mother was French?"

Her stomach flittered in anxiety at this stranger's knowledge of her family. "Do you know my French Ormond family?"

"I've never had the good fortune to meet your family, but I'd love to discuss your French heritage with you, mademoiselle." The way he lilted mademoiselle in his French accent made his interest in her too intimate.

Did the comte simply miss his homeland as many of the émigrés did and want to talk about her French connection or was there something more sinister in his curiosity?

"Perhaps another day?" Another day without Uncle Charles taking part in the conversation. "My uncle and I've one stop to make before we return home."

"May I have the pleasure of calling on you and your uncle in the near future?"

Her uncle put his arm on the stranger's shoulder. "Come to Kendal house. I'd love to discuss mummies. You said you're fascinated with mummies?"

"Uncle, we need to leave."

"Please let me escort you to the door." Comte De Valmont's tone was gracious while he directed her out of the stacks of books. She needed to get her uncle safely back to Kendal House, away from the inquisitive Frenchman.

Cord sat with Ash at his massive oak desk in the inner sanctum of the espionage offices in Abchurch Lane, the den of secret-making and code-breaking. He was much better suited to being in the action than plotting the activities of others from a desk. Nothing was as he had expected since he returned to England.

Slouched low in a leather chair, Ash held a brandy snifter and a cigar between his fingers. "What in the hell were you thinking, bringing Isabelle to Lady Wentworth's Ball last night?"

Cord didn't miss the bewildered tone in Ash's voice.

"Damn it. I didn't bring her."

Last night he had been stuck with Isabelle Villiers, playing a role that had been set in place in France. He tried not to vent his frustration on his friend. "Isabelle came with De Valmont. She and that snake are playing some kind of game, flaunting her position as my mistress in front of the ton."

His plans to pursue Lady Henrietta and to establish his respectability as the new earl had gone sideways last night. He had hoped four years on the Continent would've been enough time for his reprobate reputation to be forgotten.

"While you were busy entertaining Isabelle, De Valmont was busy entertaining the very attractive Lady Henrietta," Ash said.

He wanted to walk into the center of the crowd of gentleman surrounding her, snatch her from the French fop and the doting dandies and claim her as his own. "I hoped to make amends last night, but instead I was trapped with Isabelle." He was unable to remain seated at his cluttered desk. He moved toward the window. The London fog didn't add much light to the room.

"Does Isabelle still work for Talleyrand as well as us?" Ash asked.

In his new role as head of the office, Cord was trying to understand all the plots and subplots he had inherited from Sir Ramston.

Cord walked from the window toward Ash. "Isabelle would like me to believe that she has renounced her allegiance to the French foreign minister but Talleyrand saved her from the guillotine. She was doomed to the same fate as her husband, the Marquis de Lombard. In the last moment, Talleyrand rescued her from the blade. Knowing Talleyrand's manipulations, he most likely made a deal with Isabelle. I doubt he has rescinded the agreement."

"Does De Valmont work for Talleyrand too?"

Cord was slowly learning the machinations of his predecessor and kept nothing from his closest friend. "I thought De Valmont worked for Talleyrand. But this new relationship between Isabelle and De Valmont makes you wonder if Talleyrand is suspicious of De Valmont and assigned Isabelle to learn his secrets. There is always an objective in Isabelle's liaisons."

"Our newest information might be related to Isabelle and De Valmont's affair. The rumor is Napoleon plans to distance himself from Fouché," Ash said.

Cord sat on the corner of his desk. "It makes sense that Napoleon would like to sever his connection with the bloody past. As minister of the police, the powerful and brutal Fouché won't go down without a fight. He'll try to take his arch enemy, Talleyrand, with him. It's possible Fouché has turned to De Valmont."

"I can't keep up with the twists and turns in the French political scene." Ash shook his head. "I liked it better when we did actual espionage, not analysis."

"It was easier when we were actually at war with France and not bound by a signed treaty. This business of trying to predict what Napoleon will do and what role Talleyrand and Fouché will play is riskier than daily death threats in France," Cord said.

"But you've a far more interesting and enticing challenge in London than our French exploits." Ash waggled his eyebrows.

Cord couldn't help but smile at the thought of Henrietta as a challenge, a challenge he planned to win. And what pleasure they would have in her surrender.

"It could be worse. Your Aunt Euphemia and sister could've been at the Wentworth ball. I don't think Aunt Euphemia would believe you were working for His Majesty." Ash laughed.

"Aunt Euphemia arrived yesterday, and, trust me, the old bloodhound will know every detail by teatime.

I'd certainly like to dine out tonight and avoid her. I promised the old girl that I'd play the role of the respectable brother and escort Gwyneth this season. When she hears about the Wentworth ball, there will be hell to pay." He'd have to make amends to Aunt Euphemia, but he wasn't sure what approach he should take.

Cord sat in the chair behind his desk. "Join us for dinner. Aunt Euphemia will have to temper her comments in your presence. And Gwyneth will be thrilled to see you."

"Truly, you can't believe that I can actually calm your Aunt Euphemia? I can already hear the piercing voice: "Lord Ashworth, why is it that you're always in the vicinity when Cordelier is taking the path of a reprobate?" Ash did a perfect imitation of his aunt's imperious tone.

Cord laughed with his friend, enjoying the shared memories of their roguish past. On his return to England, he had resolved never again to be a disappointment to the grand lady. His thoughts turned to another woman he planned never to disappoint again. He'd a lot to explain to Henrietta after the Wentworth Ball, but how could he deny a relationship with Isabelle without explaining his secret work

"It's only the expectation of seeing Gwyneth after four years that keeps me from making every excuse." Ash leaned forward in his chair. "Your aunt will forgive you as she always does, but Lady Henrietta will not be as easy."

Every muscle in Cord's body tightened in aggravation. He would be repentant. Hell, he would beg if it would work. He was trapped in a twisted coil. He couldn't disclose his relationship with Isabelle without disclosing his position concerning her uncle and brother.

"Have you heard a word I've been saying?" Ash waved his cigar in the air. "Speaking of the Harcourts, have you heard anything from France? Sending a scholar instead of one of us was a mistake. I know the situation called for a linguist, but what experience does Kendal have in judging dangerous situations?"

"Sir Ramston did the best he could with the choices he had. Brinsley was sent to protect Kendal and I expect to hear from Brinsley any day," Cord said.

"Brinsley is watching Kendal?" Ash waved his cigar in the air, his voice laced with disbelief. "It's hard to imagine that Sir Ramston trusted Brinsley after the scandal with his brother's fiancée."

"Sir Ramston seems to have chosen quite a few of us to make amends in our lives by serving His Majesty on the Continent." Sir Ramston had saved Cord from a self-destructive path after the accidental death of his older brother. The former head had created a network of talented young men in France who, for various reasons, needed to take a break from their lives in England.

"Last night you didn't look like you were making amends. You looked like you'd picked up right where you'd left off."

In his isolation as a spy, he believed his fantasies of the indomitable Henrietta Harcourt had been magnified. Last night reconfirmed every yearning. There was one brief moment when his eyes had locked with Henrietta. He felt the same forceful connection, until Henrietta saw Isabelle pressing her breast against his arm and whispering into his ear. Henrietta turned away and never made eye contact for the rest of the evening.

He risked his life every day in France yet last night he felt trepidation at attempting to please one virtuous woman.

CHAPTER FIVE

"They call themselves gentleman, pshaw."
Henrietta plunked her boot into a muddy hole on the
sidewalk outside the Abchurch offices. Cold water
seeped through to her toes. "Arrogant, self-
righteous...." The unpleasant feel of wet stockings only
served to fuel her anger at the clerk and all the men in
the Abchurch office, the bastion of male superiority.

Her body shook from the insult and her soaked
clothes. The clerk, who had refused her admittance to
speak with Sir Ramston, had implied she was a
spinster worried for naught about her brother. She
bowed her head into the driving rain, glaring down at
her sodden black boots. Her dark mood festered like
the foul weather plaguing London this last week of
April.

The impact was sudden. She stumbled backward,
her arms swung in an outward arc. The slippery mud
grabbed at her boots.

The man thrust his hands into the mud, trying to
stop the impact of his large body driving her farther
down on the wet ground.

The shock of the fall left her immobile and
speechless. She was flat on her back in the middle of a
main London thoroughfare with Lord Rathbourne's
hard body pressing against her. The huge man loomed
over her, grinning with all the nerve of a blatant

libertine. Looking up into his chiseled face, she noticed the small lines surrounding his bright eyes, laughing back at her.

He had no discomfiture in his posture and took longer than necessary to right himself. He stood above her, so large, so confident and so male. "Lady Henrietta, are you injured? Allow me to help you up."

She heard amusement in his tone. Her whole body quivered with outrage, as did her voice. "I'm perfectly capable of getting up myself."

She refused the large hand beckoning to her. She tried to stand, but she was unable to gain any traction in the mud. She pushed against her wet heavy skirt, teetered a few inches from the ground and flopped. Attempting to regain some poise while lying flat on her back, she straightened her crumpled, dirty skirt, pushing it back down to cover her ankles.

Lord Rathbourne bent, grabbed her by the waist and heaved her upward.

Her body was thrust against his solid thighs and his expansive chest. Like a flash of lightning, his body heat burned into her, penetrating her soaked clothes. She felt hot, breathless, and furious. She pushed against his chest with her muddied gloves, leaving brown streaks down his impeccably cut, black waistcoat.

"Of all the rude, thoughtless behaviors. What were you thinking, plowing down the street like a bull on a rampage?"

The man had the nerve to laugh. His voice was low, gravelly. He started with a small chuckle but moved into a deep belly laugh. His giant body shook, sending waves of sensation against her.

She pursed her lips, trying hard not to smile. The absurdity of the situation overcame her. She laughed aloud. She brought her muddied glove to her lips to cover her mouth. The smell of horse manure wafted to her nose.

"Let me help you." He smiled at her in a way that felt new and heady. He had mud smeared on his cheek. He slipped his dirty glove off and brushed the dirt away from her mouth, his thumb lingered on her lower lip.

Her heart galloped against her chest.

He bent to remove her reticule from the mud. "It appears that your reticule is ruined."

Her new dress, trimmed with damask roses, worn for her meeting with Sir Ramston, was covered with mud and other unmentionable brown substances.

"It's not just my reticule that is ruined."

His eyebrows lifted slightly as if to ask a question, implying that she was ruined.

The idea that a woman's reputation could be soiled as easily as a dress was an antiquated, ridiculous concept for all free-thinking women. A man who had brought his mistress to a ball had the nerve to raise his eyebrow.

"I bid you good day."

"Allow me to escort you home."

"It's not necessary."

"I certainly wouldn't want any further misfortunes to befall you. Besides I was on my way to Kendal House."

He had been considerate after her dunking in the Serpentine, visiting her with flowers. But what reason would he have to visit Kendal House today?

Taking a firm hold of her elbow, he guided her down the street toward his carriage. "I'm sure we can forsake proprieties under the circumstances. You're completely soaked through." The timbre in his voice darkened with his close inspection of her wet dress and pelisse that clung uncomfortably to her body.

Recognition of his deepening voice and the male appreciation in his eyes raised her body temperature, despite the iciness of her wet clothes.

She continued walking, the water sloshing in her

boots. Her wet hair hung down her neck. She didn't want to think about what was sticking to her hair or her clothes. "You were on your way to Kendal House?"

"I was planning to call on you. I hoped I might take you to Hyde Park, if this rain ever lets up."

"Why would you want to do that?" Her response was rude after his timely rescue of her and Edward. But her uncontrolled attraction to a man who was arm-in arm with his mistress at the Wentworth Ball made her surly.

"I had hoped...." He appeared to be at a loss for words. "I hoped to explain my behavior at the Wentworth ball."

"Why should your behavior concern me?" Lifting her chin with the best hauteur she could muster, she turned to walk the opposite way.

He grabbed hold of her elbow and turned her toward his carriage. "Regardless of your lack of interest in my explanations, I'll escort you home today. I'll not be responsible for you catching a deathly ague."

She tried to pull away, but he tightened his hold. The wind picked up, sending a cold chill through her body. She began to shiver.

"Don't fight me on this, Henrietta."

"I didn't give you permission to call me Henrietta. And I never get ill. I need to get out of these wet clothes.'

"How is it that each time we're together you need to remove your clothes?"

Her gasp made him laugh.

She turned her head to find his face close to hers. A frisson of awareness passed down her body that wasn't due to the cold. She wanted to press herself against the warmth radiating from his body.

"We'll talk tomorrow when you're not soaking wet. You're shivering." His grip lightened as he pulled her closer to his body, guiding her into the awaiting carriage.

Heat blasted from his body like an open fire, warming one side of her. She wanted to turn and melt into the blaze. She must have hit her head on the pavement, wanting to be held by a man who hadn't changed at all since her first encounter with him.

"I also hoped to speak with your Uncle Charles. I share his interest in hieroglyphics."

Her sensual haze evaporated, suspicions flaring in an instant. She couldn't imagine him as an Egyptologist. How could she shield Uncle Charles from someone so intimidating?

She never believed the rumor that he worked for the Abchurch office as a spy, not unless he had done it as a gambling wager or on a lark. There were many stories about his high life on the Continent—gambling, duels, and women—many stories about him and women.

She lifted her eyes to catch a side glimpse of the man sitting next to her. The gloom of the day shadowed his face, giving his angles sharper edges, making him appear formidable.

She wasn't a young girl out of the schoolroom like when first she'd met him. With the death of her mother and the responsibilities she shouldered for her family, she possessed all the confidence to handle this powerful male.

"I don't recall you having any intellectual interests. Unless, of course, gambling qualifies as an intellectual challenge, since you must ponder numbers."

He twisted to look at her face. His blue eyes had darkened to the color of the storm clouds above them. "I'm impressed that you're willing to voice an opinion concerning my interests. If I recollect correctly, you were never willing to take the time to countenance an acquaintance with me to further understand where my interests might lie."

"I didn't need further acquaintance to comprehend your pursuits. They were quite apparent when we met three years ago. And by your behavior at Lady

Wentworth's ball, it doesn't seem that your horizons have expanded."

"You're clearly mistaken." His tone was dispassionate. He had an air of domineering masculinity, which might be attractive to a woman who wanted to be bullied.

She drew herself up, ready for battle. "Mistaken! I don't think anyone at Lady Wentworth's ball could be mistaken as to the nature of your relationship with the lady who accompanied you."

She revealed more than she had intended. Why did this man elicit the most overstrung reactions from her?

"I was only commenting on your mistake regarding the length of time since our first meeting. It hasn't been three years but four years since I had the pleasure of dancing with you. If I remember correctly, I danced with you twice at Lady Chillington's Ball." His gaze locked with hers and carried a distinct challenge.

Of course, it had been four years; it had been the year her mother became ill.

How did he do it? How could he so quickly turn the tables on her?

She refused to be further baited and retreated into icy silence for the remainder of the carriage ride. The ten-minute journey to Kendal House seemed like ten hours.

She had recovered her composure by the time they approached home. She had to prevent Lord Rathbourne from visiting her uncle. "I appreciate your accompanying me home. I suggest you visit my uncle on another day. He's been suffering from a mild illness and is quite indisposed."

"I'll come to Kendal House tomorrow."

She found herself backing into the corner of the carriage, unwilling to enter into another verbal contest. Like her appearance, her emotions were ruffled and messy.

The carriage stopped. She jumped forward, clearly communicating her need to remove herself from his presence.

"Good day," she said.

"Let me accompany you to your door."

"It isn't necessary. Brompton already has the door open.

Henrietta was gone without a backward glance. Cord wanted the laughing woman he had just glimpsed, the passionate woman with her green eyes flaming as she set him down for his rakish behavior.

He couldn't believe he had argued about the number of years since he had danced with her. Why did he feel that he needed to win when he was with her? His need wasn't just to win. It was to possess Henrietta Harcourt.

Four years ago, he had asked her to dance at Lady Chillington's ball because she was the only woman he didn't recognize as one of his Aunt Euphemia's potential matches. The sparks had immediately flown between them.

She wasn't pleased, like all the other debutantes he asked to dance. She couldn't mask her disdain. In frustration and in an attempt to assert his control, he pulled her too close, breaking all rules of propriety. She wasn't in any way intimidated by him, actually just the opposite. She was amused.

"Is this your only method—to bully those who won't dance to your tune?" She had laughed then, the most incredibly joyful sound. That sound had moved into every cell of his body, invigorating and calming him all at the same time.

"I didn't intend a pun, but I do like it," she'd said, continuing to smile and clearly enjoying her witticism.

She had been oblivious to his mounting awareness of her body pressed against him.

That had been the moment he'd decided she was a lady worth pursuing. Unfortunately, soon after Henrietta retired to the country to take care of her ill mother and he received his assignment in France.

Today, when she was lying under him in the mud, he had never wanted a woman more. His uncontrolled response was more than lust. He enjoyed the battle with her, the tug and pull between them. The challenge invigorated him, bringing back a youthful enthusiasm he believed he'd never regain after his brother's death.

Isabelle's appearance at the Wentworth ball had made it difficult for him to prove his serious intentions. And Henrietta wouldn't be pleased about the position he held over her uncle and her brother, especially since she considered him a rake of the first order.

Sir Ramston should never have sent Kendal into the lair of Le Chiffre. Kendal didn't have the experience to handle the intrigue. He needed to bring the young pup home before anything happened to him. He was ready to admit that his nagging worry for Kendal was because of his quick-tempered sister.

CHAPTER SIX

Lord Brinsley shivered and cursed as the icy rain soaked into his embroidered footman livery. This was Paris as Sir Ramston had promised, but he had no time to indulge in watching the exotic dancers or drinking in the outside cafes. Instead, he was concealed behind a tree, watching the Saint Germain residency of the Earl of Kendal. Sir Ramston had been succinct with his assignment. "Keep Kendal safe."

Two months ago, Brinsley had believed the life of a spy to be romantic. Now he knew better. It was tedious at best. His days were spent as the watchful footman in Le Chiffre's home, where Kendal spent his days studying Greek. At night, he played guardian shadow to Kendal. His expectation of protecting a brilliant linguist in Paris clashed with the reality of the job. None of his manly skills, well-honed after years of carousing, had been challenged.

He turned to the sound of pounding feet. A dark figure resembling Kendal raced toward Kendal's house. No more than twenty yards behind, a second figure appeared. A tall man in a long black cape chased the first man. The caped pursuer paused when the first man reached the front entrance of the mansion. The pursuer raised his arm to take aim.

Brinsley made a mad dash. The report echoed when the door opened. He was too late. A wounded Kendal fell forward into the arms of the butler then the door slammed shut.

Brinsley's heart cantered against his chest. How in the hell had Kendal left his house?

The caped assailant calmly lowered his arm and turned away from the scene.

Brinsley ran to catch the assailant who sauntered down the street as if on an evening stroll. His natural response was to tackle the man first and then figure out what game he was playing. Sir Ramston's instructions flashed through his mind. Undercover and discreet. Spying was a cat-and-mouse game and he needed to act like a cat, not the bulldog that he was. Acting the part of a cat didn't sit well. He slowed his pace to a rapid walk.

At the first corner, the assailant paused, and then glanced back over his shoulder. He anticipated the move, ducking behind one of the thick oaks lining the street.

The caped man entered the main boulevard and slowed his pace. The street was empty and there was no place to hide. The dark night afforded little cover since lanterns lit the way.

He waited, watching the man move further away. His heart raced against his chest. Every muscle tightened and strained to give chase. When the assailant turned the corner, he sprinted after him. Holding his breath, he hugged the building and edged around the corner. The man had disappeared.

He squinted hard, trying to make the man reappear on the small side street lined only with darkened houses. He swore under his breath and moved down the street. In the middle of the block, tucked between two houses, a narrow alleyway appeared. He bolted down into the smelly darkness to investigate. The slimy cobblestones were as slippery as his adversary. The alley was a dead end.

Frantic and frustrated, he retraced his steps. He

returned to the street, walking back and forth in front of the alley looking for a clue to the man's disappearance. He was hot, hot from the effort but mainly hot from the fury that seethed under his skin as he admitted the painful truth—he had just blown his first spy mission. His gut twisted in knots with the idea that Kendal might be mortally wounded because of incompetence.

He strode down the boulevard toward Kendal's house, trying to figure out a way to determine Kendal's injury without breaking his cover. Sir Ramston had directed him to keep Kendal ignorant of the intrigue that swirled around him. Sir Ramston believed that Kendal's naïveté would keep the French from becoming suspicious, but with this evening's events, all strategies were in the wind.

Kendal's house was fully illuminated and a carriage sat outside. Presumably, the doctor was in attendance and when his patient was stabilized, the doctor would depart. When the doctor got into his carriage, Brinsley would have the perfect opportunity to discover the extent of Kendal's injury.

Brinsley returned to his post under the tree in the park and waited for the doctor. Rain beat on his head and dripped into his collar during the half hour he waited.

With his bag in hand, the doctor walked toward his carriage with his head down.

Brinsley left his position and reached the doctor before he entered his carriage. "Sir, how is my good friend Kendal? I just heard the news and came as fast as I could."

The doctor shook his head. "Your friend is very lucky. A few more inches and..." The doctor raised his hand in Gallic fashion. "Unless he develops an infection, your friend will recover but he will be laid up for months."

"I'm grateful to hear my dear friend is in good

hands." If the doctor only knew the extent of his gratitude for Kendal's survival.

"It would be best to wait to visit until tomorrow. I've given him a large dose of laudanum." The doctor climbed into his carriage. "I bid you good night."

"Good night, Sir." Brinsley exhaled a slow breath of relief as the doctor drove away. But the relaxed feeling didn't last long. Guilt and self-loathing swelled into his body over his botched job of guarding Kendal and for allowing the assassin to escape.

How did it come to pass that Kendal was chased down in front of his house by a professional assassin in the middle of the night? Was Le Chiffre behind the shooting? There had been no obvious changes in Kendal's routines or the household of Le Chiffre. What had he missed?

He headed back to his rooms, where he would compose a message to Lord Rathbourne. He had no explanation for Kendal's shooting or information about the assailant to offer his new superior. The new head of espionage was known for his reckless and dangerous escapades in the spy circles. Brinsley hoped the earl would be as tolerant of his lackey's blunders.

Brinsley walked to the Tuileries at early dawn to send his message. A coded message wasn't an exposition that allowed room for excuses or explanations. The winter light gave the morning sky a pinkish hue, but the beauty was lost on him. He felt isolated and out of his depth.

He scanned the park before he moved to the tree assigned for his message. With a spade, he dug to expose the bottle from its hole under the tree. He paused repeatedly to look around the park to make sure no one observed him, then loosened the dirt around the rope and pulled up a green glass bottle from the hole. He inserted the folded message. Placing the bottle back into the ground he covered it with dirt.

Shaking the dirt from his gloves, he searched the area, wondering if the Spanish or Russians used similar methods to send their secret messages home.

On his way home, he stopped at the Café Verlet and had an aperitif, the signal that there was a message in the park. In the spy business, there was some subterfuge.

CHAPTER SEVEN

Arriving home late, Cord threw his coat on the marble table in the foyer, ignoring the footman's arm. The rumor of an attempt to assassinate Henry Addington, the prime minister, had set off a flurry of activity, keeping him at the office late tonight. Approaching the dining room, a growing sense of insecurity sat in his stomach. Aunt Euphemia had that effect on grown men.

She was going to have a bee in her turban about his mistress's attendance at the Wentworth Ball. He had compounded his sins by not being home when she and his sister arrived in London. Now, he was late for dinner. He'd gone into enemy territory with less trepidation. He entered the grandiose dining room, feigning an air of confidence, reminding himself that he was an earl.

His aunt, seated at the head of the formal dining table, was decked out in an outrageously bright green gown and matching turban. He bent down to place a kiss on her powdered cheek. "Aunt Euphemia, it's a pleasure to have you back at Rathbourne house." His nervousness disappeared at the look of fondness on the grand lady's face.

Aunt Euphemia patted his cheek affectionately. "It's good to see you, too."

Her sharp eyes were focused on his face, assessing

him, searching for clues of how he fared. It had been his aunt's support that had saved him from himself after his brother's untimely death. "You look well, my boy."

"As do you, Aunt Euphemia. You don't age. If I didn't know it was to be Gwyneth's season, I'd believe that you're the debutante," he said.

"Cord, don't try to work the Rathbourne charm on me." Her eyes warmed with the compliment. The peacock feather on her turban swayed with her head movement.

Gwyneth jumped from her seat to greet him.

He turned and swung his younger sister off her feet. Then he put his hand on his back, pretending to be in pain.

Gwyneth punched him in his arm and laughed. "I haven't gained an ounce. I think your years are starting to show. Shall I help you to your seat?" Her dark eyes were filled with the same childhood mischief he remembered.

"Gwyn, you're the one who has aged. You've become quite a beauty. Ash, what do you say about the little girl who tortured us as a child?"

Ash, seated next to his aunt, stared at Gwyneth. "She definitely has grown."

"Oh, don't let the gown and hair fool you. She's still the hoyden we knew growing up."

Cord guided Gwyneth back to her chair across from Ash.

Gwyneth wrapped her shawl around her bare arms, lowering her head coyly. "How am I going to achieve the effect of a lady in town for the season if you make such pronouncements to the gentlemen I meet?"

"First of all, Ash isn't a gentleman. Second, he has known you since you were a child in curls, always pestering us with your endless questions. Isn't that so, Ash?"

His friend was regarding Gwyneth with a

bewildered expression on his face, as if he didn't recognize the stunning woman who sat across from him. Gwyneth resembled their mother with her black hair and slanted eyes, but the liveliness and enthusiasm was clearly Gwyneth.

"Isn't that so, Ash?" Cord repeated.

"I can't think of either you or Ash as gentlemen after all I know about your exploits. Remember when you were both courting Widow Smithton?" Gwyneth asked.

Aware of Aunt Euphemia's raised eyebrows, Cord promptly changed the direction of Gwyneth's remarks. "How was your journey, Aunt Euphemia? Did the Black Swan's accommodations meet your needs?"

"The journey was fine. Let's hear about the London season. I'm ready to launch Gwyneth and hope that your most recent indiscretions won't have any effect on her reputation."

Ash stared intently down on his plate.

Cord didn't respond to his aunt's comments about his newest indiscretion. The less said, the better. As he had predicted, Aunt Euphemia was aware of all the gossip in the ton. He let most of the conversation wash over him, until the mention of Henrietta.

"Lady Henrietta Harcourt has a dashing Frenchman trailing her. Rumor has it he's smitten with her," Aunt Euphemia said.

He had trouble swallowing his bite of mutton. Henrietta couldn't be serious about the cad. Surely she could see his hypocrisy. Isabelle was De Valmont's mistress.

"Wasn't it expected that Lady Henrietta would marry the Duke of Wycliffe several seasons ago?"

He had never liked Wycliffe, just as now he disliked De Valmont.

"Cordelier, do you remember rumors around Lady Henrietta and the duke?" With her usual prescience, Aunt Euphemia perceived his interest in Henrietta.

"There were rumors that Lady Henrietta was to become betrothed to him. But her mother became ill, requiring Lady Henrietta to return to the country," he said.

Henrietta had left London before he could further his acquaintance with her, as if fate was always against him. But not any longer.

"Rumors about Henrietta? I wouldn't believe it for a minute. She is the kindest woman, and witty," Gwyneth said.

"When did you meet Henrietta?" He couldn't hide the edge in his voice.

"Henrietta?" Gwyneth raised her eyebrows. "I met her at Madame du Puis' when I went for my first fitting. She asked me to call her Henrietta." His sister's eyes sparkled with interest. "Did she give you permission, too?"

He had been with his sister and aunt no more than an hour and they had already deduced his entire private life.

"I don't recall meeting Lady Henrietta at Madame du Puis'." His aunt watched his face looking for his reactions.

"You arrived late because of your earlier commitment, Aunt. Henrietta and her good friend Amelia Bonnington were there when I arrived. I had a cozy chat with Henrietta during Amelia's fitting. Cord, did you see Amelia and Henrietta at the Wentworth Ball? They were planning to attend." Gwyneth watched his face with the same searching look as Aunt Euphemia.

If they weren't his relatives, he'd consider giving his aunt and sister positions with the Abchurch office. The only problem was Aunt Euphemia didn't take directions from anyone.

All faces were turned toward him and Ash had a ridiculous grin.

"I did see Lady Henrietta across the floor."

Cord hadn't seen her friend Amelia. All he had seen were hordes of men surrounding Henrietta, especially damn De Valmont. He was supposed to be the man taking her arm, touching her, smiling into her emerald eyes, not the entire male population of London.

"Did you dance with Lady Henrietta?" Aunt Euphemia asked. His aunt could be like a hound, relentless in her searching, pursuing.

"Henrietta told me she had danced with you in her first season. What happened the night you met her?" Gwyneth asked.

"Did she? Why would she mention that evening?" His face grew red when he remembered what an insufferable ass he had been.

"Did you dance with her at the Wentworth Ball?" His sister was becoming more and more like Euphemia.

"A colleague plagued me through the night, preventing any dancing," he said.

Gwyneth turned toward Ash when he snorted.

"Don't tell me neither of you gentlemen danced?"

"Unlike your brother, who was involved with...business, I did speak with Lady Henrietta. And she is a most pleasing lady." Ash grinned at Cord, baiting him further.

"Henrietta invited us to a soirée next week at Lady Chadwick's. I'm hoping we can attend," Gwyneth said.

"Emily Chadwick, I haven't seen her in age. Cord, will you have time to attend?" his aunt asked.

He smiled at the idea of encountering Henrietta in a crowded soiree, pressed against her soft curves. "It'd be my pleasure to attend."

When he looked up, all three dinner companions stared at him in wide-eyed disbelief.

"Is something wrong?" he asked.

Ash coughed into his napkin, barely concealing his laughter. "You surprised us with your enthusiasm to attend a soiree."

"It isn't the soiree. It's the pleasure of escorting the Beaumont ladies." Three pairs of eyes watched him as if he were the lion at the Tower of London, ready to escape his cage.

"Thank you, Cord." Gwyneth winked at him. "I'm thrilled we shall attend the Chadwick Soiree."

Darn the minx. He wasn't ready to have his privacy scrutinized by his younger sister.

The dinner felt interminable under Aunt Euphemia and Gwyneth's gaze. There was also something amiss with Ash. He was pensive and restless, not his usual bantering self. He tried to put his friend at ease. "Ash, we'll take our morning ride tomorrow?"

"Can I join you? It will be like old times, before you both left for the Continent." Gwyneth turned to Ash and smiled. "I hope you won't try to outdistance me as in the past. I believe I can keep up now."

What was the matter with his friend? Ash had such a silly look, as if someone challenged him to parade naked through Mayfair.

"I'll look forward to the challenge," Ash said.

"Cordelier, since its family, please forego the port, and let us move to the drawing room." His aunt rose from her chair and headed to the door. "I'm sure Lord Ashworth wouldn't mind if I have a few moments of privacy with you."

Aunt Euphemia knew that neither Cord nor Ash could refuse her directive.

"Gwyneth, please escort Lord Ashworth to the drawing room and summon your maid. Cord and I'll confer for a few minutes in the library."

Like a frigate to battle, Aunt Euphemia plowed down the hallway, the feather on her turban blowing like the Union Jack.

Gwyneth gave him a look of understanding when he turned and followed his aunt down the corridor to his library.

Aunt Euphemia seated herself on the settee next to

the warm fire. In its soft light, it seemed to Cord that his aunt hadn't aged a moment from his youth. Aunt Euphemia had always been part of the Rathbourne household when she wasn't travelling the world.

"Aunt Euphemia, may I offer you a sherry?"

"Brandy, my boy. I need something to take the ache out of these old bones. I can still feel that long damp carriage ride."

He poured generous drinks for himself and his aunt. Aunt Euphemia wasn't a teetotaler.

"You truly do look wonderful, Aunt Euphemia, and I'm glad you and Gwyneth are in London." He handed her the deep golden liquid.

"It feels good to be back at Rathbourne House." She took a long drink from the cut crystal glass and looked into his eyes. "How are you faring in London?" Direct as always, Aunt Euphemia wasted no time.

He wished to discuss neither his transition from spy to administrator nor his transition back into society as the new earl. Aunt Euphemia would be relentless in pursuing both.

Aunt Euphemia paused, trying to force him to answer, then she would probe to hear if his inner demons were still driving him.

He had learned a few tricks during his time on the Continent. He would outwait her.

"Are you finding it difficult to make the transition from your life in France?" she said.

"I'm adjusting. There are many challenges and responsibilities as the new earl."

"I've heard the rumors about you at Lady Wentworth's ball. Your grief drove you to outrageous behaviors in the past. I had hoped that the years in France helped you to forget."

Forget? He tried every day to forget that he had been the cause of his brother's death. If only he hadn't challenged Gray to take the jump. His return to Rathbourne house, with all its memories, stirred the feelings he kept well hidden. Anger crept into his voice. "Aunt Euphemia, I'm able to conduct myself in society."

"I know you'd never insult my dear friend, Abigail Wentworth."

"I'd never wish to insult your friend or disappoint you."

His aunt deserved an explanation, but what could he say? Protesting that he hadn't brought Isabelle would sound absurd. And the purpose of his relationship with Isabelle was to keep those rumors afloat, establishing her entrance in London society to mix with the men she was to befriend. The only glitch in the plan was Isabelle's appearance at a respectable event.

"My darling boy, you can never disappoint me. I believe deeply in you. I had hoped ..." His aunt grew quiet and gazed into the fire, regret etched on her face. She sighed. "I had hoped you might be ready to settle down. Perhaps the right woman could help you make a life. A solid marriage has been the making of many men."

If it were only that easy. His aunt loved him and stood by him, but how could he explain he wasn't sure if he was capable of happiness. Something changed after Gray's death. It wasn't just that he'd lost his brother and best friend. He'd lost his innocence, the belief that all matters could be fixed. He couldn't fix Gray's death or his parents' grief.

"Cord, you must forgive yourself."

He had nothing to say which would reassure his aunt. She was trying to shape his life into a normal existence. She had his best interests at heart.

"Is there no lady who has captured your interest? What about Lady Henrietta? I've not had the pleasure of meeting the lady, but I've known her uncle for many years."

Henrietta did give him the hope of happiness. He

was drawn to her vibrancy. She was filled with radiance, a joyfulness that he had been missing for years.

"Cord, you're looking very serious. I assume if she were the right lady you'd at least smile."

"I'm content with my work as the earl. And now I have you and Gwyneth in London."

Perhaps he should be offended that, at the age of thirty, his aunt was still interfering in his life. But he was grateful to have someone concerned about him. His aunt would be vastly entertained that the lady had captured him, and he was definitely caught. After the Wentworth Ball, he had a lot to explain to Henrietta before he could share the good news with his aunt.

"Gwyneth and I'll be busy getting ready for her presentation into society. Of course, you'll make yourself available to escort Gwyneth and introduce her to acceptable men?"

"I'm looking forward to spending time with you and Gwyneth. I can't say I'm thrilled to attend many society functions."

"Cord, you must prepare yourself for the mamas. You are a wealthy unmarried earl and a war hero. I expect you'll receive as much attention as Gwyneth."

The thought of the society mamas required fortification. He took a large gulp from his brandy glass. The smooth liquor didn't seem to be helping the tightening in his throat, as if his cravat was tied too tightly.

Aunt Euphemia rose from the settee, sweeping her ribbon-covered skirt aside to start her march to her bedroom. "I'm fagged from our long journey and will retire for the evening. We'll have time to further pursue my concerns."

Aunt Euphemia's words might sound reassuring, but the promise in her tone was familiar. *I'm not done with you, young man.*

Rising from his chair, he offered his arm. "Let me

escort you."

"Thank you. I'm able to get to my room on my own. You'd better go help your friend. He seemed to be having a difficult time adjusting to the spectacular beauty of your sister." Aunt Euphemia chuckled. "This should be a most interesting season."

CHAPTER EIGHT

Henrietta tore into the paper, too impatient to wait for a knife to open the large package from France. She needed to make this small contact with Michael. Her hands shook with the anxiety that beat through her body.

Mrs. Brompton stood over Henrietta. "Master Michael has finally sent us the silks from Paris." When excited, Mrs. Brompton reverted to her past affectations for the Harcourt children she had help raise.

"Oh, such beautiful silk... look at this purple. How do they achieve the delicate colors?" Mrs. Brompton chattered, unaware of Henrietta's heightened tension. "What about Edward's knife?"

Henrietta held up a triangular shaped, heavily wrapped object for Mrs. Brompton's inspection. "I assume this is the knife that Edward requested."

"Edward is going to be thrilled. We mustn't open the package." Mrs. Brompton was as excited by the package as her younger brother would be.

Henrietta tried to appear calm but she found it hard to breathe, as if her corset strings were tied too tight. She continued to dig through the soft material, hoping for a letter. Even the briefest note would reassure her that her worries over her wayward brother had been for naught. She felt something soft, square. Her heart beat a rapid tattoo against the whalebone. *Dear God, please....*

She peeled away a sky blue silk to find a worn, brown leather book. She tightened her grasp on the book, trying to stop her hands from shaking. She opened the dog-eared volume, looking for a letter, some word of Michael.

Leafing through the pages, she examined the columns of numbers—a code table. She immediately recognized that this extensive code table was unique. The pages had endless numbers matched to French letters and words. To the untrained eye, this table would appear no different than the one she used to decipher messages sent to Uncle Charles from the Abchurch offices.

She focused on the book trembling between her fingertips. Was this some sort of strange and oblique joke, one of Michael's McGregors? But Michael never joked about linguistics or codes. No one in the Harcourt family joked about such matters.

A memory floated to the surface—her brother's high voice fluting down the hallway, calling out to his horrified sister that he had broken one of their mother's favorite vases. "We're in a McGregor." And it seemed nothing had changed over the years. He had her involved in another McGregor.

"Just in time for the Firth ball." Mrs. Brompton startled her from her reverie. "Shall I send over the deep green silk to Madame de Puis?" Mrs. Brompton folded the silk carefully over her arm. "Remember how your mama always favored her designs? Your mama was always heads above all the other ladies."

Henrietta nodded. From the look of the cover, the book was old but why would Michael send her old French codes. Was this a book of the new codes the French were working on?

The code developed in the 1700's was too lengthy and complex to be useful at the battlefront. The

French had shortened their coded messages to track troops and communicate strategy. England and France were at peace since the Treaty of Amiens had been signed, but no one believed that Napoleon was finished in his drive for world power.

She fanned the pages of the book, looking for a letter, a note of explanation. "I must return to my work."

"So you agree? I should send the green silk?"

"Whatever you think, I'm sure..." Henrietta turned back to her desk and reached between two massive volumes retrieving a slender packet—the code table she had meticulously edited based on Abchurch's previous tables.

When he recognized her prodigious talent, Uncle Charles demanded her ability to recognize patterns, uncover subtleties the men often missed be put to use. Uncle Charles maintained she was the best code breaker in the family.

Again and again, she scanned the arrival. The French had broken new ground. She was used to deciphering with less than fifty numbers. This new table was at least one hundred and fifty numbers.

Why hadn't Michael sent the book to Sir Ramston? Nothing made sense unless Michael's work for the intelligence office had been exposed. She pressed her hand against her chest to slow her speeding heart. She needed to speak with Sir Ramston and share the codebook.

Her last attempt to gain entrance into the offices had failed dismally. Sending Sir Ramston a note for an appointment was out of the question. Women didn't communicate with men who weren't family and definitely didn't write men concerning intelligence work.

She decided to send a letter to Sir Ramston, pretending it was from her uncle. Why hadn't she considered that before?

At her appointment with Sir Ramston in Uncle Charles's place, she would be able to ask about Michael and the communications he had with Sir Ramston. Then she would give Sir Ramston the codebook.

She began the letter to Uncle Charles's old friend asking for an appointment for the following day since Lady Chadwick's soiree was tomorrow. The two-day wait would be interminable, but an unscheduled appearance at the Abchurch offices would be fruitless.

By the looks of the codebook, Michael had gotten into more than a foolish prank. Did he refer to the McGregor in the letter from her cousin because there would be dire consequences with his newest caper? A niggling uneasiness filled her body. She was going wring his neck when she saw him. Why did that idea make her eyes tear?

CHAPTER NINE

Isabelle paced in her lush sitting room, decorated with black lacquer in the Chinoisere style. The dark, exotic atmosphere with midnight blue wallpaper and japanned furniture was designed to appeal to the sensual.

Attendance at the Wentworth ball had been a miscalculation. She had followed Lucien's suggestion to distract Cord while he pursued the codebook and Lady Henrietta. But Cord's fury could jeopardize their mission of obtaining the stolen codebook.

She stopped her frantic movement. It was best not to attempt explanations but seduction. Her life had prepared her for persuading men. By the attentions of her uncle at an early age, she had become adroit at sexual manipulation. Except, now she was the victor, not the victim.

Bolton announced a visitor and ushered Comte Lucien De Valmont into her sitting room. It wasn't the arrival she had expected.

"My darling, you are enchanting this afternoon." He bowed.

She had dressed in a cornflower blue dress that made her black hair and eyes shine, creating the appearance of an innocent. Men always found the illusion of virginal innocence juxtaposed with the low-cut décolletage stimulating in a tawdry way.

Lucien raised her hand to his lips. His eyes darkened with desire as he surveyed her. "What is the English expression? You are in fine fettle today?"

Lucien was breathtakingly beautiful, every woman's fantasy. His intense blue eyes and curling blonde hair gave him the look of a devilish cherub. He slid his long narrow finger down the cleft between her breasts.

Her newest assignment from France had been to become close and intimate with the comte, a fellow agent in the service of the prime minister. She was to monitor Lucien's activities. There were suspicions about where Lucien's allegiances lay.

The irony wasn't lost on her, since she also was a double agent, turned by Cord. All the twists of her double life had gotten convoluted. She believed Cord saw past their short but passionate affair in France to know that sex wouldn't make her forget her loyalty to Talleyrand, who had saved her from the guillotine. But then men didn't believe women had the ability to separate sex from business.

"Do you not feel like playing today, my little *l'oiseau?*" His finger snaked under her breast.

In the beginning, she had found her mission of seducing the comte interesting, but now it was work.

"Or do I suspect correctly that this show of all your plumage is not for my benefit but for Rathbourne?"

Isabelle forced her breathing to slow. Maybe she wasn't as bored with her assignment as she believed.

"Lucien, *mon cheri.* I always dress to please you. You've remarked before that this gown pleases you."

"It does please me." His eyes raked her breasts. "However, I'm not sure I want to share my prize with that English prig."

He straightened and moved to the window, his cane tapping a staccato beat. He appeared to be contemplating the activity on the street below.

Isabelle prepared herself for the predictable jealous outburst. She was surprised when he continued in a mild tone of voice.

"I'll not detain you. You expect no difficulty today in dealing with Rathbourne?"

"Lucien, darling, you can have the greatest confidence in my ability to handle Lord Rathbourne." She seductively stretched on the chaise to allow Lucien the opportunity to guess how she intended to handle Cord.

Lucien's breathing became audible. He exhaled slowly. "Isabelle, my tigress, I regret there is not time for you to practice your skills on me before the arrival of Rathbourne."

He moved away from the window. He bent, taking her hand to his lips. Instead of an expected polite kiss, he slowly licked her fingers with his tongue.

"Au revoir, *ma sorciere,* until tonight."

"Lord Rathbourne, milady." Bolton announced Isabelle's next visitor in his deep bass voice. She had always known that Bolton was hired by English intelligence to report her activities, but her butler's punctilious announcement made it clear where his loyalties lay.

"Please show him in, Bolton."

"Yes, milady."

She positioned herself as a magnificent tableau. She wanted Cord to come to her. Her heart throbbed in excitement, the more dangerous the game, the more gratifying the spoils. She needed the missing codebook. Distraction and possible leads to the whereabouts of the codebook were tonight's goal. But Cord's love-making was definitely a pleasurable prize.

Cord's wavy black hair was pushed back in disarray, as if he had brushed his hands through his hair when he arrived. With his finely-chiseled features and well-formed body, Cord would make her work for France less arduous.

"Good day, Isabelle." Cord's stance was rigid, his shoulders tightly pulled back.

He was in control. The game would be easy, since it was a short path from anger to passion.

"Cordelier, *mon cheri*, are you in a snit this afternoon? Come, sit here, and let me help you relax." Using her sultry voice, she writhed on the settee, moving her hips sinuously across the cushions.

His cheeks flushed; she heard him take in a breath. The high and mighty Cordelier Beaumont was going to be an easy English whale to reel in. He cleared his throat and paused as if he could control the tension building in the room by keeping his distance.

"Please, Cordelier, come sit." Emphasizing the French pronunciation of Cordelier, she beckoned to him, like a siren from the mythical Greek Seas, swathed in her azure blue dress.

He cleared his throat again as if struggling with his breath. "Isabelle, your role as my mistress doesn't continue when we're in private."

She loved his reaction. The English were so predictable. Correct procedure, correct roles. If he needed her to clarify what their relationship could be, that was fine with her.

"Darling, I know what my role is in society, but we can have any relationship we both desire when we're together in private. Can I show you this afternoon the relationship I desire with you?"

She drew her lips into a pouty "O" shape to suggest what she could do with her mouth, and at the same time, she rubbed her breasts, tempting him with the prospect of the pleasure the perfect orbs could bring. At the young age of fifteen, she had learned the power of her breasts.

Her uncle had not been able to resist them, nor had the sixty-year-old Marquis who had purchased her from her uncle. When the guillotine had rid of her of the Marquis, Talleyrand had offered her an escape and the chance to control her fate.

She continued to stimulate herself, rubbing her breasts and slightly spreading her legs. Watching the domineering Lord Rathbourne weaken was stimulating, and her breathing became short pants. Her control over this powerful specimen of masculinity was exhilarating.

His eyes had turned steely and his voice got rough. "Stop it. Stop it, Isabelle. We're here to work together."

She couldn't suppress a laugh. Seducing Cord was enthralling, and she wasn't about to let it end. "*Cheri*, we can work together, but I don't think you'll think of it as work." She leaned toward him, removing one of her hands from her breast to reach for him. "Come here, darling. Let me do all the work." She eyed his massive erection. "You're under a lot of stress at the office. Let me help you relieve all your tension."

The mention of the office helped bring Cord back to the purpose of his visit. It would be so easy to walk the few steps and indulge in all the pleasures Isabelle Villier was offering. It had been a long time since he had a woman, and he would have a powerful release with Isabelle— but that's all it would be, a release. There was only one woman he wanted and it wasn't just for carnal pleasure. He'd had a lifetime of empty carnal pleasure. He wanted something more, something lasting.

He watched Isabella release her luscious breast from the confines of her morning dress. He'd have to be a monk or a eunuch not to respond to the performance Isabelle was enacting. His erection began to throb.

Dampening down his masculine, primitive response, he reminded himself that he had come to get information about De Valmont, Isabelle's lover.

"Isabelle, desist from this." He struggled to regulate his breathing. "I'm here about your appearance at the Wentworth ball and how you'll go on as my mistress."

She maintained a smile that didn't reach her eyes. "Cordelier, do we have to be so serious? We can play and still do our jobs."

"Isabelle, I've no need to play. Let us say I've others..." He paused. "To meet my needs."

She eyed his prominent manhood. Her lips and eyes warmed into a knowing look. "It's fine, *mon cheri.* I'll be here when the others..." She snickered, "aren't available, since I'm your mistress."

"Thank you for your concern." His voice came out harsher than he planned. "Why did you attend the Wentworth Ball?"

"You said we were to make our relationship obvious. I thought you wanted a public display to establish yourself in your old reprobate identity to distract from your more secret responsibilities."

She was lying, but why? Isabelle knew the rules. He needed to discover what she and De Valmont were planning. He assumed that De Valmont also worked for Talleyrand, but there were rumors that De Valmont also worked for another powerful person who sought to stir dissidence in the French émigrés. He wanted to know if Isabelle was involved with the subversive plot.

"The plan is for us to attend social events where men, especially foreign men, are known to relax and confide secrets that they wouldn't consider speaking in a respectable setting."

Isabelle leaned back and sighed, fully aware that doing so enhanced her breasts and wouldn't go unnoticed. "How absolutely boring. I can think of more entertaining ways to establish our relationship."

He needed to get out of this space. Isabelle had perfected the art of tempting a man. He would do better questioning her away from her planned seduction. "Let us take my phaeton around Hyde Park to reinforce what you started last week at the ball. Let's make a spectacle at the park."

CHAPTER TEN

Cord drove his matched set of black horses through Hyde Park and acknowledged that Isabelle played the role of mistress sublimely. No one would guess that he had just rejected her sexual advances and that their relationship was platonic. She flirted lightly with him, publicly allowing herself to be seen gazing at him as if he were the center of her universe. He never underestimated anyone who was so adroit at changing their roles.

"Cordelier, smile fondly at me. Here comes the biggest gossip in the ton, Lady Billingsworth."

Hildegard Billingsworth was worth her weight in innuendo. And if the size of the turquoise dress she wore today was any indication, she was going to be going full steam by teatime.

Lady Billingsworth spoke loudly enough for him to hear when her carriage passed by them. With just the right amount of practiced outrage, she intimated that the old Earl of Rathbourne would be shocked to see his son, the new earl, with a French... The last word was lost, as it was intended to be. Her companion ladies tittered at the implication.

So much for his new image. He didn't want to guess what his father would've thought. He was lost in musing about his father when he saw Henrietta. The sunlight shone on her golden hair, giving the red streaks the effect of fire. She rode upon a mammoth horse, not a tame mare that ladies were supposed to ride. The silence in the park was peppered with her laughter, sending anticipation through his body. She was riding with Edward and a gentleman whom he couldn't identify.

With the gentleman's back turned, his face remained hidden, but his posture and stance looked familiar. He couldn't believe it. Ash was riding with Henrietta. He was going to mutilate his friend.

In his annoyance, he inadvertently pulled too tightly on the reins. The sensitive horses reared, thrashing against their confinement.

Henrietta and Ash wheeled their horses toward the sound. They both stared at him, watching him pull in the horses. Ash laughed loudly. He watched Henrietta's tight intake of breath when she recognized his companion.

Her younger brother said loudly, "What a fine pair. Have you seen any better?" The innocent innuendo wouldn't be lost on Ash, who snorted.

Isabelle, sensing his discomfort, joined in the fracas, primed for retaliation after this morning's rejection. "Cordelier, darling, do you want me to help you?" She pressed herself closer to him, running her hand along his leg.

He thought he heard Henrietta gasp, but perhaps it was only his guilty imagination.

Isabelle was laughing gaily when they drove by the group.

He shot Ash a look that promised retribution. An unrepentant Ash smiled back.

Henrietta bent down to speak with her brother, avoiding them and effectively distracting her brother from the improper scene unfolding.

"Isabelle unhand me this instant," he said *sotto voce*.

"Lady Henrietta Harcourt?" She laughed heartily.

"Is she the other who offers you comfort?"

Outrage coursed down into his gut. "Keep silent." He did want Henrietta to be the one who brought him comfort, but after today's foray with Isabelle, it was going to be almost impossible to convince Henrietta that Isabelle wasn't his mistress.

Henrietta wasn't making it easy for him to tell her about the Wentworth Ball and now this newest escapade would be hard to explain without revealing his work. He planned to clarify his position with the Abchurch office and his relationship with Isabelle but he had deep fears that Henrietta wouldn't be receptive to his role over her family. She hadn't been home to him all week, however Henrietta Harcourt wouldn't be able to outmaneuver him much longer. The Chadwick soiree was tomorrow.

Henrietta and Edward had paused on their morning ride to greet Lord Ashworth. The friendly gentleman had been regaling them with hilarious anecdotes about Lady Billingsworth.

"Hen, look at that pair," Edward shouted and pointed. The thunder of hooves, snorting, and clatter of wheels came from behind her.

She wheeled Minotaur toward where her brother gestured. Lord Rathbourne, moving in a phaeton toward them, fought to control a magnificent pair of black horses. Seated next to him was Isabelle Villiers, amused at his difficulty.

Anyone looking upon Isabelle Villiers's décolletage didn't have to make a big leap to know why Lord Ashworth coughed into his hand to hide his amusement about Edward's innocent comment.

"Hen, isn't that Lord Rathbourne?" Edward inquired when the couple passed them.

She tried to appear disinterested, adjusting her

riding skirt over her sidesaddle.

"Hen, why didn't you speak to him?" Edward asked in a loud voice. "I'd really like to learn more about his horseflesh."

Henrietta bit the side of her mouth, suppressing her need to say anything about flesh in front of her younger brother. "Lord Rathbourne was fully occupied." She looked directly at Lord Ashworth, challenging him to make any further comments.

"His wife is a looker, isn't she, Lord Ashworth?" Edward's whisper was fully audible. He was imitating the banter he must have heard many times among Michael and his friends.

Lord Ashworth leaned over to speak to her, out of Edward's hearing. "This isn't what it appears." He gestured to the couple who had passed them.

Trying to feign indifference, she spoke with the right amount of insouciance. "He's planning on marrying her, then?"

Lord Ashworth chortled loudly. Lord Rathbourne turned back when he heard his friend laugh.

Bored by the adult conversation, Edward and Gus, his stout, four-legged companion, continued to the Serpentine to throw and retrieve sticks, the favorite activity of the boy and the yellow dog.

"It looks like Cord has returned to the reckless life he led before he went to the Continent, but he has changed. He'll never return to the life of dissolution." Lord Ashworth watched her closely, gauging her response to his disclosure. "He suffered terribly after his brother died."

Her gaze drifted upward, taking in the brilliance of an almost opal sky. She remembered the pain, her deep anger and bewilderment when her mother died. Could Cord's wild behavior have been a reflection of his grief? His controlling, cold manner a defense to protect himself from the pain?

Lord Ashworth leaned over his roan. "He's my

closest friend and I want to see him put the past behind him."

"You're a good friend, but I'm unsure what this has to do with me."

"You held his interest before he left for the Continent and he hopes to further his acquaintance with you now that he has returned." A wide grin spread over Lord Ashworth's boyish face. "He was ready to kill me just now for talking with you." Lord Ashworth's smile widened, enjoying his friend's wrath. "He isn't the easiest man."

"I'm sure Lord Rathbourne has many endearing qualities."

Lord Ashworth laughed loudly, his head thrown back. "I'm sure his mother would've found him endearing if she were still living, but I'm not sure I can think of anyone else who would find Cord endearing. Uncompromising, stubborn, controlling would be how I'd describe him and a courageous and loyal friend."

What could she say after such a heartfelt testimony? "Lord Ashworth, it's been most enlightening to hear about the gentleman. But you're under a misapprehension about Lord Rathbourne's feelings for me. We're mere acquaintances."

"Hen, come and see Gus try to catch the swans!" Edward's voice traveled the distance. After their last excursion, she didn't trust Edward and Gus at the Serpentine.

"Excuse me, Lord Ashworth. I must attend to my brother and his dog."

Lord Ashworth tipped his head in a bow from his horse and said under his breath but loud enough for her to hear, "Not mere acquaintances for long."

She turned Minotaur toward the path leading to the Serpentine. She was a grown woman with many responsibilities, but when it came to understanding relationships between women and men, she was ignorant. She wished there were a book that dissected men and their behaviors like Greek participles. She was brilliant at dissecting Greek participles.

Four years ago, Lord Rathbourne had approached her at Lady Chillington's ball with an air of superiority and haughtiness. His dark aristocratic features and powerful muscular physique created a commanding presence, but his distracted and insincere gestures annoyed her. For him, asking a young debutante to dance was sport, nothing more than a form of entertainment, simply something to laugh about with his jaded friends.

Soon after their dance, she caught a glimpse of him leading Lady Atherton, a widow of some repute, into a curtained alcove. His fingers trailed along the woman's neck. His other hand gently moved her into the hidden area. She might have been an innocent, but she knew there was only one reason for Lord Rathbourne to lead a lady into a cloistered area. Her suspicions were confirmed when she heard the gentleman near her chortling about Rathbourne and his newest paramour. The gentleman, unaware of Henrietta, described in scathing details Lady Atherton's known appetites.

Lord Rathbourne had the nerve to come back and ask her for a second dance after his exploits with Lady Atherton behind the curtain. Unable to refuse a gentleman, she was forced to dance with him again. She never admitted that a tiny, a very tiny part of her fantasized about the pleasurable activities in the alcove. And she never, ever admitted that in her fantasy she was the captivating woman led behind the curtain by the experienced rake.

From that night forward, she had spent her first season avoiding Lord Rathbourne. She wasn't sure if it was because of his insincerity or her own frightening fantasies. A few weeks later, her season ended prematurely. Her mother had fallen ill and, for the next years, she had no time for a young woman's

fancies about captivating lords and secret pleasures.
Her time was spent tending to her dying mother.

CHAPTER ELEVEN

Henrietta stood with Mrs. Brompton at the top of the stairs. "Please remind Uncle Charles that I've gone to Lady Chadwick's soiree this afternoon."

"A soiree? You're going to a soiree?" Mrs. Brompton didn't try to hide her surprise. The housekeeper didn't hold back her feelings or opinions concerning the Harcourt children. Having grown up in the Harcourt household as a young maid and been with the children through the death of their parents, Mrs. Brompton acted more as an elder relative than a servant.

"The soiree is to solicit support for the French émigré community." Her mother had worked tirelessly for the émigrés and Henrietta had taken over the cause. If this were merely a frivolous social event, she wouldn't have been attending

"Ahh, the French émigrés." Mrs. Brompton raised her eyebrows but chose not to comment.

"The French émigrés are experiencing a backlash in England." She channeled her frustration into her hands by waving them in the air. "The English fear Napoleon and project their anger onto anyone who is French."

"Napoleon is the devil, causing all those young men's deaths."

"Why can't the English people see that the émigrés aren't at fault for Napoleon's ambition to take over Europe?" Henrietta stooped to collect two partially gnawed sticks peeking out from under the heavy mahogany console in the hallway. "How is Gus able to unearth so many sticks from our garden?"

"Our Gus is a retriever of the best sort," Mrs. Brompton replied affectionately. Gus was held in the highest regard by all for his constant devotion to Edward after their mother's death.

"Uncle Charles may forget that I'm at Lady Chadwick's and ..." She paused.

Mrs. Brompton patted Henrietta on the arm. "Don't worry about your Uncle Charles. I'll not let him get into a dither about your whereabouts."

"Uncle Charles and I've already discussed the plans for the afternoon. Edward and Mr. Marlow are planning to have tea with him. Military strategy will be the topic."

"Master Edward loves all the talk of guns and soldiers as much as Uncle Charles."

"It sounds as if Amelia has arrived." Henrietta and Mrs. Brompton moved down the main steps toward the peals of laughter.

"Brompton, I'm convinced you've discovered the tonic of youth," Henrietta's childhood friend teased the elderly man.

"Thank you, my lady. It's marriage to a fine woman that keeps me young." Brompton spoke loudly, insuring his approaching wife would hear him.

"Alfred, don't try to sweet talk me." Mrs. Brompton's words were matter of fact, but the wrinkles around her eyes crinkled.

Henrietta embraced Amelia. "What an interesting ensemble you've donned for the soiree." Amelia wore a flowing, white gown with the fabric tied in knots at her shoulders.

"Do you like it? I've been experimenting with less structure. Our clothes should enhance movement, not hinder it. I've taken inspiration from the talks I suffered through with you on ancient Greece."

"That you could be inspired to create this stunning gown from Professor Hardwick's discussion of ancient Greek choruses is mind-boggling."

Amelia examined the modified pale green muslin that Henrietta wore. "What have you done to your beautiful dress?"

She must have been crazy to believe for a minute that Amelia wouldn't notice the changes she had made to her dress. "I had all the frippery removed. It was too much." She had Alice, her maid, remove the large sash and bow in the back of the gown.

"Sometimes I don't believe you're French. Even Michael shows appreciation for fashion. Has he sent you the silks from France? He promised me a daring shade of purple."

"He didn't forget. They just arrived." Hard as it was to hide her emotions from Amelia, Henrietta kept up the banter about Michael. "We're late, but when we return I'll give you the silk. I can't wait to see what gown you'll create from purple silk—not the color of choice for an unmarried woman."

"Exactly why I choose it."

As much as she wished to confide in Amelia, she couldn't share her worries about Michael's safety. Amelia had no idea of the secret work the Harcourt family did for the crown.

Linking arms, the friends departed Kendal House.

Henrietta and Amelia entered the crowded ballroom, maneuvering their way to the hostess. The scent of blooming hothouse roses and freesia filled the air in the heavily decorated room. Crocodile-footed couches, columns, and statues of Egyptian goddesses crowded the space. It seemed she couldn't escape the Egyptian madness.

Lady Chadwick turned toward Henrietta, a huge smile encompassing her round face. With her arms outstretched, the portly woman gathered Henrietta close to her. "My darling girl, I'm so glad you've come. You're as beautiful as your dear mama, with the same magnificent green eyes."

Henrietta curtsied to her mother's friend. "Thank you, my lady. I'm honored by the comparison."

"Your mother would be very proud of your endeavors to carry on her cause," Lady Chadwick said.

Henrietta scanned the crowd of the stylish ton. "Congratulations, Lady Chadwick. It's quite a crush." A distinctive large male head with ebony hair stood above the crowd.

"I'm pleased by today's turnout." Following Henrietta's gaze, Lady Chadwick added, "And pleased that Lord Rathbourne has joined us. His presence gives our cause great credibility."

Henrietta was having the opposite reaction. Watching him carelessly run his fingers through his tousled hair caused warm sensations to flitter along her skin as if someone ran a feather along her arm.

"Oh my goodness, another dashing gentleman. I must welcome him." Lady Chadwick moved to greet Comte De Valmont who stood at the entrance to the ballroom.

Henrietta turned toward Amelia. "I can't believe he's here. I hoped not to have to converse with him."

"Already tired of the wondrous blond deity's devotion to you?"

Henrietta did wonder about the comte's interest in a bookish, non-stylish woman like herself. "Be serious, Amelia. Not Comte De Valmont. Why would Lord Rathbourne be at a soiree? I'm sure this isn't his usual social fare."

"Have you forgotten that you invited his sister? Gwyneth said she and her aunt were going to be looking for a bride for him and he looks quite interested in the lady with whom he's talking."

Lord Rathbourne's broad shoulders blocked a view of the woman he was bent over. Henrietta refused to acknowledge that Lord Rathbourne or his behavior could upset her, but the heavy lump of her morning crumpet sat uneasily in her stomach as she watched his obvious interest in the unseen woman. "The man's a reprobate. It'd be just like him to be courting a young innocent woman and still make an appearance at Hyde Park with his mistress. I feel sorry for the young woman."

"Really? You needn't feel sorry for the young woman. I can see the lady. It's Gwyneth. Let's greet her."

"I'd love to visit with Gwyneth, but unfortunately it would mean speaking to her brother, and I've no need to speak with him."

"The lady doth protest too much." Her friend couldn't resist teasing her.

"Lord Rathbourne isn't a respectable gentleman." She delivered her standard response about Lord Rathbourne. But neither Amelia nor she believed the words.

"Pshaw. You'd be absolutely bored with a respectable gentleman. He seems to have seen you, Henrietta, and the scandalous gentleman is headed our way."

Lord Rathbourne with his compelling opalescent eyes stared across the room at her, causing her body to tremble as if she were stricken with a mysterious malady. "I don't want to speak with him."

Lord Rathbourne wound his way through the crowd. His progress was slowed by the admirers who stopped him to deliver greetings.

"We can't just run out of here," Amelia said.

She didn't want to face Lord Rathbourne or the confusing, angry feelings she'd battled since seeing him with his mistress. Scanning the crowded room for

an escape, she spotted the conservatory. She navigated
through the crush, smiling on her route to the opposite
side of the room, passing no one she immediately
recognized. With the conservatory in sight, she began
to relax. Amelia had deserted her to talk with Lady
Mountlake.

To her right, the shrill Lady Billingsworth called
out to her.

Not slowing down, Henrietta raised her hand,
attempting a small wave. Her hand connected with the
bottom of the tray held by a footman who was passing
champagne. The flutes flew off the tray, spraying
champagne over the ample Lady Billingsworth.

The lady screamed and screamed. The cold liquid
dripped down Lady Billingsworth's thickset face onto
her mauve dress, revealing her oversized bosom in a
most unflattering manner. The unscathed footman
stood frozen as if in tableau.

"You idiot!" shrieked the lady at the hapless
footman.

The entire room, witness to the unfolding drama,
became silent.

Henrietta's indignation at the treatment of the
innocent footman made her speak. "Lady
Billingsworth, I am at fault. I am truly sorry."

Lady Billingsworth ignored the apology and
blustered about the stupid footman and her dress.

The situation was growing into a comical farce when
Comte De Valmont moved to Henrietta's side. "Excuse
me, Lady Billingsworth, may I be of assistance?" The
perfectly formed man who resembled an archangel on
a medieval icon, graced Lady Billingsworth with such
a charming smile that the lady became befuddled and
stopped shouting.

The comte's charming smile didn't affect her as it
did Lady Billingsworth.

"Oh, Comte De Valmont, as always the perfect
gentleman," Lady Billingsworth crooned. "How

delightful of you to come to my rescue."

"Shall I escort you to a retiring room so a maid can attend you?" offered the gentleman in the slightest French accent.

"Lady Billingsworth, please allow me to help," Henrietta said.

"I'll have my maid sponge my dress in a moment." Lady Billingsworth, oblivious to the improper manner in which her dress was clinging to her breasts, moved closer to Comte De Valmont. "Tell me, Comte, have you been traveling? I haven't seen you in society for a few days."

A flash of annoyance crossed Comte De Valmont's face, but his full lips tightened into a smile. "I'm flattered that you've noticed my brief absence. I've been visiting friends in the country.

He took Henrietta's hand and kissed it, holding her hand longer than was proper. "Lady Henrietta, a pleasure."

She tried to pull her hand away.

His bright eyes darkened and he squeezed her hand firmly before releasing her. "Lady Chadwick shared how you've taken it upon yourself to continue your mother's unfailing commitment to our people. I hope you'll allow me to help in your noble efforts."

Disarmed by De Valmont's effusive compliments, Henrietta felt warmth move to her face and neck. Her passion for the cause of émigrés didn't usually inspire a flood of praise.

"Thank you. I'm one of many who support our displaced compatriots. My French mother was my inspiration."

Lady Billingsworth, distracted by the footman attending to her, leaned toward the comte, trying to hear the conversation. "I remember your dear mother," Lady Billingsworth interrupted.

"Your mother must have been a woman of great compassion and sympathy," De Valmont continued.

A delightful pleasure coursed through her. She didn't often get to speak about her mother. "Our household was filled with French émigrés and my father would tease that one wouldn't know by our home that we were English.'"

"Not English? By Jove, your father was a scion of English aristocrats. And your Uncle Charles, a renowned scholar and your brother. Not English?" Mrs. Billingsworth puffed up like a hen about to expel an egg. "What an absurd idea. The men in your family are the best of what England has to offer."

"Thank you, Lady Billingsworth." Bemused, she looked at Comte De Valmont for a shared understanding. His face tensed in a calculating expression.

"My heavens!" Lady Billingsworth bellowed when she stepped on a broken champagne flute. "Footman, sweep this mess up immediately."

"Lady Billingsworth, may I assist you to the retiring room?" Henrietta asked again.

"Child, I don't need your assistance. Footman!"

De Valmont moved closer to Henrietta. "How's your brother enjoying his days in France?"

Henrietta stiffened. Although it wasn't a secret, why did he probe about her brother?

"Footman!" Another screech by Lady Billingsworth resounded in the space.

"My brother is enjoying his holiday with our relatives now that we are able to visit France with the Treaty of Amiens," Henrietta said.

The comte's light eyes examined her closely. "Your brother is a brilliant linguist."

Cold pinpricks scattered along the surface of her skin from his icy inspection. "You're interested in linguistics?" She wasn't going to share anything about her brother.

"I dabble a bit. As I told your uncle, I'm interested in Ancient Egypt and hieroglyphics.

What was the relationship between attractive men and hieroglyphics?

"Everything Egyptian is passé," Lady Billingsworth interjected.

"Do you also share the talent in your family for linguistics?" He was standing uncomfortably close, studying her as if she were an exotic species.

Since women weren't supposed to acknowledge their intellectual pursuits, no one had ever asked about her abilities. Instead of being flattered, she found the comte's question intrusive. Why his interest in her mother, her uncle, her brother, and now herself? She experienced the same disquiet in his questions as when she had first met him and when she had ridden with him in Hyde Park.

Henrietta felt Lord Rathbourne's approach behind her before she saw him or inhaled his distinctive masculine scent of lime and starch.

Soaking wet, standing in broken glass, Lady Billingsworth wasn't going to budge when the two most handsome, titled gentlemen in London converged. "Lord Rathbourne, how lovely to find you back in English society."

Lord Rathbourne maintained his usual arrogant hauteur, peering down at Lady Billingsworth's less than decorous appearance.

The older woman wasn't deterred by Lord Rathbourne's silence. "Your father would be pleased to see you taking your expected place in society."

Ignoring Lady Billingsworth, he turned to Henrietta and lifted one eyebrow. "Lady Henrietta, I'm glad to see that you are drier than Lady Billingsworth." A true gentleman would never mention her mortifying dip in the Serpentine or her fall in the mud or the state of Lady Billingsworth's dress.

Lady Billingsworth gasped when she looked down. Her face became mottled. "I can't believe the French idiots Lady Chadwick employs." She swept past Lord

Rathbourne, continuing her tirade about French servants.

Henrietta was considering a scathing response when De Valmont spoke. "I didn't think soirees—and ladies—were your usual afternoon pleasures, Rathbourne." De Valmont's emphasis on ladies obviously referred to Rathbourne's new inamorata.

Lord Rathbourne's face flushed a bright crimson.

Henrietta wasn't sure if he was embarrassed or in a rage. It was hard to imagine Lord Rathbourne embarrassed by censure of his behavior.

Lord Rathbourne answered in a soft, menacing tone, "I find it unusual, De Valmont, that you take an interest in my pleasures."

She was missing part of the innuendoes that were being sallied between the two men. She didn't think this was only over Isabelle de Villiers. "Gentlemen, please excuse me. Lady Chadwick is signaling me."

Whispering close to her ear, De Valmont intoned in French that the English had no sense of humor about love affairs.

In a feigned whisper, she replied that some English didn't possess a sense of humor. She turned to walk past Lord Rathbourne, still smiling at De Valmont.

Lord Rathbourne gripped her elbow. His face was impassive but the clenched muscle in his right cheek ticked. "Humor is in the eye of the beholder," he answered in a perfect French accent. "I shall escort you to our hostess, safeguarding you from any further disasters."

"I'm totally capable of walking without your assistance," she said.

His hand tightened on her elbow, guiding her away from De Valmont. "As you demonstrated in the rain or today with the champagne?"

He turned her toward him, his back toward De Valmont.

Lord Rathbourne believed he could steer her willy-nilly like a child.

He loomed over her in his tightly-fit black morning coat. "Lady Henrietta." He paused as if considering his words. His face was tight with suppressed emotions she couldn't read.

He stood close, too close. She could see the black prickly stubble growing on his chin when she stared at his cravat. She avoided looking into his eyes since she knew they would be steely gray.

"De Valmont is not the type of man you should associate with." He growled each enunciated word. "His reputation is well known."

Her entire body tightened in anger. She didn't have any trouble looking at him now. "You've the audacity to speak to me about another gentleman's reputation?" Her voice shook. "What about your reputation? What about your behavior at the park?" Her face was heating up from a fury she didn't understand. People were turning to stare at them. She lowered her eyes as if she could hide the outrage pulsating into every cell of her fuming body.

"I told you I'd call on you today," he said between clenched teeth.

"And when I wasn't home you sought other company?" She tried to control her bewildered feelings. Why was she so angry?

"Isabelle isn't anything to me. Is that why you're allowing that French fool to follow you? Make no mistake, I've little patience with the game you're playing."

"You think I'm playing a game?" Aware of the looks they were receiving, she tried to control the rage rising in her chest, giving her the sensation that she was a hot air balloon about to burst.

"If you would give me the opportunity, a private moment to explain, I'm not the man you met four years ago." He stepped closer, his large frame towering over her.

Henrietta backed away from his intimidating posture. She couldn't think when he was near her, her feelings got all befuddled.

"I admit to a certain recklessness when I was younger, but De Valmont...he's of another ilk. He's..."

He was warning her away from De Valmont, as if she was the same naïve girl he'd met four years ago. "I'm quite capable of judging gentlemen and their worth."

She turned and walked away from the exasperating *gentleman*.

CHAPTER TWELVE

Cord rejoined Gwyneth, forcing a smile toward her and some young pup.

Gwyneth gently touched his arm. "Cord, are you ill?"

"It's insufferably hot in here. Excuse me."

He walked to the open French doors, avoided the gaze of the sophisticated women who sent him subtle and not so subtle messages. Outdoors, he inhaled the warm spring air. Above the din inside, he could hear Henrietta's hearty laugh, so unlike the proper ladies, who tittered at best.

He had lost control again. He, who never lost control, a man admired for his logical demeanor, unflappable under duress. Because of his rampant jealousy, he'd acted like an idiot accusing her of playing games.

Couldn't she see he was a grown man with sincere intentions toward her? She viewed him as the young man he had been, struggling with remorse over his brother's death, numb to all emotions.

Her laughter as she pressed against him in the mud, their limbs intertwined, revived him as if he had been asleep for the last four years. He had been too long without any genuine happiness in his life. When Henrietta was near, his world became a brighter place.

He had attended the soiree to arrange a time when

he could speak with her. He had felt a rush of anticipation when he saw her across the room but then realized she was trying to escape him. It amused him at first to see her darting through the crowd, as if she could hide from him. He understood her avoidance. She wanted to deny the magnetism, the sexual tension that flared between them, ready to combust. It was a rare occurrence to feel a deep connection with another person, and he wasn't going to let her deny what lay between them.

The thrill of her lush body under his kept him awake last night. He envisioned removing the wet, molded dress clinging to her abundant curves to expose the soft, sensual woman. Under the prim exterior, Henrietta was a fiery, passionate woman, just waiting for him.

Henrietta laughed too loudly at Amelia's joke, but her latest altercation with Lord Rathbourne was taking its toll. The man was impossible. He had the nerve to accuse her of playing games. He had the ability to upset her equanimity each time they met. She moved toward another of her mother's friends, Baroness Lemieux.

An unknown matron in an outrageous outfit approached her. The beaming lady's entire ensemble was a clash of purples and greens. The lady must've walked into her dressmaker's establishment and blindly selected the brightest colors possible.

"Lady Henrietta, I presume?" The lady's eyes twinkled in amusement. Her face creased with laugh lines from years of happiness.

"I'm Lady Henrietta Harcourt, my lady." In deference to the older woman, she curtsied.

Breaking all manner of propriety, the woman

embraced Henrietta, pulling her against her billowy bosom. "I'm pleased to meet you, my dear. I'm Cordelier's Aunt Euphemia."

Aunt Euphemia smelled of roses. The mauve feather topping the lady's shocking headdress tickled Henrietta's cheek. Lady Beaumont, like her impossible nephew, obviously didn't bother with decorum.

"And I to meet you, Lady Beaumont." There was something familiar about the lady, her posture, her horrendous fashion style. Lady Beaumont was the woman in the alley who accosted the man with her umbrella. Henrietta was speechless and shocked.

"The pleasure is all mine. I haven't enjoyed myself this much in ages. I've been waiting a long time for this moment, to see my nephew abandon his self-possession. I hope you won't mind me calling you Henrietta and you must call me Euphemia."

"I'd be honored, my lady." Henrietta was perplexed by the lady's implications.

"How's dear Charles? Aunt Euphemia asked. "I'd like so much to have you both for tea."

Henrietta's heartbeat missed a beat or two or three. "You know my uncle?"

"I've known Charles since my debut a few years back." She guffawed in a very unladylike manner.

Henrietta twisted the cords of her reticule. "My uncle isn't able to do the social rounds. He's been battling a head cold. I don't think it is advisable for him go out." She hated to lie to one of her uncle's acquaintances.

"I'm sorry to hear that. I'd love to visit with him." Lady Beaumont's pointed look made Henrietta's stomach twirl with anxiety.

"You must bring your uncle to Rathbourne House when he's feeling better. We'll have many occasions to be together."

Henrietta placed her hand on her chest, trying to soothe her racing heart.

"Oh, I didn't mean to shock you, but I've seen today the way my nephew behaves around you," Aunt Euphemia said.

There was an awkward silence as Henrietta grasped Lady Beaumont implications. "My lady, you're mistaken. Lord Rathbourne extended his assistance to me and my brother. I'm grateful for his help, but there is nothing more."

Lady Beaumont's eyes flashed in keen intelligence. "My nephew isn't the man he presents to society. I knew when the time came for him to settle down, he'd show good sense. I'll look forward to our next chat." With that shocking pronouncement, the stout lady swept past Henrietta.

Henrietta took several slow breaths, trying to calm herself and her galloping heart. She wasn't sure if her heart galloped with fear because of Uncle Charles or the idea that Lord Rathbourne was serious about her.

Lady Beaumont and Lord Ashworth—both had implied that Lord Rathbourne planned to court her. It was reminiscent of Chillington's Ball when Lord Rathbourne had disappeared with Lady Atherton, courting a respectful lady while dallying with a mistress. She clenched the strings of her reticule.

She would never consider such a man for a husband. Her short courtship by the Duke of Wycliffe had been enough for a lifetime. Her father had died two years before, leaving a young Michael to make family decisions. The duke, sophisticated and powerful, was able to convince all of them, including her mother and herself, that he would make a wonderful husband.

She hated to recall her own naiveté at the age of eighteen when she had been enthralled with the striking duke's presence and flattered by his attentions. She believed he wanted an intelligent, strong woman as his duchess. How shocked she had been to learn he had no interest in sharing his life with a woman with independent thoughts or feelings.

He wanted a woman of the correct bloodline to bear his children.

His words would always be burned in her memory. He saw "no need to change his life or his mistress" upon marriage. He didn't need a companion; he needed a wife to provide him with heirs.

Cord's aunt was most ill-informed. She would never contemplate another match with a man who wanted a lady for heirs and a mistress for his pleasure.

CHAPTER THIRTEEN

Henrietta gazed up at the darkening sky and picked up her pace, hoping to miss the imminent downpour. She usually didn't mind the circuitous conversations at the Society of Ladies of Classic Greece meetings but today she had little patience for the usual social patter. She was wound tight with worry and with the slightest provocation, she might shatter.

It had been two days since she had sent the letter to request an appointment with Sir Ramston and she still hadn't received a response. The large drops began to fall on her bonnet when she climbed the steps of Kendal House. With each passing day, her fear for her brother's safety grew unrestrained.

Before Henrietta had reached the top step, Mrs. Brompton opened the door. Her hair hung out of its usual tight chignon—testimony to her distress.

Possible news from France. Henrietta's heart galloped in apprehension.

"Brompton couldn't stop her. She sailed right past him into the library for tea with Lord Harcourt."

"There's a woman having tea with Uncle Charles?" Henrietta asked.

"No, she sent Lord Charles up for a rest and is awaiting your return."

Confounded by the shocking news, Henrietta pointed to herself. "Waiting for me?"

Mrs. Brompton shook her head. "Like the Queen of England, she awaits your pleasure in the library."

Henrietta's heart rate sped up in her chest and into her eardrums, beating with a relentless boom.

Mrs. Brompton spoke in a heated voice behind Henrietta who walked briskly toward the library. "I tried to stop her from visiting with Uncle Charles, but she said they were old friends."

Lady Beaumont plowed forward from the library, encased in an asparagus green gown with her bosom barely covered by a fichu of lace. The lady wore a matching putrid green turban with a purple feather. "I'm glad you've arrived before the rain."

The years of training by Miss Hartshaw didn't fail her. Henrietta curtsied. "Lady Beaumont, what a pleasure."

Had Lady Beaumont discovered Uncle Charles' difficulty? The lady spoke, but the pounding beat in Henrietta's ears prevented her from registering the words.

"As I said at Lady Chadwick's, you must call me Euphemia or Aunt Euphemia." Lady Beaumont took Henrietta's arm and began to steer her into the library. "You look a bit fagged out, my dear. A spot of tea will bring you around. Let us retire and have a cozy chat."

Mrs. Brompton muttered under her breath, "Of all the nerve."

Henrietta allowed herself to be taken to the library. It was easier to be led than to fight against the tidal current of Aunt Euphemia.

The older woman guided Henrietta to the settee next to the roaring fire. "Please sit down. I pace and move about when I've things to say."

The rain pelted at the windows, beating a steady soothing rhythm. The candles flickered, spreading shadows on the high, vaulted ceiling and the endless shelves teeming with books. Everything in the library appeared the same, but nothing was the same. Had Lady Beaumont discovered Henrietta's deception?

Henrietta fingered the pleat in her muslin dress, avoiding Lady Beaumont's gaze to hide her fear. This exceptional lady wouldn't be easily fooled.

Lady Beaumont stood over Henrietta. "My dear, I can see you're shocked by my presence."

The biscuit Henrietta had ingested at the ladies' meeting twisted and turned in her stomach. She adjusted her position on the settee, hoping the unbearable rolling sensation would cease.

"Let us be frank, shall we?"

Alarm as ponderous as a boulder sunk to the bottom of Henrietta's stomach.

"How long have you been deciphering the codes for your uncle?" Lady Beaumont's tone was relaxed, as if she asked Henrietta whether she wanted sugar in her tea.

The question Henrietta had dreaded for years had been asked aloud and the gates of hell didn't open, the world didn't stop spinning. She had never imagined the question would come from a woman, a woman she barely knew. She had always thought Sir Ramston would eventually discover the deception.

"I respect your loyalty to your uncle, but Charles isn't the man he used to be and clearly has been declining for a while."

The pain of hiding her uncle's worsening condition was palpable, making it hard to swallow or speak. "The change has been gradual." She had never spoken with anyone outside the household about her uncle. "I've been assisting my uncle for several years."

Lady Beaumont settled next to Henrietta and enfolded Henrietta's trembling hands in her own. "My poor child, you've been carrying this burden far too long." The older woman's voice filled with warmth and compassion

Henrietta fought the burning ache gathering behind

her eyes. "It hasn't been a burden. It's the least I could do for my uncle."

"Of course, of course. You wanted to protect him."

"He's a gentle, sweet man." Her voice broke. "He's taught me so much."

Lady Beaumont's only response was to tighten the hold she had on Henrietta's hands.

The sympathetic gesture made Henrietta want to throw herself into the arms of the older woman and confide all her worries for the Harcourt men, especially her pressing fear for Michael. She realized how long it had been since someone comforted her. She had been alone for so very long.

"You've done an excellent job assisting your uncle."

She was barely able to get the words out, to ask the feared question. "Are you going to inform Sir Ramston?"

Lady Beaumont patted Henrietta's hands. "We need to think this through."

"I need to continue to do this work," Henrietta said. "The pressure to decipher and analyze anything coming out of France has intensified during this lull with the Treaty of Amiens. No one believes Napoleon has slowed his plans for world domination. We must continue to monitor France and Napoleon's activities."

The shrewdness in Lady Beaumont's eyes sharpened. "Go on."

Henrietta wondered how Cord's aunt had known her uncle assisted the Abchurch offices. She looked directly at the older woman. "I'd like to continue to decipher codes in my uncle's name. The office will continue to get what they need and Uncle Charles' world won't be torn apart."

"We need to use all of our resources at this critical time to protect England," Lady Beaumont agreed.

Lady Beaumont seemed to have a keen grasp of the war strategy.

"I couldn't bear to see my uncle suffer the

embarrassment of..." Henrietta swallowed the quiver in her voice.

Lady Beaumont pulled a handkerchief out of her reticule and handed it to Henrietta. "I'm close friends with Sir Ramston and know he'd never want Charles to suffer any public embarrassment or to have our enemies discover that our greatest code breaker is incapacitated. My nephew is associated with Sir Ramston but he can be a bit of a stickler for rules."

Henrietta wiped her nose and eyes. "I'm not convinced your nephew would be supportive if he became aware of my role."

Lady Beaumont guffawed, causing her fichu to flutter. "Henrietta, you underestimate your power to influence my nephew. Although quite controlling, Cord's still a man."

Henrietta, who never thought of herself as a blushing woman, felt the heat move into her cheeks. In her recent dealings with the Beaumont family, her face was red more often than not, especially in her interactions with the exasperating earl.

Lady Beaumont patted Henrietta's hand. "You remind me of myself in my younger days, trying to take care of everyone. I see no reason why you can't continue as you are. I'll keep your secret, but we must agree you'll inform me if you've any concerns or the burden becomes too great."

"Thank you." Henrietta wanted to hug the older woman but instead patted her eyes with the handkerchief. "I can't tell you how grateful I am."

Lady Beaumont jumped from the settee. "Now that we've got that settled, I must be getting on with my calls. I still expect you to bring Charles for tea. You don't have to continue with the story of his head cold. You're both welcome at Rathbourne House and bring your younger brother. I had the pleasure of meeting him this afternoon."

With Lady Beaumont's abrupt exit, Henrietta

stared at the closed door. Lady Beaumont descended upon Kendal house like a fiery crashing comet and then disappeared as quickly as she'd arrived—leaving only a trail of unanswered questions behind.

CHAPTER FOURTEEN

Two hours and Cord had barely made a dent in the pile of estate papers stacked on his desk. Unlike his usual work mode, he couldn't stay focused, all because of one woman. Again and again he flashed to the events of the last weeks—Henrietta trying to save her brother in the Serpentine, Henrietta furious in the mud, her green eyes aflame, Henrietta trying to elude him at the Chadwick Soiree.

He tossed the document down and threw open the French doors from his library to the garden. The sun shone on the spring flowers. The fresh scent of new grass and budding flowers filled his senses. He inhaled deeply. If he didn't know better, he would think he had spring fever.

Returning indoors, he moved across the gold and crimson Aubusson rug to open the library door and achieve a cross breeze. His aunt and sister were out on their social calls, giving him a chance to work on estate business. He moved back to the pile of papers and began to read the next document but was distracted by the distant sound of Sloane admitting someone into the house.

He couldn't hear the conversation, but the visitor was a lady seeking his aunt. Something in the woman's voice sounded familiar. He rose and crossed to the doorway, peering down the hallway to see the visitor.

Henrietta, in a yellow and green ensemble, stood in a swash of sunlight from the opened door. Her surprise arrival suffused the darkened hallways with the promise of spring, like the budding daffodils in the garden.

"It's vital that I see Lady Beaumont." Her voice was insistent. "Please if she is truly home, can you tell her it is I, Lady Henrietta, with an important message."

Sloane, in his usual frosty manner, ignored the desperation in the lady's voice. "Lady Beaumont isn't at home."

She wasn't to be deterred. "Fine. I'll wait."

She looked around for a place to sit. Her reddish blond curls poked out of her bonnet. He couldn't see her eyes but knew the green would've darkened like the deep waters of the stormy Serpentine.

Cord stepped into the hallway. "Lady Henrietta, what a pleasure to welcome you to Rathbourne House."

She stood abruptly. By the astonished expression on her face, she hadn't expected to see him. "My lord..." she mumbled, looking down at the floor. She fingered a necklace hidden under her pelisse, an anxious gesture, he was coming to recognize. "I've come to see your aunt." Her chin went up in defiance.

He knew nothing of her friendship with his aunt. He glanced behind her to see if her maid accompanied her. She was alone.

She didn't offer any further explanation but bit on her lower lip.

A very sensual lower lip, now that she had called attention to it. He found himself riveted to the pink plump lower lip. "My aunt is out on her social calls with Gwyneth. May I assist you?"

It didn't matter what brought her here today. He wasn't going to let her leave until he had time to probe the mystery of her unaccompanied appearance.

She stood motionless.

The air filled with expectation.

"Is your need to see my aunt concerning your uncle? I know they're close acquaintances."

It was hard to imagine that her large green eyes could get any larger, but they seemed to grow.

"What do you know of my uncle?" Her strident voice and stiffened stance challenged him. She was absolutely compelling with her fiercely determined eyes.

"I don't believe I've yet had the honor of meeting the gentleman."

She studied him, weighing his answer.

"I'm trying to understand what would cause you to arrive at Rathbourne House, seeking word with my aunt."

"My visit is of a private nature."

His impulse was to take her into his arms and console her about whatever problems she faced, to kiss away the anxiety furrowing her forehead. "May I offer you tea while we wait for my aunt?" He gestured with his hand to the marble staircase, which wound grandly up to the second floor.

She gazed upward toward the staircase. Her slender fingers caressed the hidden necklace.

Warm arousal ran through his veins with the vision of her pale fingers touching him.

"Please I don't wish to interrupt you. I'm content to wait for your aunt in the parlor."

"I was finding it difficult to concentrate on estate business." He attempted to bring some normalcy to this strange, wonderful interlude. "Would it be too cold if we took tea on the terrace?"

"Thank you." Her words and body were taut as if any sudden noise or movement would cause her to flee out the front door.

His attempt at the social niceties did nothing to reduce the strain she was suffering. She continued to chew on her lower lip.

"Let us go through my study to the terrace," he said.

Sloane appeared from a closed door.

"Sloane, Lady Henrietta and I'll take tea on the terrace." Cord took her elbow. Her arm was tight with tension. "Right this way." He guided her down the hallway to the library door. He paused, hesitating to enter the library. Few were allowed to enter his private space.

When his brother had died, he had abandoned the solitary enjoyment of his scholarly studies, unable to tolerate the stillness. Instead, he had sought endless activities and nameless crowds to dull the acute pain of grief. Since his return to England, he began to find contentment again in his books.

She peeked through the doorway. "What an extraordinary room. You've as many books as we do in Kendal House."

He watched her scan the two walls overflowing with worn books. Afternoon light shone from the large windows onto Henrietta, surrounding her in a warm halo. She turned a full circle, noting his massive mahogany desk scattered with papers, the stacks of his favorite books on a round table next to the two high back chairs situated in front of the fireplace. Her sensual lips turned up at the corners—her first smile of the afternoon.

He wanted her to see more than the books; he wanted her to see the man who engaged in intellectual pursuit. He wanted her to sit with him in front of the fireplace, sharing the fire's heat and the magic of literature, of a good story told. He wanted her in his house, in his life.

"Is there someone in the family who is a scholar?"

"My father was a scholar. He loved to spend all his days studying history, never tiring of ancient worlds."

The tilt of her head, the sparkle in her eyes showed her appreciation of his description.

"Was your father a member of The Odd Set of Volumes, a club devoted to the love of all books? He sounds like he would've made a perfect member."

"I don't know. I was away the last years and missed the opportunity to know many details of my father's later life."

"Was your father's death was recent?"

"Fourteen months ago. He wasn't ill for long. I came as soon as I could from the Continent, but I was too late."

"I'm sorry." Her voice filled with compassion.

Her calming, gentle voice soothed the rough edges of the pain; he had been too late to say goodbye.

"I've also lost my parents. There are many times I wish I could talk with my mother, share my concerns about my brothers, my..." Red patches graced each of her cheeks. She quickly turned and walked toward the gilt-framed picture above the fireplace. "Is this your father as a young boy?"

"No it's my older brother, Grayson." He didn't mean to sound abrupt, but he wasn't ready—he might never be ready to discuss his brother, despite the warm intimacy growing between them.

She wandered closer to the shelves, running her fingers along the leather binding. She kept her back to him.

"Are the Greek books your father's?"

"No, they're mine. I went through a Greek phase during my youth."

She turned to look at him, her eyes and lips were rounded with astonishment. "You read Greek?"

He could hardly control the urge to press her against the bookshelves and kiss her surprise away. "You're finding it hard to believe I studied Greek? You should speak to old Mr. Thornton, my tutor. I was crazy with everything Greek."

He could feel her veiled scrutiny, her attempt to reconcile this new revelation about him with her perceived notions of his character.

He couldn't stop gazing at her, enjoying her confusion. He wanted to kiss the surprise out of those luscious lips.

Aunt Euphemia swept into the library like a northern windstorm. "Henrietta, is something wrong?"

"Lady Henrietta is here to see you, Aunt Euphemia." He raised his eyebrows.

"Sloane told me of Henrietta's arrival." His aunt gave him a sharp nod and moved toward Henrietta. "My dear, has there been a change in Charles?" Aunt Euphemia took Henrietta's hands into her own as if they were closely acquainted.

"No, he is the same as when you left." Henrietta exchanged a knowing glance with his aunt.

"Your visit is one of urgency?"

"My visit pertains to the matter we previously discussed." Henrietta's answer was barely audible.

Neither lady paid any attention to him. He was puzzled by their secrecy.

"Has there been something of importance in the packet of messages that you and Charles were going to decipher?" Aunt Euphemia asked.

Henrietta bent her head toward his aunt and whispered, "A most disturbing message."

"My dear, you needn't worry about Cord knowing you assist your uncle. He works for the same office as you... your Uncle Charles does." Aunt Euphemia gave him an expectant look, as if he should know about Henrietta assisting Charles Harcourt on highly secretive work.

"Why don't you share the message with Cord while I freshen up? He'll be able to make sure the message gets to the right place. Isn't that so, Cord?"

"Of course, I'll assist you in any way, Lady Henrietta."

When had his aunt had time to make Henrietta's acquaintance, and why was his aunt meddling in intelligence office business?

"You can trust Cord." His aunt again gave Henrietta an encouraging nod, as Henrietta was obviously hesitant to share the code her uncle had deciphered.

"Gwyneth and I'll join you and Lady Henrietta for tea, Cordelier." And in a breath, Aunt Euphemia was gone, leaving him to assist Henrietta.

Henrietta again fingered the hidden necklace, her composure shaken by his aunt's abrupt manner and high-handed directions.

"Why don't we go out onto the terrace and you can share your uncle's concerns about this latest message?"

Sloane and a footman had already laid a white damask tablecloth and placed the silver tea service. Sloane nodded to the footman to place the platter of scones and sandwiches.

Cord helped seat Henrietta in an iron garden chair.

"Lord, would you like me to pour?" Sloane asked.

"It isn't necessary, Sloane. I'm sure Lady Henrietta or my aunt will do the honors." He dismissed the butler and seated himself directly next to Henrietta. She sat so close he could see flecks of amber in her green eyes. He spoke in soft tone as he did with Gwyneth when she was a young child and upset. "Tell me about the message."

Henrietta took a deep breath. "My uncle and I believe there is a plot brewing to assassinate the Whig candidate for Prime Minister, James Fox."

He exhaled a long breath between his teeth. Only last week he had dealt with threats against Henry Addington, the Prime Minister.

"James Fox has been threatened many times before for his radical views and his support of Napoleon. Does your uncle believe this is a credible threat?"

"This message is very different than previous threats." She leaned toward him and took a folded sheet of parchment out of her reticule.

He got a whiff of something fresh, of spring—Lilac. It suited Henrietta. He felt the blood pumping through his body as he imagined his lips tracing the path of scent to the warm soft space between her breasts. He shifted, uncomfortable on the metal chair.

She carefully spread the creased paper on the white tablecloth. "This message is unique, unlike any other we've deciphered... I mean my uncle has deciphered. The pattern is new and has a new code name—*asuto.*" She paused and looked expectantly at him. "The French have changed Fox's code name. He has been *renard* for several years."

He found it endearing the way she gave her uncle the credit. But caught up in the moment, she revealed her role. He didn't feel threatened in the least by his future wife's prodigious abilities, emerging right in front of him. Clearly she worked with her uncle. "*Asuto* means clever, if my Spanish doesn't fail me," he said.

"Clever, cunning. Descriptions of a fox? A new code pattern, a new code name in Spanish for James Fox. What do you deduce from this?"

Her eyes were bright with intellectual curiosity. She waited for his response. He basked in the moment of having Henrietta's full attention focused on him. He tried to hide his inner turmoil between admiration and lust.

"My belief...my uncle's belief...this is from a splinter group with an intelligent leader and code writer. The message was very difficult to decipher. I struggled but finally recognized that the code writer used Hittite."

"Hittite? Unbelievable. How many people can write Hittite?" He tried to make sense of today's turn of events—somehow he was on his terrace with Henrietta discussing ancient languages and assassination plots.

"You know what Hittite is?" Her pupils dilated and her mouth formed a plump "O".

Warm arousal pulsed through his body when he looked at her alluring lips. The idea of pink moist flesh caused the blood to pump harder through his body. "The oldest known language and the basis for the current Greek language. I believe it was the Hellenization of Anatolia in 1600 BC that brought the change in language, if I'm not mistaken."

"Amazing." She gaped, her most alluring mouth hung open.

He wanted to laugh out loud and kiss her at the same time. He had discovered the way to win Henrietta's heart. Not through bouquets and afternoon calls but through his knowledge of dead languages.

"Then you can appreciate the skill of this astounding code writer," she said.

He wanted to choke the clever code writer who now had Henrietta's eyes filled with admiration. Jealousy of an unknown enemy twisted his gut.

"Their plan is to have the Spanish look responsible for the attempt. Can you imagine our response if we believed one of the insurgent Spanish groups assassinated James Fox for his pro-France, pro-Napoleon views?" Breathless, Henrietta's eyes shone with passion. She was in the chase and enjoying it.

He was dumbstruck. An impassioned Henrietta made his usually detached heart fill with longing, longing to be loved by this most unusual woman. His world just turned upside down and inside out.

"An English invasion would give Napoleon the perfect pretext to also move into Spain and Portugal,too," he said.

She smiled at him as if he were a prize pupil.

"Fox must be warned. I'll send the message immediately to the Abchurch office."

"Thank you." She folded the paper and paused. "This code is almost too clever. What if this is a ruse? To make us jump to the conclusions we have to distract us from something else?"

He followed her succinct logic but was struggling to overcome the hypnotic effect of lilac and amazing woman. "An interesting theory, to keep us focused on Spain and away from France."

"Or away from the unrest surrounding our upcoming election?" Henrietta asked. "Napoleon would benefit from the political chaos in our country."

His mind raced with the repercussions if Napoleon interfered with the election of the Tory Prime Minister? But how? Last week they had dismissed the threat against Henry Addington because of lack of evidence. But with this credible threat against a candidate for prime minister, was Napoleon attempting to interfere with the election?

It was his turn to stare at her in wonder. "You're a remarkable woman."

She folded the message and handed it to him without raising her eyes. "Thank you, Lord Rathbourne."

She had resumed her formal manner. Had he embarrassed her with his admiration? Why would she be embarrassed by her obvious phenomenal talent and why did she deliver the message to Aunt Euphemia instead of asking Charles to send it directly to the intelligence office? He wanted to ask Henrietta a thousand questions, but he heard his aunt and sister approaching the terrace.

Today wasn't the day to press his questions. Discovering the secrets of the enigmatic Lady Henrietta would be the most pleasurable aspect of his new job.

CHAPTER FIFTEEN

Henrietta arrived at the Abchurch offices in her best bonnet, adorned with a jaunty peacock feather that curved on her cheek. She wore her favorite dress and pelisse which matched the forest green in the feather. Dressed in her most ladylike outfit, she was ready to storm the male citadel. She needed the Abchurch offices to see her as Charles Harcourt's niece—a respected lady of the ton, not as a worried spinster.

She exhaled deeply and ascended the stairs.

A footman opened the door to a cavernous room filled with rows of wood desks. Clerks dressed in dark suits that matched the mahogany paneled walls were bent over their work. The room smelled of wood, fire, and tobacco.

She made no eye contact and proceeded to the next office. "Oh, darn, darn." It was the same blasted clerk who guarded Sir Ramston's office at her last futile attempt.

The clerk stood from his desk and blocked access to the anteroom of Sir Ramston's office. "May I be of assistance, my lady?"

In her most haughty voice she said, "I've an appointment with Sir Ramston. Please announce me— Lady Henrietta Harcourt."

"I'm sure you're mistaken. Sir Ramston doesn't have any appointments with..." The older gentleman's face colored crimson. "Aren't you the same...person?" He said "person" with thinly disguised sneer. "You tried to see his lordship last week."

She mentally kept herself in check. She needed to use her feminine allure, not her usual direct manner. "I'm aware that you're charged with the grave responsibility of guarding Sir Ramston and his schedule. My uncle, Lord Charles Harcourt, had an appointment with Sir Ramston today. Due to my uncle's illness, I'm here in his stead."

Warring emotions played across the clerk's mottled face. He would never want to offend Lord Harcourt or his family, but obviously he had never admitted a woman to this office.

"Please excuse me, my lady. I'll announce you to Sir Ramston." He rushed to a large oak door and knocked discretely before entering.

Seconds later, Sir Ramston came out to greet her. "Lady Henrietta, I hope that nothing is wrong with Charles." Concern darkened his eyes.

"Uncle Charles has a head cold which, of course, Edward gave to him. It's nothing serious and I'm sure Uncle Charles will be back to his old self very soon." Lying to Sir Ramston, a trusted family friend, felt terrible. She couldn't stop babbling. "He asked me to come. I hope this isn't an imposition for you."

"Of course not, my dear. Please come in and give me all the news of my friend and your brothers."

Her confidence soared. She gracefully swept past Sir Ramston into his office.

"Please sit down. Shall we have tea?" Sir Ramston gestured to a leather settee by the fireplace. His dark hair was now streaked with silver and he moved slower than she remembered.

"Thank you, Sir Ramston."

Seated together in front of a warm fire, Sir Ramston asked the details of Uncle Charles' illness and Edward's progress with his studies. Just when she thought Sir Ramston would finally ask about Michael, the tea arrived.

Sir Ramston then discussed his estate, bordering near Kendal land. When he began to describe his hounds in great detail, Henrietta became impatient. She mentally tapped her foot.

He drifted on to memories of his days at Oxford.

"Michael also attended Oxford," she interrupted, crashing her teacup down on its saucer, most unladylike.

"Well, of course, I remember. I can assume that Edward will follow in the Kendal tradition? Does young Edward show the same capacity for linguistics?"

Was Sir Ramston purposely avoiding discussing Michael?

"Sir Ramston, I came today, I mean, Uncle Charles asked me to come today. We're concerned about Michael. We haven't heard from him in weeks. Please, has this office had any word of him?"

Sir Ramston cleared his throat, fingering his signet ring. "I did wonder the purpose of Charles' visit today. He hasn't been to the offices in at least two years."

More like three years.

"I assume Charles told you the circumstances of Michael's role in France, or he wouldn't have sent you today?"

"I'm aware that Michael's unique linguistic talents are being used in our espionage efforts."

"I haven't been able to keep up with Michael's assignment in France since I've been spending my time more in the diplomatic channels. You might say, retired to home pastures."

She knew better than to believe that Sir Ramston wasn't still exerting a major influence in England's intelligence.

"A younger man has stepped into my position. He played a central role in our dealings with Napoleon. Unfortunately, the death of his father required his return to England. No one has a more outstanding record of bravery."

She wanted to scream in frustration but politely asked, "Sir Ramston, what does this gentleman have to do with my brother Michael?"

"I think its best, Lady Henrietta, if I summon my replacement so he may give you and Charles the reassurance you're seeking."

Henrietta tried to hide her rising panic at the idea of a new man in charge of her brother. Her heart thumped and her stomach churned.

Sir Ramston rose from the settee and moved to the door. "I'm sure he'll join us if he's available."

Who was this esteemed gentleman and why hadn't she heard anything about him? How could she trust an unknown man with her brother's safety? The panic penetrated her chest then skittered along her nerves.

The door opened behind her.

"Lady Henrietta, Lord Rathbourne has just told me of your previous acquaintance."

Lord Rathbourne, impeccably dressed in a superfine dark blue coat and a crisp white cravat, followed Sir Ramston into the office.

The air seemed to have left her lungs, as if someone had crushed her chest. She blurted, "You're a war hero?"

Lord Rathbourne bowed. "Lady Henrietta, a pleasure. I don't believe I've ever been referred to as a hero, but I did spend time in the service of His Majesty."

"You can't be the person in charge of my brother. Sir Ramston has always been in charge." She tried to take a deep breath, but to no avail.

"Lady Henrietta, I can reassure you that Lord Rathbourne has an outstanding military record and truly is my replacement. I can't think of a more highly-capable man to take my place."

His outraged masculinity filled the office, his anger

well-suppressed except for the change in his eye color. The bright blue had deepened to a steely gray. "Thank you, Sir Ramston. Perhaps we could move to the reason for your visit today, Lady Henrietta?"

"I meant no offense, sir. I just hadn't expected..." She needed to get a hold of herself, but she struggled with this dramatic change.

"It's clear to all present that you've been caught unaware. How can I be of service?" His voice was crisp, bordering close to punctilious.

He was different in this office, a commander, not the warm man she had confided in at his home. Could she turn to him for reassurance that her brother Michael was safe or share her concern that her brother might have gotten himself into a sticky situation?

She fingered her mother's locket, trying to calm herself against breathlessness and her runaway heartbeat. She wanted to dart to the door, hoping that this was all a bad dream. Lord Rathbourne's overbearing presence could never be confused with a dream, more like her worst nightmare. He was too masculine, too capable, too controlling. Too everything.

"I understand that your uncle was unable to make the appointment. I'm sorry that I haven't yet been able to meet him. His reputation as a brilliant linguist is well known in this office," he said.

Why did he mention Uncle Charles at this point? Was he implying that he would reveal her role in assisting her uncle to Sir Ramston? He had lied to her when they were tangled in the mud. He had said he had an interest in hieroglyphics, but he knew Uncle Charles worked for the Abchurch offices, in fact, for him. He hadn't said a word about his position when she had brought the message to his aunt. The arrogant man acted if he would be sending the message to someone, when in truth it was for himself.

Her spine stiffened. Betrayal and anger supplanted her distress. "Sir Ramston has been a trusted family friend for many years. I'm sure your qualifications are exceptional for this position, but you can understand my shock at your appointment."

His aunt had warned her that he was a stickler for the rules. Lord Rathbourne wouldn't be tolerant about the change in her uncle or the possibility that her brother had landed himself in misadventure. She hated to be deferential to the despot but Michael took priority. "We haven't heard anything from my brother. We're a close family and it is so unlike him not to correspond."

Her voice began to quiver when she described their closeness as a family. She wouldn't show how frightened she was and toll upon her for not to sharing her fears. She raised her eyes and looked directly at him, daring him to comment.

His eyes weren't steely gray any longer but had returned to the warmth of a summer sky. "Let me reassure you. Your brother's position as a linguist doesn't carry a great risk to his safety." His tone was authoritative but not in the least bit reassuring. Lord Rathbourne didn't know Michael or his capability for escapades. "I'm surprised that your uncle, with all his years of service, has been influenced by your feminine imagination to actually be concerned. Please, my lady, do not be alarmed. I wouldn't want you to be distracted from the season's requirements."

Angry rage burned through her body like a forest fire igniting. She wanted to wrestle the clod to the ground and pound him with her fists for his condescending reassurance.

"You believe that if my feminine brain is filled with shopping and attending balls, I'll forget about my brother?"

He stepped toward her.

She was quicker and moved close enough for their toes to touch. She wasn't afraid of the insensitive brute. "By your conduct in society, you must be harboring a great deal of family concerns?" She wished she were a gentleman and she could've accompanied her verbal attack with her fists.

His face colored. He took an audible breath, as if ready to refute her.

"Lady Henrietta, I'm sure Lord Rathbourne understands your concerns about Michael. Cord, you don't want Lady Henrietta to worry about her brother. What have you heard recently from Kendal?" Sir Ramston asked.

Cord's eyes never left her face. She was getting good at reading the change in his eye color that signaled his mood change. His eyes were glacial, like the frozen water of the Serpentine.

He held his jaw tight, the muscle in his right cheek twitched. "I'd never wish Lady Henrietta to worry. I can vouchsafe that nothing untoward has happened to her brother."

He leaned closer. She backed up. He bent forward as if he might take her in his arms. "I hope this reassures you."

No, that didn't reassure her. She wasn't going to allow him to pat her on the head and send her home. "Have you had any contact with my brother in the last month?"

"No, I haven't, but he's well protected in Paris."

"I'm sure Lord Rathbourne would share more about your brother's position if he were able. It sounds like Michael might have been too busy to write to his family."

It was easier to rail against Lord Rathbourne than to delve into her reaction that Michael hadn't been in communication with anyone and what it must mean. Fear blasted through her body. She felt shaky, as if she might swoon. She had never swooned. It was too much, too much filling her mind, too much filling her heart. She had to get out of the office.

"Thank you, Sir Ramston, Lord Rathbourne." With a

curt nod of her head, she escaped.

"Lady Henrietta, let me escort you out," Lord Rathbourne said.

She didn't care about proprieties. She shook her head without looking back or replying.

She descended the steps, thinking of all types of torture she would like to inflict on the mighty Lord Rathbourne, who wouldn't trust her with the truth about her brother.

"Lady Henrietta, what a surprise to run into you."

She squinted in the sunlight to see the striking comte's smiling face. Her brain began to ache with the idea of having to deal with another overbearing gentleman.

Comte De Valmont moved with feline grace across the sidewalk to assist her with the last steps.

A burgeoning tension ran through her body when he pressed his lips to her fingertips. Although she was half French, she wasn't comfortable with his overly affected manners.

"What brings you to these offices? You aren't being harassed by the pompous English because of your French connections, are you?"

"I was returning a military history book for my uncle." She was grateful for the excuse she had prepared in advance for such a chance meeting with an acquaintance. "As you know, my uncle is fascinated with war history and prolific in his reading."

"May I escort you home? I've my curricle and the change in the mercurial spring weather is to be enjoyed."

The sun was shining after a cloudy morning. *Darn!* In her rush to get out of the office, she'd left her umbrella in Sir Ramston's office. Nothing would cause her to go back into those tyrannical offices.

"Lady Henrietta, are you all right?" His voice was filled with concern.

"I was remembering a trying task at home. A ride in

your curricle is just what I need."

Cord flew down the steps to give Henrietta her umbrella. It wasn't the umbrella that caused him to dash out without a word to Sir Ramston. It was the pained look on Henrietta's face when he had no word of her brother. But he couldn't let her get involved. Too much was at stake, and this was too dangerous.

He came out of the building as De Valmont assisted Henrietta into his curricle. Henrietta smiled down at De Valmont when she took her seat. She was radiant in the sunshine with the silly feather flapping in the wind.

Why was that damn Frenchman always in the vicinity of Henrietta? Red-hot fury burned in his chest. He retreated up the steps. His pounding feet matched his rising anger. When he came around the corner to his office, Sir Ramston stood waiting outside the door.

"What is the situation with Kendal? I assumed you've had bad news that you weren't willing to share with Lady Henrietta?"

He opened the door to allow Sir Ramston to enter the office ahead of him. "I don't have any news, which makes it bad news."

"No messages from either Brinsley or Kendal?"

"None."

"Damn, I knew there was a risk sending Kendal into Le Chiffre's den. But he was the best man for the job, a brilliant linguist with impeccable French connections."

"You made the right decision. There are no easy choices during wartime," Cord said.

"If anything happens to young Kendal, I won't be able to forgive myself. I've known the boy since he was in leading strings."

Cord felt the same way. If anything happened to Kendal on his watch, he would never be able to forgive himself and most likely Henrietta would feel the same way.

"And you've no word from Brinsley?"

Cord shook his head. Having Kendal guarded by an untried and inexperienced agent was a problem that kept him awake at night.

"Brinsley doesn't have field experience but he has good instincts," Sir Ramston said. "But to assure that young Kendal was protected, I placed Denby, an ex-military man, in Kendal's household. Denby can handle himself and any threat. He'll get Kendal out of France if it becomes necessary."

"I didn't see anything in Kendal's file about Denby."

"Denby's acting as Kendal's valet. Denby's been in many tricky situations."

With the knowledge that an experienced military man guarded Kendal, Cord was able to take his first deep breath since Henrietta had arrived in the office. When she voiced his exact worries about her brother, he couldn't share any of his concerns or uncertainties. He didn't want to fuel her anxieties. His only response was a primitive need to protect her.

"I suggest you pay a call on Lady Henrietta and Charles and smooth the stormy waters. I don't think the lady was pleased with your response?" Sir Ramston made his comment a question and waited like a good, intelligent officer for Cord to reveal his relationship with Henrietta.

Cord had been trained by Sir Ramston and wasn't fooled by his predecessor's tactics. "I had nothing to share that would alleviate her concern." He almost took her in his arms to comfort her and would've if Sir Ramston hadn't been present. She looked fearful and lost.

"Your purpose in encouraging the lady to take in the season was a ploy?" Sir Ramston raised his eyebrows. "Lady Henrietta has never struck me as a woman who cares about the social goings on."

Cord shrugged his shoulders. "I didn't know what to tell her." His tactical skills got muddled, interacting with a woman like Henrietta—a woman who helped her uncle decipher codes, a woman who was now infuriated by his callous response. When she left looking so vulnerable, he felt like a cold bastard. And now De Valmont was offering her consolation.

"I'm sure you'll find a way to comfort Lady Henrietta." Sir Ramston smiled and walked out of the office.

CHAPTER SIXTEEN

Henrietta threw her hairpins down on the vanity. "What male balderdash—that a lady must be protected from the truth." With a neat flip of her ivory comb, she secured the wayward curl to her upswept hair. Why couldn't her unruly hair behave tonight? Her hair, like her tongue, seemed to go its own way.

She had every right to challenge the mighty Lord Rathbourne yesterday. Typical of men of his station, he had treated her as a mindless woman who should be sheltered from real life. She was disappointed. She had begun to soften toward him when he had listened respectfully while she explained the threat against Wellington. He had asked her opinion on the workings of the cipher. In the Abchurch offices he was a different man—a controlling despot.

She took the codebook out of the drawer, where it had been hidden between scarves and shawls. She ran her fingers over the worn cover. It was her only connection with her brother. Touching the book didn't bring any comfort, only a sense of impending doom.

In the midst of another sleepless night, she came to a solution of how she could provide the Abchurch offices with the codebook and avoid possible censure of Michael. She would give the book to Sir Ramston at this evening's ball. Sir Ramston had been very kind yesterday, trying to convince Lord Rathbourne to share information about her brother. Sir Ramston, who had known Michael his whole life, would tell her what Lord Rathbourne had refused to confide. She hoped Lord Rathbourne was too busy working to attend tonight's ball.

She tucked the book into her green silk reticule. The decision against giving Lord Rathbourne the book hadn't been easy for her. She couldn't allow her conflicting emotions about the enigmatic lord to influence her decision. She wouldn't jeopardize Michael's safety and his position with the intelligence office.

Since her last disastrous meeting in the Abchurch offices, Lord Rathbourne had called at Kendal House twice. Both times Brompton had deflected him, feigning her absence. She didn't want either her brother or her uncle to be under Lord Rathbourne's scrutiny.

Touching the golden locket around her neck deepened her sense of isolation. A month with no word from her errant brother left her exhausted, her emotions frayed.

Mrs. Brompton knocked on the door. "Henrietta, Miss Amelia and the comte have arrived."

Henrietta draped a paisley shawl over her bared shoulders. The amber in the pattern of the shawl matched the same copper hues of her hair.

Henrietta stood slowly when Mrs. Brompton entered the bedroom, allowing the housekeeper a full view of the new gown. The ruche green silk crisscrossed over her breasts in a daring décolletage, then dropped into a flowing, full skirt.

"*Ooh la la* as the French say. You'll put all those young misses to shame. I can't wait to see the flowers the comte will send after tonight."

Since the Chadwick soiree, the comte De Valmont had become quite attentive. Bouquets of fragrant flowers arrived every day.

"He shares my interest in the French émigré problems."

Mrs. Brompton laughed out loud. "The comte and Lord Rathbourne definitely aren't interested in the problems of the French émigrés."

Henrietta refused to respond to Mrs. Brompton's teasing. "I wish Michael were here to escort me." Henrietta placed the reticule over her wrist as she and Mrs. Brompton moved into the hallway.

"You stop worrying 'bout Michael. He's a grown man, and can get himself out of any scrape he has gotten himself into. He wouldn't like you worrying about him. Go to the ball and have a good time."

Comte De Valmont and Amelia waited at the foot of the stairs. The comte had volunteered to escort both Amelia and Henrietta to the ball.

"Amelia, Lucien, I hope I haven't kept you waiting," Henrietta said.

"No, we've just arrived." Amelia walked in a full circle around Henrietta to inspect the new gown from different angles. She carefully examined Henrietta's dress, not missing any details. "Madame de Puis did a fabulous job with the silk Michael sent you. Green is your color.'

"As lavender is yours," Henrietta said.

Amelia's purple gown had simple lines with one shoulder bared, a testimony to Amelia's newest obsession with Greek designs.

"Lady Henrietta, you'll outshine all other ladies at the ball tonight. Except for Miss Amelia who is also exquisite in her new gown. Do I understand that you received the silks from your brother in Paris? What a thoughtful gesture. What else did he send you?"

The hair on Henrietta's neck prickled. "Michael sent a knife for my younger brother."

"Didn't he send Uncle Charles brandy, too?" Amelia asked.

"Oh, you're right. I'd forgotten," Henrietta said.

"Shall we depart?"

Henrietta entered the ballroom on the arm of Lucien. Dark blue velvet and pale pink rose garlands were intertwined and draped around the ballroom's white columns. Crystal vases filled with the same heavily-scented roses sat on velvet-covered tables throughout the sparkling candlelit room. Aware of the evening's mission, she didn't enjoy the room filled with merriment and grand decorations. Instead she searched the crowded room for Sir Ramston.

After greeting their host and hostess, Amelia left Henrietta and Lucien to mingle with friends. Ignoring the women's enraptured glances and open stares, Lucien paid close attention to Henrietta.

She had attracted many men in her first season, but she found Lucien's determined interest in her unnerving. He was trying to be a part of her daily life and tonight he was trying to claim her publicly by remaining at her side.

Pretending a thirst, she sent Lucien for champagne. She didn't trust him. She wasn't sure if her distrust was due to her past courtship by the deceitful Duke of Wycliffe or the result of the comte's chameleon-like personality.

As if she had conjured him, the Duke of Wycliffe pressed through the crowd, moving toward her. She blinked her eyes to make sure she hadn't imagined her former suitor. And right behind him was Lord Rathbourne. Could the evening get more complicated?

"Lady Henrietta. It's been too long." The duke brought her hand to his wet lips.

She hadn't seen Marcus Blenseim, the Duke of Wycliffe, since his courtship four years ago. And four years wasn't long enough.

The duke's hawk-like features had softened over the last years, the angular lines were filled in with puffiness and bloating, likely from dissipation.

"Your Grace." She curtsied.

He lifted his eyebrow with the affectation that at one time Henrietta had thought to be charming. She now felt otherwise.

"You've grown into a most beautiful woman." His eyes remained on her décolletage. "I was sorry to hear of your loss. It must have been very difficult for you."

Henrietta was on the verge of uttering a very unladylike response. What a hypocrite he was to pretend any concern for her or her family. He had been furious that Henrietta had chosen to retire from society and take care of her ill mother, furious that she didn't remain in London to be courted by his grandiose self.

Lord Rathbourne stepped toward her, pressing the duke aside. "Lady Henrietta, a pleasure." He bowed over her hand.

The heat of his hand penetrated through her glove. He smelled fresh, like the outdoors, unlike the duke who smelled of musty furniture.

Lord Rathbourne nodded toward the duke but kept his eyes on Henrietta. "I hear congratulations are in order. A second son, I believe, Your Grace? How is your duchess?"

The duke stiffened, his tone prickly. "You're well informed, Rathbourne. Lady Wycliffe is fine."

"Rathbourne, excuse us. Lady Henrietta and I have much to catch up on." The duke took Henrietta's elbow.

"I would never interfere with friends reminiscing. Lady Henrietta, may I have the honor of the next dance?" Lord Rathbourne asked.

Lord Rathbourne had left for the Continent before she returned to the country to take care of her mother, but he remembered her past relationship with

Wycliffe.

Both men stared at her, waiting for her reply. "Yes, thank you."

"I'll return shortly." Lord Rathbourne turned and strolled back into the crowd without further acknowledgement of the duke.

"Is Rathbourne pursuing you?" The duke's squinted eyes followed the earl.

She pulled her arm away from him. "You assume too much, my lord. Please excuse me. I see my friend Amelia."

When she attempted to pass by him, he grabbed her arm. "You're ravishing, Henrietta. I was a fool to let you go."

Bursts of his wine-sodden breath grazed her neck, causing her body to shudder in revulsion. She tried to pull her arm away. He tightened his grip.

Lord Rathbourne's menacing voice came from behind her. "I'm sure you won't importune the lady any longer."

The duke immediately released her arm. Henrietta turned. She didn't know how Lord Rathbourne managed to be behind her, but she was grateful for his presence.

"And I'm sure Lady Henrietta is too occupied for the rest of the evening to be bothered by old acquaintances." He emphasized the word "bothered."

Wycliffe's puffy face contorted like some giant sea creature. He bowed to Henrietta. "I bid you good night."

Lord Rathbourne took her arm and directed her to the open French doors leading to the balcony.

She went from one gentleman's strong grip to another. She had been at the ball less than an hour and her entire time was spent escaping gentlemen—the comte, the duke and now Lord Rathbourne. Her purpose in attending the ball was to talk with Sir Ramston.

"I believe a breath of fresh air is needed," he said.

They stepped out into the balmy evening.

"I wasn't sure if you would be glad to be rid of the duke?" He pressed close to her side, his arm and leg brushed hers. "At one time you had formed a tendre for the gentleman?"

She stopped abruptly. How dare he speak to her about other gentlemen? But when she looked up at him, the moonlight had softened the hard angles of his face and his eyes were warm with concern. Was this the same authoritative man from Abchurch offices?

His voice was quiet but insistent. "I couldn't allow him to use his past acquaintance to ingratiate himself."

Lord Rathbourne didn't seem like the cold and unfeeling man when she gazed into his understanding eyes. "I never developed a tendre for the duke. It was assumed that we would become betrothed, but my mother became ill."

"You had to leave London to care for her?" He seemed genuinely interested to know about her life in the intervening years since the Chillington Ball.

"My mother developed a fever, and I took her to our country estate to recover."

His head was tilted toward her, his full attention focused on her. He stood too close for propriety's sake, but she didn't move away. No one had looked at her with such intense interest.

"Your mother never recovered from the fever?"

She wasn't intimidated by Lord Rathbourne's large size or the way he loomed over her. She felt only his quiet concern. "I thought she would. We all did."

He turned to face her, as if he might take her into his arms. "It must have been devastating." His words were quietly spoken, but she felt as if he understood all that she had suffered.

"The fever was the beginning of what the doctor called a wasting disease."

"I'm sorry."

She had never shared with anyone the experience of the awful years before her mother's illness—the agony of watching her mother weaken each day, the glow diminish in her eyes.

"You never returned to London to finish the season?"

"No, I couldn't leave her." Her mother had encouraged her to go to London and enjoy the season. The pursuit of social pleasures had never held interest for her. And she wouldn't leave her mother alone.

"You were very young to lose your mother."

"Not that young. I was twenty-two years."

"I remember the night I met you at the Chillington Ball. You were young and exuberant."

"I wish that I had the same fond memories of you."

His deep laugh resonated in his broad chest. "You weren't impressed, but I was entranced by you."

She searched his face to see if he was sincere. His eyes were focused on her lips.

"I thought of you often when I was in France."

"You did?"

"Thought about what it would be like to kiss you." He cradled her chin in his hands.

Pinpricks of anticipation skittered along her skin like the moonlight floating on the balustrades and balcony.

He lowered his head with infinite slowness and touched his cool dry lips to hers. He tasted her as if she were a sweet to be savored, nibbling on her lower lip. He played and pleasured her mouth until a trembling moan rose from her throat.

She had never imagined kisses like these tender caresses, that made the lonely space around her heart swell with joyful need.

The tip of his tongue played along the edges of her lips in sweeps of moist heat. She arched her body toward him reaching for a promise of what she did not know.

Brushing the tender skin of her throat with open-mouthed kisses, he traced the edge of her gown with overwhelming care.

Shivers of white-hot heat danced on her skin. She threw her head back giving him access to her vulnerable flesh.

His mouth broke from hers. "My God, this is madness." He dropped his hands from her quivering body. "I'm not usually this clumsy, but I've waited so long for you." He sounded winded, as if he had been running.

His palpable need fed her growing desire. She didn't want him to stop kissing her. And for once in her life, she was lost for words. "I...I..."

He stared at her as lost as she was. "I never..."

Neither moved, not wanting to break the wondrous moment.

"Lady Henrietta." Lucien's sharp tone interrupted their interlude in the shadows.

She moved quickly away from Cord. She couldn't think of him as Lord Rathbourne after their enthralling kisses.

"Lady Henrietta, I've been looking for you all over the ballroom."

Cord stepped out of the darkened recesses.

"Rathbourne." Lucien paused as if digesting the implications of Rathbourne's presence. "Why are you here? Have you lost Isabelle?"

Henrietta flinched as if she had received a physical blow. The mention of Cord's mistress brought back the reality of whom she had been kissing on the balcony for anyone to see, her fear for Michael forgotten in the arms of the man who wouldn't confide her brother's whereabouts.

"I've searched everywhere for you." Lucien stepped closer to her. "I didn't think to look here." He emphasized here with a flick of his lace-covered wrist.

She wasn't fooled by the French aristocrat's offhand manner.

"Lady Henrietta, a footman has arrived with an urgent message from Kendal House. Let me escort you to him."

She gasped. "What's happened?"

"I didn't speak with the footman. Lady Firth asked me to find you."

"Mrs. Brompton would never send for me unless..." She shuddered with fear.

Cord reached for her but she took Lucien's offered arm. "Please take me to the footman."

CHAPTER SEVENTEEN

Cord ignored his need to pummel De Valmont into the ground and followed behind the departing couple. It wasn't the time or place to demonstrate who would be the victor with Henrietta. He needed to find out whether the urgent message contained news of Kendal. Since Henrietta's visit to his office and no word from France, his worries had heightened exponentially.

De Valmont's blond head was ahead of him in the crush of people. The bastard had deliberately mentioned Isabelle to get Henrietta to react. It had been effective. Henrietta had stiffened with De Valmont's accusation. Just moments ago, she had been on fire for him; now she wouldn't look at him or let him touch her.

He had never intended to kiss Henrietta in a public setting, but when she looked at him, her green eyes wide open with a mix of innocence and frankness, he couldn't help but respond. He hadn't exaggerated when he said he couldn't resist her. She looked at him in her off-kilter, appealing way, and he was lost.

In his hurry to follow Henrietta, he stepped on poor Lady Billingsworth's dress. The dress flowed in large waves of purple ruffles. He made his apologies to the lady, never taking his eye off the back of De Valmont's head. He heard the outraged lady bellow, "The nerve of some people!"

He pushed his way through the last crush to reach the foyer as a young boy approached Henrietta.

Not more than fourteen years old, the messenger spoke in a cracking voice, "Mrs. Brompton sent me to bring ya home." He stared at his feet when he delivered his message.

"It's all right, Robert. What has happened?" Henrietta's voice trembled and her face had lost all color.

With the attention of two lords and the lady focused on him, the boy stammered and continued to stare at his feet. "Lord... Lord Harcourt was attacked by thieves in Kendal House. He got a good knock on the head. Mrs. B sent for the doctor and for me to get ya straight away."

Henrietta couldn't move air in or out of her lungs. "Uncle Charles was attacked?"

The candles in the hallway flickered in the periphery of her vision. She felt light-headed. Someone had hurt her sweet, gentle uncle.

Cord wrapped his arm around her waist, supporting her upright. "I'll take you home."

Lucien stepped forward. "I'll accompany Lady Henrietta." He took her hand.

Lucien's cold grasp shook her from the shock. She didn't want a stranger to witness her uncle in a vulnerable state. She withdrew her hand from his tight grip. "I don't need an escort and we're wasting time. Robert, please get my wrap."

"I'll take Lady Henrietta home." Cord pulled her closer to his body.

Lucien turned slowly to face Cord. "I'm the lady's escort for the evening." His French accent intensified with the strain.

She pulled away from both men and took her wrap from Robert's arm. "I'm leaving." She was outraged that these men continued to argue over who would accompany her while Uncle Charles was hurt and most likely confused.

Cord stepped in front of her to stop her progress toward the door. "Lady Henrietta, as a close acquaintance of your uncle and dear friend of Sir Ramston, I should be the one to accompany you and assess Charles' injuries."

The reminder of Uncle Charles' injuries caused her knees to buckle. She willed herself to take small breaths and moved toward the door.

Cord took her arm and pulled her close to his body to steady her. "Let me help you."

She spoke over her shoulder. "Lucien, would you notify Amelia of my hasty departure because of..." Her voice broke.

Cord placed her shawl around her shoulders. His warm hand on the small of her back guided her to the carriage.

She offered no conversation during the carriage ride. The thought that her uncle had been assaulted in his own home was too difficult to grasp, too difficult to believe. Why would anyone want to hurt a bumbling linguist? Unless of course, the French realized he was England's code breaker, but England had been at peace with France since March.

She rummaged through her reticule for a handkerchief to dab her tears and touched the worn leather book. Michael was the only one who knew she had the French codebook. No one else could possibly know about the codebook, could they?

CHAPTER EIGHTEEN

"*Petite garce,*" Lucien uttered the expletive under his breath and bowed to Lady Henrietta. No one dismissed Lucien De Valmont. She treated him as if he were a servant. He, the Comte de Valmont, had been pursuing the bitch for weeks and her response was to have him fetch and carry while she departed with Rathbourne.

He couldn't imagine why she wasn't succumbing to his Gallic charms. She was part French. It must be her emotionless English blood.

He scanned the ballroom, searching for her friend as he reached for the glass of champagne from the footman in blue velvet livery. He needed something stronger than champagne.

Later he'd have to clean up the mess his men had made at Kendal House. He wasn't going to pay the agreed sum for a botched job. He shouldn't have employed the dockside gang known more for brawn than finesse, but he didn't want anyone French connected to the break-in.

"*Quel idiots.*" He should be cursing the day Fouché decided to seek revenge for his father's errors. His father would disown him if he knew his son was forced to work for the peasant Fouché. Lucky for him, his father had lost his head and would never know what happened to his heir. He gulped the champagne and reached for another.

He walked outside, ignoring the beckoning looks from the ladies. He needed a break before having to work his charm on another frigid English woman. Couples mingled on the brick terrace in the warm night air. Descending the candlelit steps, he sauntered toward a darkened area of the manicured garden.

De Valmont sensed him before he heard the rustle of the bushes and then the barely audible heavy breathing. He was tired of the bastard acting as if he were in charge of their mission. His title was as high as the fucking English mongrel. It was bad enough that they worked together for Talleyrand, but now they both were caught in Fouché's Machiavellian game of bringing Talleyrand down.

"I'm hoping that those weren't your thugs who perpetrated this stupidity—assaulting a peer of the realm in his own home." His words were spoken in a menacing taunt.

The sounds of the ballroom could be heard in the garden, giving the English lord's voice an eerie, otherworldly quality. Laughter and the clinking of glasses made a strange backdrop.

"Your silence is answer enough. You and your incompetents have drawn attention to the Harcourts. This is most indiscriminate."

De Valmont almost smiled at the typical English understatement. He might have been amused if he weren't wary of the violent mood swings of his associate. He had wondered at first what Fouché held over the mighty English lord, more than his astronomical gambling debts. But it didn't take long to recognize the English lord's opium addiction.

"Worst of all, your assault on the old man has alerted Rathbourne. He was already sniffing around Lady Henrietta's skirts. Now he'll be at Kendal house searching."

No one could say that Lucien De Valmont was a

coward, not after he had survived the Reign of Terror. He turned to face his accuser. "I should kill you, right here."

The light from the ballroom reflected on the opium addict's oblivion. Lucien recognized the detachment of someone with nothing to lose. He had seen the same detachment in the French aristocrats who had lost their families to the guillotine. "And what do you think would happen to your sweet, virginal sister?" An unnerving chuckle echoed in the silence.

De Valmont could hardly contain his burning need to grab the bastard by the throat and squeeze hard, hard enough for the son of a bitch to turn purple, his eyes bulging. He would enjoy watching the haughty bastard gasp his last breath. He gripped his hands into fists. He had to know that his sister was safe and out of France before he avenged her and father's honor.

"I'll return and make it look like a break-in," he said.

"No, don't go near Kendal House. You won't fool Rathbourne. You'll do as I say this time. I need that book."

De Valmont made no reply. His French ancestors would be proud of his dignified self-restraint.

In the shadows, the corpulent, over-indulged Englishman created a menacing aura. "I'm sure the idiot Kendal sent the book to his uncle or his sister."

Having Talleyrand's agents acquire the lost codebook was the type of sadistic twist that Fouché thrived upon. Fouché also took pleasure knowing what would happen to them once Talleyrand discovered that his agents had given the missing book to Fouché.

A woman's laughter broke the silence between the men.

"Use your charms on Isabelle; get her to do your dirty work. Obviously your Gallic charms aren't working on Lady Henrietta." He commanded Lucien as if he were a French dog then walked back toward the ball. His voice grew quieter when he moved away. "I'm sure the luscious Isabelle can succeed where you fail. I've heard she is quite the resourceful woman."

Lucien wished he had brought his pistol. He would finish it now. Fouché be damned, he would've killed the English bastard. No one spoke to Lucien De Valmont in a disrespectful manner and lived. He would make both the English bastard and Fouché pay. Fouché would regret taking his sister. Survival always came down to the superior bloodline.

CHAPTER NINETEEN

Henrietta dashed from the carriage and bounded up the front stairs of Kendal house. Brompton stood ready at the door. "How is he?"

"The doctor is with him in the library. We were afraid to move him..." The unflappable Brompton cleared his throat to hide the break in his voice. "Until he could be examined."

Her stomach pitched and rolled as if she would be sick. She ran to the library and burst in before the footman could open the door. Uncle Charles lay next to his desk on the floor. She dropped to her knees. "Uncle Charles." She could barely get out the words.

His face was ashen, his breathing shallow, his hands ice cold. "Uncle Charles, it's me, Henrietta. Oh, please wake up, Uncle Charles."

He seemed to have shrunk in size, his face was colorless. An ache started in her chest. She pressed her hand against the pain, to stop her heart from shattering.

"Uncle Charles, please open your eyes. It's Henrietta. Please Uncle Charles, wake up." Her voice trembled with each plea.

"Henrietta?" Her uncle's voice was so quiet she needed to bend close to his face. "Tired..." He didn't open his eyes.

A throbbing started behind her eyes. She swallowed

hard to hold back the tears. "Of course, you're tired. You need to rest."

A brisk, efficient voice interrupted her. "Lady Henrietta, your uncle needs to be moved to his bed chamber. He has a large gash on the back of his head that needs attending."

Henrietta looked up from her kneeling position to see Doctor Hadley. She hadn't noticed their family physician when she rushed to be next to her uncle. The white-haired doctor stood at the desk, gathering his instruments. Doctor Hadley was of the same age as her uncle and had been the Harcourt family's physician for years.

"Is it safe to move him?" She placed her hand beside her uncle's head and felt the moisture of his blood. She gasped. "He's bleeding."

Mrs. Brompton came to her side. "There, there…Uncle Charles is going to be fine. A knock to the head won't stop him."

Henrietta might have been comforted by Mrs. Brompton's words if she didn't hear the quiver in the steady woman's voice.

Doctor Hadley's tone was precise and professional. "Head wounds always bleed copiously. The bleeding has slowed down, but I need to attend to the wound."

Henrietta struggled to keep her composure. She put her shaking hands over her mouth to stop the emotions from spilling out. Her dear uncle lay injured in the library where they had spent long hours together. She couldn't stop the shaking which moved from her hands to her arms and legs.

"Charles will have a massive headache, but after a few days of rest he'll be back to discussing hieroglyphics." Doctor Hadley's confidence and total understanding of her uncle lessened the alarm that engulfed her.

Mrs. Brompton leaned over and gently grasped her arm. "Let Brompton and Robert move Uncle Charles to his room. Polly will assist Dr. Hadley. You've had a shock and need to sit down."

Brompton directed Robert and two of the footmen to carry Uncle Charles to his room. Henrietta wanted to hover, but Mrs. Brompton was adamant that she was to remain seated and warm herself. Once Doctor Hadley finished his treatment, she would go to her uncle.

Henrietta couldn't stop the shaking, though she was seated close to the fire. Mrs. Brompton had cleaned Henrietta's hand and given her a glass of brandy to sip.

She raised the glass. Her motions were deliberate and slowed as if someone else inhabited her body. She took a large gulp and choked on the strong spirits.

Gus, lying underneath a side table next to the settee, whined when Henrietta coughed on the brandy.

"Come, Gus," she called to him, but he wouldn't budge.

His mournful eyes stared at her from under the table.

Henrietta walked to the table and bent over to speak to the distressed animal. "It's okay, Gus. Uncle Charles is going to be fine."

The dog whined louder.

Gus' painful cry raked along her jangled nerves, causing the shakes to start again. She knelt next to Gus. On the top of the dog's head was a swollen lump. She crawled farther under the table to assess the soft mass. "They hit you too."

His dark russet eyes were filled with sympathy when he licked her face.

A battered Gus trying to console her snapped her fragile control. It was too much finding her unconscious uncle and an injured Gus. The tears couldn't be held back. "Who could be so evil?"

Once Cord had been reassured that Charles Harcourt wasn't seriously injured, he interrogated the staff with little success. No one had seen or heard anything unusual. Charles Harcourt was alone, working in the library during the break-in. Cord had found two sets of footprints next to the library window.

With everyone attending to Harcourt, Cord went to the library to search for clues to the thieves' purpose in breaking into Kendal house. Papers and books were scattered in disarray on two large oak tables that faced each other in the center of the room. The assailants had definitely been searching for something in Harcourt's work.

Someone spoke in a low, crooning voice from behind the settee. Proceeding tentatively, Cord peered over the couch. Henrietta was sprawled underneath a side table with tears streaming down her cheeks, petting the family dog. She was unaware of his presence.

He bent on one knee next to her. "Henrietta?"

She tried to jump to her feet but her skirts got tangled. Cord caught her and gathered her close to him. He breathed in the lilac scent of her hair and pressed a fallen curl behind her ear.

"They hurt Gus, too." Her eyes were bright with tears. Blood was streaked down her evening gown. "He must have tried to protect my uncle."

"I'll take a look at him, but Labradors are a sturdy breed."

"After they carried Uncle Charles..." Her voice shook, she swallowed and tried again to speak. "I found him here with a large bump on his head."

Cord didn't want to let go of Henrietta, but he needed to reassure her about her dog. He stooped over the dog. "I'll try not to hurt you old boy, but let's make sure you don't have any other sore spots." He ran his hands along the dog's back, stomach, and legs. The Lab didn't react to the exam.

"Gus has no other injuries—only the bump on his head. I'm sure he'll be fine."

Henrietta nodded.

He wanted to kiss away the tears on her flushed cheeks, to hold her in his arms until the shattered look on her pale face disappeared. Instead he handed her his handkerchief.

"Hen, where are you?"

Her body stiffened against his side when her younger brother entered the library.

"Edward, I'm here with Gus." Her tone changed with a false cheerfulness.

"Everyone's in an uproar. They won't tell me anything," the young boy said.

Henrietta handed Cord the handkerchief. She smiled at her brother. "Someone broke into the house and surprised Uncle Charles in the library."

"Mrs. Brompton sent me to say Doctor Hadley has finished with his examination of Uncle Charles. Why does Uncle Charles need a doctor?"

"Uncle Charles was injured by the thieves." Her voice quivered and her chest moved in painful breaths, as if each word was an effort.

Cord couldn't watch her excruciating struggle to appear calm for her brother. "Dr. Hadley has reassured us your uncle will be fine, except for a headache."

Henrietta gave him a grateful glance over Edward's head. The young boy nodded but said nothing until Gus whimpered.

"What's wrong with Gus?" Edward dropped to all fours to talk with his dog. "Gus, why are you under the table?"

Henrietta bent over her brother. "The thieves must have tried to stop Gus."

"They hurt Gus?" Edward's voice trembled, his

green eyes widened with horrified shock.

Henrietta's face contorted in pain for her brother's anguished plea. She gave a deep exhalation. "I'm sure Gus attacked the men. You know what an amazing watchdog he is. He's very protective of you and Uncle Charles."

Witnessing Henrietta and Edward's suffering caused Cord's rage to surge. No one would get near them or hurt them again. He would do a better job of protecting them. "Edward, can you help me get Gus to the kitchen."

Gus sat up at the mention of the word *kitchen*.

Edward laughed. "Look, Gus is ready to go to the kitchen. He knows he'll get a bone."

Gus thumped his tail with the promise of a treat.

Henrietta put her arm around her brother's shoulder. Her face was soft with nurturing tenderness. "Gus is going to recover nicely."

An area around Cord's heart, an area he didn't know he had, filled with longing.

"It falls to us men to take care of Gus since your sister needs to attend to your uncle." His voice was husky with emotion.

"Thank you." Her smile was wan, her hair had come loose and strands hung around her face. He thought she never looked more beautiful—a warrior woman who battled to protect her family.

"I can't let Gus be alone when he's injured. May I stay with him?" Edward asked.

"It will be a great help to me to know you're taking care of Gus," Henrietta said.

She brushed at her blood-smeared gown then her eyes darted around with panic. "I've misplaced my reticule in the chaos."

She started to search, behind the chair, under the cushions, on the desks, under the cushion again. Speaking to herself in rapid French, *"Ah, Zut alors, où est mon sac?"* Unaware of him or her brother, she continued to hunt frantically for her bag. "*Oh que c'est penible.*"

"Is it possible you left your reticule in the carriage or at the ball?" Cord asked.

She startled at the sound of his voice, as if she had forgotten he was in the room.

"Shall I send a footman for it?" He asked.

She searched his face. "I'm sure it was on my wrist when I came into the library. In all the excitement, I seem to have misplaced it."

"I'm sure the maid will locate it tomorrow."

Her eyes narrowed and two bright red spots appeared on her checks. "I don't want the maid to find it. I need it now—not tomorrow."

Her anger over a missing reticule packed with a handkerchiefs and hairpins was out of proportion but she had endured a traumatic evening. If finding the missing reticule would relieve her distress, he would find the bag. In less than a minute, he spotted the green reticule under an armchair by the fireplace.

He picked up the flimsy silk bag. "Here it is." Surprised by the reticule's weight and oblong shape, he ran his hand over the bag. There was a book inside the reticule. Why would she bring a book to a ball?

Henrietta rushed toward him and grabbed the bag out of his hand. "Thank you, Lord Rathbourne, for all you've done tonight." She didn't meet his eyes as she touched the reticule. "I must go to Uncle Charles."

She turned toward Edward. "I'll come to the kitchen to check on Gus once I'm sure Uncle Charles is settled." Her voice got shaky and she swallowed hard. "Uncle Charles and Gus are tough. Both will soon be fine and ready for military strategies and scones." She departed the library without looking at him.

Cord spoke with the staff, after settling Edward with his dog in the kitchen. He wasn't taking any further chances concerning Henrietta and her family. He posted men to guard the house.

Assaulting an old man and a dog was the work of thugs. But the thugs were definitely looking for something in Harcourt's work. His years in the business had taught him to listen to his gut and his gut was twitching with suspicion. He wished Harcourt was well enough for him to question. Sir Ramston, a family friend of the Harcourts, could answer some of his questions about the family's potential enemies.

He departed without getting to say good-night to Henrietta.

Traffic across Mayfair was clogged with society, retiring in the early hours of the morning. He sat in the carriage, impatient to speak with Sir Ramston. In all his years of spy work, he could think of no evening quite as tumultuous as tonight. Hard as it was for the seasoned campaigner to accept, he teetered close to the edge of losing control over a green-eyed enchantress.

At the ball, seeing Wycliffe and De Valmont touch Henrietta, Cord had wanted to beat the men into a heap and claim her for himself. He had come close to ravishing her on a balcony when she'd responded passionately to his kisses. Then seeing her vulnerable, crying over her dog, he wanted to be her protector. Within minutes of possessing strong chivalrous feelings toward her, he wanted to wring her neck for keeping secrets from him. He had never experienced such a see-saw of emotions. And his little code breaker was hiding a book in her reticule. What was so important about the book that she had taken it to the ball and was there any connection to the break-in?

He should have set aside his feelings for Henrietta and acted like an intelligence officer. He should've questioned her when she was most vulnerable. Instead, he had been agitated to see her upset and all he could think about was how to comfort and protect her. In the morning, he would insist on answers, answers about the mysterious book.

CHAPTER TWENTY

Cord stood outside Sir Ramston's house, waiting for Kemble to answer the door. He was eager to review the evening's events with Sir Ramston but expected a long wait to talk with his mentor. The lateness of the hour shouldn't be an imposition since Sir Ramston barely slept. Agents, diplomats, and ambassadors called upon Sir Ramston at all hours of the day and night.

The energetic and solidly-built butler and Sir Ramston's body guard greeted Cord as if it were mid-afternoon. Kemble's exacting manners and pressed black suit couldn't disguise his bowed legs or his past in the cavalry.

Kemble led Cord into a small drawing room away from the main hallway. The location allowed for ultimate discretion as neither arrivals nor departures could be viewed. As Cord had expected, Sir Ramston was meeting with someone. He'd have to wait.

The delay was fortuitous as it gave him time to rethink the evening's events. When he presented his report, he wanted to be precise and logical about Charles Harcourt's assault. His thoughts were muddled all due to a combustible red haired, green-eyed lady.

Cord was surprised when Kemble returned immediately to lead him to Sir Ramston's library. Cord's Hessian boots tapped crisply down the brightly lit corridor hung with epic paintings of battle scenes. Familiar with Sir Ramston's taste, he gazed at the mix of bloody Roman battles and English triumphs.

Kemble announced him in a cultured, aristocratic voice, barely betraying his Yorkshire roots. Sir Ramston stood at the fireplace, the fire to his back.

Cord moved toward Sir Ramston. "I apologize for the late hour, sir."

He was so focused on making his way to Sir Ramston that he almost overlooked the figure seated on the couch. Noting the back of a woman's head, he felt self-conscious that he had interrupted what appeared to be a romantic interlude. Fumbling for words, he was shocked to hear a familiar voice.

"Cordelier, my boy, what a pleasant surprise."

"Aunt Euphemia?" His aunt was seated on the couch, one leg crossed over her knee, in a very unladylike posture. His face heated with the implications of his aunt's presence alone with Sir Ramston at this late hour. Red-faced and embarrassed, he felt like a young boy caught snitching tarts out of the kitchen.

His aunt sat with a wide grin on her face, clearly enjoying his discomfort.

"Ramsey, dear, I think we've done it. I never thought I'd see the day this arrogant buck would be speechless."

"Effie, don't torment the boy. He's obviously uncomfortable and must have important matters to discuss."

His aunt and Ramsey? And they spoke of him as if he were a lad of fifteen years.

"I apologize, Cordelier, for enjoying your confusion, a little revenge for all the years of your mischief."

"Aunt, I'm surprised to find you out at this late hour."

"You can't hoodwink me. I know what thoughts are racing through your mind and they aren't related to the time of night." His aunt's belly laugh dislodged the lace fichu that decorously fluttered with each guffaw.

Sir Ramston moved away from the fireplace. "Cord, a brandy?"

"He looks like he could use a large one. Ramsey, I could do with a wee bit more myself." His aunt's voice had a warmth that he had never heard before.

Sir Ramston handed Cord a snifter of brandy.

"Thank you, Ramsey... uh, I mean Sir Ramston." Cord coughed to hide his mistake.

He had just called Sir Ramston *"Ramsey."* Could this night get any more bewildering? He sat across from his aunt in his usual chair.

Sir Ramston walked to the table to pour himself brandy.

It was the same library, the same chair, the same excellent brandy; everything was exactly the same as all the other evenings he conferred with Sir Ramston. All the same except his world and his stomach were now spinning out of control.

"Ramsey and I were just discussing that it was time to reveal our secret when Kemble announced your unexpected arrival. As the new head, I hope that you've come to the correct conclusion about my late hour presence."

He had come to the correct, shocking conclusion. Using the French word *affaire* didn't make it less shocking that his aunt and Sir Ramston were romantically involved.

"Aunt Euphemia, I'm sure I don't know what conclusion you expect me to make by your presence here."

"Dear boy. I work for you. I mean I would work for you if I weren't retired."

"What?"

"I'm a spy...was a spy."

"You're a what?" He tried to sound reasonable, but his tone came out outraged. "How can that be? How can I not know?"

Still spinning from the thought of his aunt as Sir Ramston's paramour, he now had to digest that his aunt had been a secret agent. His mind wouldn't work. He couldn't believe what his aunt was saying.

Sir Ramston patted him on the shoulder before sitting next to Aunt Euphemia. "I know it comes as a shock, but Effie just returned to town. I felt it was important that she be the one to tell you of her work."

He knew his aunt to be a voracious reader and traveler with great insight into the political realm, but a spy? He gulped the brandy, enjoying the fast burn down his throat to his stomach. He waited for the heat to soften his agitation and shock.

"Effie is a gifted tactician—England's best secret. You've known her by her code name, *La Bataille*."

His Aunt Euphemia was *La Bataille*—the battle. Of course, he knew *La Bataille*. The name was revered throughout intelligence circles. She had saved hundreds of lives during the Reign of Terror, going into an insane France to rescue aristocratic women and children from the guillotine.

He must have looked bewildered, because his aunt's voice softened and she spoke without her usual teasing tone. "I'd always planned to tell you when you got older. But after Gray's accident, I had to get you away from England and your parents."

What did she mean, she had to get him out of England? Sir Ramston had been the one who approached him at his club when he was in his darkest hour of grief, in the depths of despair over the death of his brother.

Sir Ramston spoke to him of his loyalty to England, the need for men of his ilk. Cord would like to believe he also felt a duty to his country at the time when he had agreed to go to France and become a spy. But in his heart he knew it was the promise of facing death that had caused him to escape England.

"I never thought you would stay away so long. How could I've known how well you would take to the spy game?" His aunt tried to tease, but the wistfulness in her eyes betrayed her.

He was great at espionage because it gave him a legitimate reason to take deadly risks and squash his guilty feelings. He had become a master at controlling and suppressing his emotions.

"I'm struggling with tonight's revelations, Aunt Euphemia." He hadn't understood that it was his aunt who intervened to save him from himself. "Am I to understand you engineered my position with His Majesty?" Had she known the self-loathing in which he had been mired, how destructive he had felt?

"I never imagined you wouldn't return before the death of your parents." Her face was partially hidden in the shadows, but his vibrant aunt looked drawn and tired.

"I did have something to do with it, but you became one of the best agents we've seen in years. I'm very proud of you, my boy, and the contribution you've made to our country." Her eyes were bright with tears, but the familiar twinkle wasn't diminished. "We can talk later about the past. I expect you came tonight to talk with Sir Ramston about the assault on Charles Harcourt."

She already knew? Of course, she was *La Bataille* and Sir Ramston had people placed throughout London, reporting any unusual activities.

"I did come to discuss Charles Harcourt. I'm trying to figure out why he would be violently assaulted in his home."

He recounted to his aunt and Sir Ramston the details of what had occurred at Kendal House that evening. Had it really been earlier this same night that he had been at the Firth ball? His thoughts drifted when he remembered the heated interlude with Henrietta on the balcony.

His aunt looked at him speculatively. Her lips curved up in a small smile. "Has your man reported anything from Paris concerning Kendal? Is the assault on Charles connected to the brother's activities in Paris?"

Her brain quickly made the same connections he had. Tomorrow he would send someone to find Brinsley and bring Kendal home.

"There has been no communication from Brinsley. Lady Henrietta approached our office with concerns that she hadn't heard from her brother," he said.

"I did tell Effie about Lady Henrietta's visit to the Abchurch offices. The young woman has a great deal of fortitude. She was very direct about her concern." Sir Ramston didn't look at him when he spoke nor mention how disdainful Henrietta had been of Cord and his new position.

Aunt Euphemia didn't seem to notice anything amiss. "I've always liked the Harcourt family, though they're all a bit too brilliant. Henrietta tries to hide her abilities, but she is as talented as both the Harcourt men. She has tried to blend into society."

Aunt Euphemia never stopped amazing him. She was correct about Henrietta trying to escape notice.

"What about De Valmont courting her? Is it part of his work for Talleyrand or is he truly courting her? Cord, do you know?" His aunt asked.

"I can't believe Henrietta would consider such a reprobate." He couldn't keep the antagonism out of his voice.

"You've indicated that De Valmont continues to be involved with Isabelle Villiers," Sir Ramston said.

His aunt hadn't missed any part of his vehement response or his inability to control his jealousy.

"Are they involved like you and Isabelle are? Or is it a true affair?" His aunt was well informed for being retired.

"From my understanding, De Valmont and Isabelle

are involved."

"Do you think De Valmont knows that Isabelle works for us?" Aunt Euphemia probed.

"I wouldn't think Isabelle would allow anyone to know about her work for our office. But I've wondered why she appeared with De Valmont at the Wentworth Ball. She maintained she was assisting me in keeping up my rakehell reputation, but it just didn't make any sense. Why jeopardize her position with me?"

"I can't see a real threat in her appearance, but I'm sure it didn't help your relationship with certain members of the Harcourt family." His aunt chuckled.

"It definitely hasn't helped."

Sir Ramston, who had been quiet during the discussion, spoke. "Judging by Lady Henrietta's response to your new position, I'd say you've got your work cut out for you. Effie, the chit couldn't countenance Cord as head of the office. Oh, you would've loved the fireworks on the day of her visit."

His aunt smiled at Sir Ramston's recital but responded thoughtfully, "I do believe Henrietta has suffered with the loss of her mother. She has had too much responsibility for someone so young and now she must deal with violence against her uncle in their home."

Henrietta and her family had to be protected. "I've posted a guard for the remainder of the night, but I'm planning on arriving early tomorrow to search Charles Harcourt's work."

"Cord, I've no doubt you will get to the bottom of the threat against Charles Harcourt and protect the entire Harcourt family. But I'm more interested in how you plan to convince Henrietta that you've changed your rakish ways." His aunt laughed and then patted her dislodged fichu into place.

CHAPTER TWENTY-ONE

Joseph Fouché, the Minister of French Police, strode across the room, his black polished boots leaving a trail in the thick Flemish carpet. The room was bare except for the exquisite rug, a desk, and a Fragonard pastoral. Nothing about the raw-boned man gave the slightest hint into the sentimental depiction of the French countryside that dominated the Spartan interior.

Sensing his superior's mood, Giscard Orly tried to control the twitch that caused his eyelid to tremor. Fouché, an impatient man who struck out violently when displeased, was in a fever. His dark eyes were dilated and his face flushed. He continued to pace as he beckoned for Giscard to be seated.

"I have him...I have him where it will hurt when I squeeze," his superior said.

Giscard knew immediately that Fouché referred to Charles Talleyrand, the foreign minister. Obsessed with humiliating Talleyrand, Fouché, the most feared man in Paris, was animated with another vindictive plan for his enemy.

"I'll crush him."

Talleyrand wasn't the only one who Fouché had by the balls. His body clenched in anticipation of Fouché's punishment over his failed mission to kill Kendal. Fouché had ordered Kendal's death to incite English fury against Talleyrand and his man Le Chiffre—all in his pursuit to find favor with Napoleon.

Rumor had it that Napoleon was distancing himself from Fouché and his brutal past.

Fouché was desperate to discredit Talleyrand, a favorite of Napoleon's.

An unprivileged man, Fouché had risen from the ranks, driven by his lust for power and a blunt, ruthless personality. Opposite in style, Talleyrand, an urbane master, excelled in gamesmanship and crafty manipulation.

"I've waited a long time for this moment. I've discovered the name of Talleyrand's secret agent, *Le Couteau*, the knife."

Fouché finally sat at his desk, his block-like body tilted forward so his angular face jutted close to Giscard. "I'm depending on you."

It seemed he was being given a last chance to redeem himself—his mistake in not killing Kendal could've been his death warrant.

"I'll not fail." He spoke calmly, ignoring the blood thundering in his chest and ears.

"It will give me great pleasure to foil Talleyrand's grand scheme to cause havoc around the English election."

"Yes, sir."

"Kendal sent a codebook to England after he took it out of Le Chiffre's home, probably the night you shot him. That codebook represents two years of ground breaking work. Kendal has fled France, pursued by Talleyrand's and my men," Fouché said.

Fouché leaned back in his wooden chair. The gold buttons on his stark black uniform gleamed in the morning light. "I've found a way to get rid of Talleyrand's *Le Couteau*. He's dangerous and not just another pampered English aristocrat who sold himself for gold."

Giscard remained silent, awaiting the details of the

dirty work. He had no illusions about what part he would play. He was an assassin.

"By my orders, De Valmont was to charm the book from Lady Harcourt, give the book to *Le Couteau* and then expose the English aristocrat as working for the French. After De Valmont has done my work, he'll receive my full mercy."

There was no misunderstanding what Fouché's full mercy meant. His assignment was to kill De Valmont, a distinguished French aristocrat.

"I thought De Valmont worked for Talleyrand?"

"I've secured De Valmont's cooperation using his sister, who he thought was safely hidden in a convent."

Giscard felt a moment of sympathy for the young woman caught in the devil's web.

"You'll then stage *Le Couteau's* downfall after the scandal erupts. He'll be accused of stealing the book from the English for the French. Then you will leak Talleyrand's plan that *Le Couteau* and De Valmont have been working on a violent rebellion to prevent the English election. You won't mention Talleyrand's name," Fouché instructed.

Of course, Fouché wouldn't want any of his plans against Talleyrand to get back to the Emperor.

Now that Fouché's wrath wasn't focused on him, Giscard perceived the twisted machinations of Fouché's revenge against De Valmont and the unnamed English Lord.

"You'll need to make the murder look as if the *Le Couteau* took the honorable way out as the English bastards like to do."

"Yes sir, but how will these two deaths lead to the downfall of our foreign minister?"

Fouché jumped violently out of his chair, causing it to teeter. "Giscard, you haven't discerned the crux of this affair."

"The emperor will be furious to be linked with a plot aimed at the English election. French spies in England causing disorder contradict the image that the emperor has been presenting to the English as a meek lamb under the Treaty of Amiens. He'll be quite displeased." Fouché chortled. "The emperor's faith in Talleyrand will be destroyed."

Fouché smiled broadly, revealing his large yellow teeth. "Of course, I shall report all of these disgraceful events to the emperor. Talleyrand's career will be finished."

Giscard had never seen Fouché in such a mood. If the commander were a child, he would have been jumping up and down like the children at the guillotine watching another aristocrat's head roll.

"You must leave for England immediately." Fouché stood, dismissing him. "Notify me of your success."

When he stood, Giscard felt the pain in his injured leg from his last assignment. He held his leg stiff to disguise the weakness when he walked out of his superior's office. Fouché didn't tolerate any flaws.

Killing De Valmont wasn't going to be that difficult. He found masquerade balls quite conducive to his work. Dressed in a black domino mask, he'd look like any aristocratic buck, seeking a bit of dalliance. His hand touched the stiletto hidden in his boot. A slender dagger thrust at the right angle and then he would slip into the night. Staging the suicide of an English aristocrat would require more planning.

Giscard limped down the austere hallway. He was to kill a scion of a French aristocratic family and an English lord to oust the foreign minister. This was the new order of France.

CHAPTER TWENTY-TWO

Fortified by a cup of strong tea, Henrietta was ready to return to her uncle's bedside. Mrs. Brompton had relieved her at dawn for a brief nap after her night-long vigil. She walked down the long corridor to her uncle's bed chamber. She was weary but hopeful. The doctor believed that Uncle Charles's concussion wouldn't have any long-term, deleterious effects.

Henrietta bent over her uncle, gently touching his face. She whispered, "Good morning, Uncle Charles."

Her uncle opened his eyes, searching her face in confusion. "What's happened?" With the slight turn of his head, he winced in pain.

"Oh, Uncle Charles, I've been so worried. You've had an accident, but Doctor Hadley says you'll be fine." She didn't share any of the ghastly details, hoping he had forgotten. She wanted to spare him further distress.

Dark circles ringed his eyes. Pale and gaunt, he looked frail—so different from when she left him last night for the ball.

"You need to rest," she said.

"I might nap a bit more."

"I'll sit right here and when you awaken, we'll have tea."

"That would be nice. A buttered scone sounds wonderful." His eyes fluttered, but there was a smile in his voice.

Henrietta pulled her chair close to the bed. She took his hand into hers and massaged. Speaking quietly, she told stories of her parents, of Michael, of happier times. She had just begun on Edward and his love of military strategy when Mrs. Brompton knocked at the door and then entered.

"Lady Henrietta, Lord Rathbourne has arrived and wishes to speak with you."

After a sleepless night, she wasn't ready to fence with Cord. "I promised Uncle Charles I would be here when he woke."

"I bet his lordship has already caught the villain. He's just the kind of man to make short work of the criminal. I hope they'll hang the scoundrel at Newgate." Mrs. Brompton's face flushed with intensity. "I'll sit with Lord Harcourt until you return. He may sleep for hours."

Cord might have news, but, drained and exhausted, she didn't want to face his questions. Stamping down her strong need to fling herself into his solid arms and confess the entire Michael mess, she stood. "Where is he?"

"Lord Rathbourne asked to be shown to the library."

She didn't want Cord in the library where he might deduce her uncle's incapacitation and how she had taken over her uncle's work. "I'll go down to hear if there is any news but have Brompton interrupt my meeting with Lord Rathbourne after a quarter of an hour. I want to return to Uncle Charles."

Mrs. Brompton hesitated, as if to speak. She took the opportunity provided by her housekeeper's moment of uncertainty to rush to the door and hurry down the steps.

When she entered the library, Cord was rifling through the papers that were strewn about from last night's break-in. Her usually orderly desk was a mess. Her worry about her uncle, fear for Michael's safety, and her lack of sleep, all fused into a boiling sense of rage.

"What are you doing?" She demanded.

Preoccupied, Cord didn't register her outrage. He spoke matter-of-fact. "I'm trying to find a clue to the thief's intentions. Does your uncle have a secure area for his confidential work? There are two different sets of handwritings on these notes. Is this your handwriting?"

Her heart thumped loudly, as if it might leap out of her chest. "Yes, it's my handwriting. As you know, I help my uncle with his work. Do you need to go through my uncle's papers at this time?"

She had almost slipped and called them "her papers." She needed to be careful not to reveal anything that might hurt her uncle.

Cord stopped his search and came around the desk. His face was creased with concern.

"How is your uncle this morning?"

His quiet strength made her want to confide all the secrets that she had just sworn not to reveal. She was drained. If he so much as touched her, she would cave. "He's napping but awoke earlier with a headache."

He stepped closer and his voice softened. "You're exhausted. You mustn't worry. Lord Harcourt will recover and return to his normal brilliant self."

She longed to tell him that her uncle would never return to the man he had been; he hadn't been that man for years. But once informed, how could he, as the head, ever allow the situation to continue with her uncle?

He took her into his arms, pressed his mouth against her hair, and slowly rubbed her back in slow circles. His touch was gentle and loving. "You've had a hard night."

She inhaled his smell, an earthy mixture of lime and starch. Tilting her head upward, she looked straight into his intense blue eyes and was lost in the deep tenderness.

He cradled her face in his hands and kissed her forehead, her eyelids, her cheeks. "You're not alone. I'm here."

Henrietta relaxed into his strong hands. This is how it feels to be cherished. It was a feeling she had never experienced and it filled her with longing and hope.

She leaned into him and pressed her lips against his cool lips, needing him. His hands at the nape of her neck supported her head.

With her tongue, she outlined his lips, touching then retreating. He groaned. The primitive sound enraptured her.

"Henrietta." His voice was low and rough.

She put her arms around his neck and pulled on his lower full lip as he had done to her the night before. She nibbled, tasting him, anticipating his next primal response.

His groan became a growl. The deep sound reverberated against her chest and she pressed against his strength, melting into his hard body.

His arms clamped around her, tightening her against his firm length.

His kisses became demanding, desperate. His tongue thrust in and out of her mouth.

She was swept away in a flood of feminine sensation. She returned each kiss with a need she didn't understand.

His hands went down her back to her bottom. He lifted her against the full length of his swollen erection. Her body throbbed against him.

She heard a whimper, which must have come from her. She fought to get closer, climb into his body. She could feel his heart beating rapidly against her chest.

His hands dropped to his sides. He exhaled loudly while his whole body shuddered. He kissed her gently on the lips, on her eyelids.

She was breathless, her face was burning, her body shivered in expectation. Embarrassed by her lack of control, she didn't know what to do, where to look. Dazed, she looked into his darkened eyes.

"You're exhausted and have had a shock. My lack of restraint is unpardonable." His voice was husky and his breathing ragged. "I seem to have no control when you're near."

"You needn't apologize." She touched her finger to her burning lips. "I needed…"

Brompton tapped then entered the library. "Lady Henrietta, the doctor will be arriving soon to examine your uncle."

She tried to focus on what Brompton was saying, but she was only aware of Cord, his scent, his heat, and every breath he took. "Thank you, Brompton. I'll return to my uncle's room." Her voice was shaky. A warm blush covered her face.

She had forgotten her instruction to Mrs. Brompton. She had forgotten everything once she started kissing Cord, kissing him in the library with everyone in the house. What had come over her? It must be the shock of the assault on Uncle Charles. Yet she wanted to return to Cord's arms.

His breathing remained irregular, his voice strained. "You need not worry about anything. I'll find whoever did this to your uncle. You need to rest while I examine your uncle's work to make sure nothing is missing."

The vision of Cord searching through her desk, discovering her secrets, hit her like the dunking in the Serpentine. Shocked out of her body's glorious languor, she moved in front of her desk. "You don't believe it was a house burglary?" She tried to sound nonchalant, but her heart sprinted. "How will you know if anything is missing?"

"I've spoken with the Bromptons. They find no valuables are missing."

When did he speak with the Bromptons and why didn't she know that nothing had been missing? Her mind wasn't reacting quickly enough. "Can't you wait until my uncle is better?"

"Your uncle works for my office. I'd be remiss in my responsibilities if I didn't pursue an investigation." The warmth in his voice vanished. "Until proven otherwise, I have to assume the break-in is related to the sensitive messages your uncle deciphers."

"Oh." She hadn't had time to consider the likelihood that the break-in wasn't a burglary but espionage. She had been too consumed with worry over her uncle's concussion.

"I'm not sure if I'll be able to tell if anything has been taken without your uncle's assistance."

"Can't you wait until my uncle is able to direct you on the order of his desk?" She fingered the ribbons in her skirt. "I find it disturbing to go through my uncle's work when he..." She hesitated. "When my uncle is unwell."

He stepped toward her. "Until I can figure out what the thief was looking for, your safety and the safety of the household are my top priorities. There will be a man in the household, guards around the house." His directives flowed in the staccato rhythm of one accustomed to commanding. "You're not to go anywhere without an escort."

She didn't want to think about possible danger to her uncle or Edward. Gesturing with her hands like her French mamma, she said, "Isn't this a bit extreme?"

"Whoever had resorted to such violence might not be easily deterred." He made no attempt to hide his exasperation. "You're to comply with my directions."

She was too tired to think about all the ramifications. She longed to share her burdens with him. But would he be understanding of her uncle's illness or her brother's capriciousness?

He moved closer, looming over her, his arms folded across his chest. "Don't be foolish. You're a woman alone. With your uncle indisposed, who'll protect you?"

As in his office, he treated her as if she wasn't capable of managing a crisis without a man's direction. She had taken care of the entire Kendal household since her mother's illness. "Your man in our household should reassure you that I, an unprotected woman, will be safe."

He looked baffled at her response and clearly wanted to say more, but Brompton stood at the door.

"Lord, I must return to my uncle." Without looking back, she quickly hastened out of the study—her secrets safe for one more day.

He had gone to Kendal House resolved to ask Henrietta questions about the book in her reticule and to examine her uncle's study. Instead, he'd acted like an unrestrained youth, coming close to taking her in the library. His blood heated with the memory of the wet tip of her tongue teasing him, her plush backside in his hands. She had taken them to a passion that he had never experienced and never wanted to end.

He rubbed the stubble growing along his chin. He had foregone shaving this morning in his rush to return to Kendal House.

Who was he kidding? He had rushed to see Henrietta. Since he had returned to England, he was either worrying for her family's safety or wanting to make love to her. He was beginning to need her more than he had ever allowed himself to need anyone. Since his brother's death, he hadn't allowed anyone to get close.

He recognized himself in her stubborn refusal to acknowledge that she needed anyone. They were alike, afraid to become close to anyone for fear of losing them. They were both used to managing alone but not any longer.

Again this morning, she dismissed his concerns for her safety. He had come off sounding a bit dictatorial when he directed her on the measures that were necessary to keep her safe. Henrietta didn't take directions easily. She was used to managing the household without male intervention. She must run circles around the elderly Harcourt.

The arrival of the fierce Talley Swanson to stand guard over the Harcourts helped lighten his irritable mood. He departed for his office.

It was time for her brother to come home. He understood the young man's need for adventure; he had done the same, escaping England and the pain of Gray's death. But it was time for Kendal to return from Paris, face his responsibilities, and relieve his sister. Henrietta's pallor and the dark circles under her eyes belied her resolute façade.

She wasn't going to be pleased with his interference, but it felt right for him to take on the ordering of her life. It also had felt right to comfort and kiss her passionately. Everything about Henrietta felt right to him. Unfortunately, the lady wasn't ready to admit she felt the same.

Climbing out of his carriage, he ascended the steps to the Abchurch offices.

The clerk moved deftly to take Cord's wool overcoat. "Lord Ashworth is waiting for you in your office. He has been most anxious for your arrival."

"How could this day get any worse?" Cord muttered under his breath.

"Excuse me, my lord?"

"Pay me no mind, Witherspoon."

"Would you like your tea now?"

"Yes, and sandwiches. I'll be damned if I didn't miss breakfast."

A tense Ash stood at the window.

"What's happened?" Cord asked.

"We've received word from our man posted in

Talleyrand's office."

Cord sat at his large desk and braced himself for the bad news. His empty stomach filled with dread. He prayed Kendal wasn't dead.

"A codebook was taken from Le Chiffre's library."

Cord exhaled the breath he had been holding.

"Our man knows nothing more about the book but it must be significant since Le Chiffre demanded to immediately see the foreign minister. He heard Kendal's name mentioned by Le Chiffre when the door to Talleyrand's office was opened."

Cord leaned forward. "Go on."

"Kendal must have recognized that the book was important and took it."

Cord jumped up from his seat. "Damn it, what was that young fool thinking? Does he know what danger he's in?"

If Ash was startled by th outburst, he gave no indication.

"The codebook had to be what the thieves had been looking for last night. It's the reason for Charles Harcourt's assault," he said.

"Charles Harcourt was assaulted last night?" Ash asked.

"There was a break-in. His study was searched. Charles Harcourt is too ill to tell me what is missing from his papers."

Cord didn't like the conclusions he was drawing about the book in Henrietta's reticule and why she had taken it to the ball.

The clerk arrived with a tray filled with cold sandwiches and scones. He hoped the hearty sandwiches and hot tea would revive him.

"How is Charles Harcourt faring?" Ash asked.

"He took a blow to the back of the head. The doctor said he has a mild concussion."

"My God, violence wouldn't be necessary to subdue the elderly man," Ash said.

"Not unless you're trying to obtain something you believe the man is hiding, possibly a codebook?"

"Men in our line of work don't require force to achieve our goals," Ash said.

Neither man needed to acknowledge their familiarity with the techniques of coercion. It was a past they shared and would rather soon forget.

Ash spoke with his mouth full of the egg sandwich. "This doesn't sound like spy work. I suspect the work of thugs."

"Last night's violence toward Charles Harcourt was confusing. But if the French believe Kendal sent his uncle the codebook, it makes sense. Send someone down to the docks to find out who's been hiring."

The tea helped Cord focus after his sleepless night, but he didn't want to acknowledge what he'd already concluded. He had believed last night that Henrietta had been upset by the loss of her reticule because of Lord Harcourt's traumatic assault.

He continued to chew, unaware of what he was eating. Her brother took the book from Le Chiffre and sent it to his sister, not to Sir Ramston or the intelligence office. Why? He didn't believe for a minute that the Harcourts were traitors. They had been loyal subjects for hundreds of years. The Kendal title went as far back as the Rathbourne title.

Who did Henrietta plan to meet at the ball with the codebook in her reticule? He had only seen her in the company of De Valmont and Wycliffe.

"Are the rumors still making the rounds about Wycliffe's debts?" he asked.

Ash didn't seem to react to his abrupt change in topic. "He has come into a great deal of wealth recently, supposedly a death in his wife's family. He has already gone through his wife's vast fortune."

Cord hadn't forgotten the way Wycliffe looked at Henrietta, as if she was a delicious dessert for his consumption. He slammed down his teacup. "Find out

what Wycliffe has been up to and where he has gotten
his money. I have never trusted that bastard."

Ash reached for another sandwich.

"Have we had word from Brinsley? I want Kendal
on a ship back to England."

Cord wasn't ready to confide in Ash. He couldn't
reconcile his suspicions about Henrietta. He really
didn't believe Henrietta was involved in anything
treasonous, but why was she secretive? He was going
to wring her brother's neck for involving Henrietta in
his dangerous escapade. He was prepared to teach the
young Kendal a painful lesson.

"Cord, are you all right?"

He hadn't heard anything Ash had said but saw the
speculation in his friend's eyes.

"I was thinking about Kendal."

"You mean Kendal's sister?" Ash teased.

When women were involved with disreputable plots,
there usually was a man behind it. He didn't believe
Henrietta was involved in anything perfidious, but he
could believe Wycliffe was. He considered the idea that
Henrietta was Wycliffe's lover. Had Henrietta been
feigning passion to manipulate him? She had
responded passionately to his kisses at the Firth ball,
but her responses were those of an innocent. He hoped
she was protecting her brother. If it was Wycliffe...
The rushing blood started to throb in his temples.

He had acted like a love-stricken fool, deferring to
her wishes not to search the library because she was
upset. Consumed with passion, he'd forgotten to ask
her why she carried the book in her reticule.

"You're giving a lot of thought to the Kendal family,"
Ash said.

Ash's jest wasn't lost on him, but he wasn't in a
joking mood. He was onto the lady's games. Since she
didn't seem to trust him to share her secrets, he would
use his own methods of learning the truth. He wasn't
above using her blooming physical attraction to him to

unveil her secrets. In fact, he was going to enjoy every moment of exploring her passionate nature.

"Send another urgent message to Brinsley to bring Kendal home. Where in the hell are those two?"

Ash nodded, understanding the dangerous game Kendal had precipitated by taking the codebook.

"I'll deal with Henrietta and her uncle." He ignored the smirk on Ash's face.

CHAPTER TWENTY-THREE

Reclining on the black settee in her sitting room, Isabelle stretched her arms over her head, lifting her breasts to awaken Lucien's appetite. She presented herself as a tableau in the slick black furnishings accentuated with crimson pillows and drapes to stir his dark erotic tastes.

Earlier today she had received a message from Talleyrand. Two of his agents in London were suspected of changing their allegiance to support Fouché. She still couldn't believe Lucien was one of the agents. Lucien hated the peasant Fouché.

Her sheer black negligee matched the Chinoiserie bric-a-brac lining the lush sitting room and fell at mid-thigh, exposing her legs to Lucien's inspection.

She had never trusted the highly placed English aristocrat's motive for treason. But Lucien was a totally different matter. The possibility that Lucien was collaborating with Fouché was more upsetting to her and Talleyrand than if Lucien had defected to the English.

Trained as a female agent to use sex, she would have Lucien's secrets before the night was finished.

"Take that damn ensemble off." Judging by Lucien's harsh command, he hadn't retrieved the book from Kendal house. Their mission of recovering the codebook remained a failure.

She hadn't expected words of love. "Lucien, darling, what is wrong? I'll do whatever you need, but tell me what has happened." Isabelle knew Lucien to be unpredictable, yet she never could comprehend what drove Lucien's volatile sexual hungers. There were nights when he was almost a considerate lover. Not tonight.

Fortified with brandy, she stood before him. She slipped off her negligee slowly and provocatively, hoping to diffuse his foul mood.

"Damn it. I've no need for seduction. Take it off, or I'll rip it off."

Having just spent a fortune on the little black frippery, she quickly discarded the lace piece. She took a deep breath while mustering her composure to approach the man who towered over her. She had learned never to reveal her fear to any man.

"Bend over the settee. I'm in need of a good fuck from a French whore."

If Lucien knew she favored this position, he wouldn't have allowed it. She found control by avoiding her aggressor's face. As an adolescent, she had learned to escape to another world. As an adult, she had mastered her repulsion and fear.

A sated Lucien lounged on the settee, his mood almost giddy. "You seemed a bit less enthusiastic tonight."

"Lucien, how can you say that? No one compares to you." She kept her back to him.

"God, I needed that. I don't know how much longer I can tolerate living among these barbarians. I need to get out of this forsaken country or I'll kill someone."

She heard his desperation mixed with anger. "Why Lucien, what has happened?" She asked nonchalantly while her instincts ran wild.

"*Quelle garce.*" He spat the words.

She slipped on her robe. "Lady Henrietta isn't cooperating?" It was hard to believe that Lucien's abundant charms weren't working on the English prude.

"Don't you tire of the endless manipulation? We're puppets on a string, dancing between Talleyrand and Fouché's game," he said.

She didn't have any idea of Fouché's plans or the devious methods that he had used to persuade Lucien to betray Talleyrand. The police minister was perverse in his need to discredit Talleyrand.

"If we don't recover the codebook, we'll be swept away with one pen flourish by Talleyrand to prevent him any public embarrassment," Lucien said.

She straightened the pillows, pretending the conversation was of no importance. "Talleyrand won't discredit us over the codebook. The minister has weathered much bigger controversies. Talleyrand's focus is on the upcoming election. The English government is close to financial collapse with the war expenditures and two failed harvests. You should stay focused on your work amongst the disgruntled citizens of London."

"Working with the wretched poor isn't as gruesome as pursuing an English virgin." He snorted. "What a farce, chasing after a frigid virgin with no style, no flair. I'm pretending to pant over her while Rathbourne is dying to get under her skirts."

She ignored the painful reminder that Cord lusted after a timid, pale English woman. If Lucien or Cord ever realized she was capable of caring...

"I've been following that English shrew around like a love-sick dog, trying to gather information. I can't believe she has any French heritage." Frustrated, he ran his manicured fingers through his blond curls. Everything Lucien did was with style.

Isabelle poured Lucien a large brandy and seated herself across from him. "Lucien, what about the brother?"

"He escaped Paris. No one knows whether he sent the book to England or not. What a debacle."

"Did the men find anything when they searched Harcourt's study?"

Lucien didn't reply, but the cold fury in his eyes told her enough. She knew better than to probe further. "I'm sure we can devise a way to obtain the book." She needed Lucien to believe she wasn't suspicious of his changed allegiance.

He took a large gulp of brandy. "I loathe the English. They lack sophistication, *savoir faire*. They've none of the French insouciance."

She found it hard to stifle her frustration. Men were such infants. "Darling, what would make the lady be willing to part with the book?"

Lucien stood up, fastening his breeches. "I'm tired. Thank God, my Father, the Marquis, didn't live to see what happened to his only son, scurrying after the English, searching for stolen codebooks." Disgust punctuated his words. His movements were abrupt when he pulled on his boots.

She waited for the tirade to end. She refused to remember France or her relatives. Nothing could come of yearning for what had been. "Lucien, what if I promise Lady Henrietta her brother in exchange for the book?"

He turned suddenly. His eyes narrowed and focused on her. "It's...a possibility."

"I could intimate that I'm holding her brother captive."

"How?"

She hadn't thought it through, but it seemed easy enough to get a message to Lady Henrietta for a rendezvous. "I'll send her a note to meet privately."

"You would need to get her away from Kendal house

and Rathbourne's watchdogs. You'll need to meet her in an isolated spot."

A shiver of dread raised the tiny hairs on her neck and on her arms. She ignored her instincts. Lucien wouldn't risk harming Henrietta Harcourt.

"Yes, to speak with her in private, early tomorrow morning at Hyde Park."

"But how will you get the book when you don't have her brother?"

"I'll barter for the book with the information of where her brother is being held. I'll tell her that her brother is in Winchester. It's far enough away to give us time."

"You think she'll believe you?" he asked.

"These English women are raised to breed, not think."

"But what if she goes to Rathbourne?"

"What if she does? It's the perfect distraction from your real mission of stirring dissidence around the election," she said.

"And when they don't find Kendal in Winchester? What will you tell Rathbourne?"

She laughed. "I'm sure I'll think of something. I'll tell Cord my source was wrong. I'm sure he suspects that I'm not a totally dedicated English spy."

"Make it the Serpentine. I like the irony that it is the place where Rathbourne saved her from drowning." He stretched into his tight blue coat and continued to instruct her on how she should proceed. As if she needed his instruction. She hid her irritation and listened with feigned interest.

"Tell her to meet you at first light, so there is no chance of any other riders."

"Yes, Lucien."

"I wish I could be there to see you in action, but I should remain as the lady's suitor. Why don't you come to my rooms after your little tête-à-tête? We'll celebrate your success."

She had never been invited to Lucien's rooms.

He stroked her cheek with cold fingers. "Very clever of you, Isabelle, to think of pretending to know the whereabouts of the brother. You should bring your pistol. It could get dangerous."

A frisson of fear shot down her spine to the back of her knees.

CHAPTER TWENTY-FOUR

Henrietta secured her thick braid in a blue ribbon and left her bedchamber. She had no time to spare to get to Hyde Park. The note she'd found under her door late last night was brief but clear.

Proceed to the Serpentine at dawn with the codebook. Come alone, if you want to see your brother again.

Her palms felt cold and unpleasantly moist when she tucked the codebook in her reticule. She needed to rescue Michael.

She longed to share the note with Cord, but she couldn't risk her brother's safety. Cord would never allow her, a mere woman alone, to approach Hyde Park and French spies.

Working through the night, she'd created a false codebook. Her plan was simple. She would give the real codebook in exchange for Michael, but if anything had happened to Michael she would give them the counterfeit.

Her stomach plummeted with the idea of an injured Michael. Her entire body trembled with the possibility of her failure. Her riding boots clicking, she descended the marble steps.

Brompton stood at the door. "No tea or breakfast before your ride, my lady?"

"There is much to be done today. I'm already late."

She swept out the front door.

"But Lady Henrietta..."

Henrietta crossed her garden to the stable. The sun peeked through the intense cloud cover. Without sleep and tea, she was ragged, frightened but determined.

She flicked her riding crop against her sapphire blue skirt and focused on the next obstacle to her mission, how to escape Tom, the stable master. A fixture in the family since her childhood, Tom would be dogged in carrying out his duties to accompany her.

"Lady Henrietta, how is Lord Harcourt feeling this morning?"

"Better, Tom. But I'm in need of a brisk ride to clear my head after the terrible assault." She kept her eyes downcast.

"Minotaur is always ready to run. Shall we head to Rotten Row as usual?"

She had taken over the task of exercising the stallion after Michael had left for the Continent. She believed the immense horse shared her loss after Michael's departure.

While Tom held Minotaur in check, she mounted. "I'll take Minotaur alone for a fast gallop and be back in time to break my fast."

"Now, Lady Hen, that gentleman, Lord Rathbourne, was very clear. He required that you be escorted at all times. He's a man I don't want to cross."

"Pshaw, Tom. Lord Rathbourne isn't in charge. Uncle Charles is, and, since he's indisposed, I'm in charge and I shall ride alone."

She had spurred Minotaur to move before Tom could respond. She turned and gave Tom her most winsome smile.

She had left both Brompton and Tom flummoxed in her wake, but she hadn't been able to keep her movements secret as the note had instructed. Cord had the entire household watching her.

She did feel bad for implicating Tom in defying

Cord's directive, but she was committed to act alone. The instructions had been very clear that she was to come alone or her brother would suffer the consequences.

The streets were already clogged with drays and wagons starting the London morning commerce. Henrietta guided Minotaur around the parked wagons, overflowing with vegetables and chickens from the countryside. Focusing on the traffic helped her settle to the next task but didn't allay her stomach's somersaulting and flipping in fear.

Cord, swathed in a crimson velvet robe, descended the stairs. After a long night of escorting his sister and aunt to all the ton balls and routs, he had been dragged out of his bed at dawn. Had Sloane really said it was the Harcourt's stableman?

This new development didn't add to his less than sparkling mood about Lady Henrietta Harcourt and her refusal to confide in him. Deep inside, what really rankled him was that she didn't trust him to protect her or her family. He didn't see any problem that he hadn't confided in her about his role with her family or his relationship with Isabelle. It was his job to keep secrets.

Henrietta, Wycliffe, and De Valmont. What was their connection? Was the connection the French émigrés? The duke was under suspicion for involvement with a dissident group of French émigrés and Henrietta supported the plight of the displaced French. What part did De Valmont play?

He rubbed the fine stubble that had grown on his chin overnight. Talley would've sent one of his men if there was danger, not the Harcourt stableman.

Tom spoke, wool cap in his hands. "My lord, Lady Henrietta refused to allow me to accompany her to Hyde Park."

"She did what?" Cord bellowed. "How did you give her a choice? Why didn't you follow her?"

"She was on Lord Kendal's stallion, the fastest horse in the stable. I'd never be able to catch her."

"Did I not make myself clear? I gave you explicit directions to accompany Lady Henrietta whenever she rode." Cord could barely restrain himself from grabbing the older man.

"I've known Lady Henrietta since she was a little girl and she can be darn mulish when she gets an idea in her head."

Mulish wasn't the word that came to Cord's mind. "Does Talley know she left unaccompanied?"

"Yes, he sent me to tell you. He rode after her to Hyde Park."

Cord let go of the breath he had been holding, knowing that Talley was protecting her.

The slow grin on Tom's weatherworn face further enraged Rathbourne.

"The old Earl would get as mad as you are now. He would rant and bellow, but eventually he found it much easier to allow the lady to go her own way."

"Thank you, Tom. I appreciate your insight." His voice was the only calm part of him. "It's time to find out what important errand the lady had at such an early hour."

Cord summoned his valet, butler, and stableman with terse commands while Tom waited.

Five minutes later, he and Tom were on their way to the stable. "Did the lady give a reason for her early departure?" Cord asked.

"She didn't. She just told Brompton she was going to be late."

Why did Cord feel as if he was missing something? Why would she put herself in danger? He didn't

believe for a minute that Henrietta was a spy involved
with French subversives but it was possible that
Wycliffe or De Valmont had threatened her. Or they
were blackmailing her? All the muscles in his body
tightened with the idea of Wycliffe hurting Henrietta.

He blew air out of his mouth. He didn't want Tom to
hear the expletives he was muttering under his
breath.

CHAPTER TWENTY-FIVE

Minotaur strained at his bit, impatient and irritable, picking up on her frantic mood. It took all of Henrietta's skill to guide him out of the congestion and finally break free, heading toward Hyde Park. They left the Curzon Gate and galloped toward the Serpentine, the site of her dramatic rescue by Cord.

She spurred her horse on, not willing to think of Cord or his reaction to the clandestine meeting. She gave Minotaur his head, allowing him to move quickly through the open green before reaching the lake. On sunny days, the lake's water was a crystalline blue. This morning, reflecting the heavy dark skies, the lake was the color of pewter and a portent of doom.

Approaching the water, Henrietta slowed Minotaur to a walk. In the shadows of the trees, she glimpsed the movement of a dark silhouette.

Mounted on a diminutive mare, a woman dressed in black with a feathered hat tipped at a jaunty angle emerged from the trees. Could this be her contact? Black netting hid her face, but it didn't hide the impressively revealing décolletage of Isabelle Villier.

As if coming for a tête-à-tête, Cord's mistress rode slowly out toward Henrietta. Isabelle Villier was a French spy? It was rumored that her parents had met their fate under the guillotine and her loyalties were now with the English.

"Lady Henrietta, I'm pleased you've followed my instructions. Did you bring the item?"

Henrietta nudged her giant stallion closer. "What possible use could you have for the item?"

"As predictable as your brother."

At the mention of Michael, Henrietta tightened Minotaur's reins ever so slightly. The horse began to back up. "Where is my brother?"

Isabelle edged her horse forward. "Like you, he rushed into peril, heedless of the consequences. Cordelier told me he wasn't an agent, but a scholar."

Minotaur, increasingly tense with Henrietta's nervousness, froze when the mare approached. With his ears plastered against his head, he bared his mammoth white teeth and tried to bite the mare.

"Cord told you about my brother?"

"He is 'Cord' to you?" Isabelle's tone had shifted to mocking.

"What does Cord have to do with this?" Henrietta feigned a sense of calmness while she tried to deduct why Isabelle mentioned Cord. Did she know he was the head of Abchurch? Oblivious to the horse's flattened ears, Henrietta instinctively tightened his reins.

"Cord didn't tell you?" A faint smirk crossed Isabelle's lips.

"Tell me what?" Henrietta held firmly to the reins while peering down upon the French woman on her small horse.

"Cord and I work together for the intelligence office."

"You work as his mistress." Henrietta used her most haughty voice. She didn't want Isabelle to suspect that she didn't know anything about the inner workings of the Abchurch offices.

"How long do you think you will keep Cordelier in your bed?"

What was the woman talking about? Isabelle was

trying to distract her by pretending the role of a jealous lover, but for what purpose?

"You think you are so clever, so smug. Let me warn you. You're not the type for these dangerous games. You need to find yourself a nice vicar."

"You have no idea what my capabilities are."

A faint smile crossed Isabelle's lips. "Mademoiselle is fiery like her hair. I can see why Cordelier is drawn to you."

"For the last time, where is my brother?" Henrietta tried not to sound desperate but her throat constricted around the words. Her heart skipped and fluttered frantically against her chest.

Isabelle muttered under her breath in French, something about the English being *ridicule*. "Your brother has put you and your uncle in a very dangerous position."

Henrietta drew in the reins, starting Minotaur on a side step. "I'll not give you the book until I see Michael."

"Your brother made a deadly mistake by putting your family between Talleyrand and Fouché." Isabelle's eyes darted toward the woods behind Henrietta.

Henrietta followed Isabelle's gaze. She saw nothing in the woods behind them.

"*Mon Dieu*," Isabelle snarled.

Turning back toward Isabelle, Henrietta looked into the barrel of Isabelle's pocket pistol. She swung her riding crop at Isabelle's hand.

"You idiot," Isabelle shrieked.

With the impact of her riding crop, the quicksilver trigger of the gun released. The ball flew past Henrietta's right shoulder. At the same time, Minotaur lurched forward with the sound of the loud blast.

Unbalanced from hitting Isabelle's gun, she couldn't regain her seat when the panicked Minotaur took off.

With one final effort, she pitched forward, trying in vain to grab the horse's mane. She hung suspended for a few seconds before she was thrown through the air.

Cord couldn't shake a sense of foreboding as he rode toward Hyde Park. Harcourt's stableman rode next to him exuding a quiet confidence that this was another misadventure by his mistress. But Cord's uneasiness grew. There was something entirely wrong with Henrietta's early morning ride.

The people who worked with him on the Continent had developed great respect for his instincts. He tried to convince himself that it was the lack of sleep that caused the anxiety growing in his gut.

Talley waited for them at the Curzon Gate. Cord had the highest regard for the young man he had assigned to guard the Harcourts.

"Tom was able to rouse you for the lady's morning tête-à-tête?" The bulky man didn't try very hard to hide his amusement.

"I'm glad you find this morning's adventure entertaining. This isn't a time for jokes. Where is she?"

"She rode to the Serpentine on that massive black stallion she treats like a kitten. I followed her there and then doubled back to direct you to her location. I didn't see the man she was in such a rush to meet." The giant of a man raised his eyebrows in question.

Cord didn't want to consider Talley's conclusions about Henrietta's early morning meeting. But, if she was meeting a lover for an affair of the heart, he would...

"Lead us to the willful lady." His voice echoed his determination to censure the lady whatever her activity.

He heard Tom snort when they galloped to the Serpentine.

Cord was anticipating giving Henrietta a dressing down about this morning's excursion. He liked challenging the lady, watching her fine green eyes get fiery with the provocation. He thought of what other ways he would like to provoke her into submission. Blood pulsed through his body and pooled in uncomfortable places. This wasn't the time to consider the pleasurable ways of igniting Henrietta's fire.

A gunshot erupted, destroying the morning quiet.

"What the hell?" Talley shouted.

The three men spurred their horses on to the Serpentine.

"No it can't be." His voice vibrated with a hoarse cry. The scene in front of him replayed the recurring nightmare of his brother's deathly fall.

Henrietta made futile attempts to regain her balance while the colossal horse sped out of the woods, out of control. Hanging half off the horse, she fought to grab the stallion's mane. She was thrown into the air, suspended in space, and then she landed with a heart-wrenching thud. The horse's hooves pounded the ground with skull-splitting force, missing her by inches.

He couldn't breathe. Crushing pain pressed against his chest.

Henrietta lay still, crumpled, lifeless just like Gray. His vision narrowed down a long, black tunnel and the only sound he could hear was his own rapid breathing.

"No, God, it can't be..."

The nightmare had him in its grip. He struggled to move but his arms and legs wouldn't comply.

Everything and everyone slowed.

Talley was bent over Henrietta's motionless body.

"Quick, Tom, summon a doctor." Talley's voice sounded muffled, as if he spoke underwater.

Cord's body shook in panic. Cold sweat ran down his

neck and back. He fought the nausea and the need to scream in agony. He jumped from his horse and knelt next to her. She lay deathly still. "Henrietta, please."

He rolled her gently over onto her back and took her cold hand to feel for her pulse.

She gave a small sigh.

"Thank God." His hands trailed along her body. He told himself that he was checking for injuries, but he was massaging life back into her body.

He pushed back the hair that covered her eyes, tucking it behind her ear. He kissed her forehead, her temple, her eyelids, whispering endearments.

"Cord?" She wheezed.

"Yes, my darling." He feathered kisses along her chin, her jaw. And he kissed her mouth, warming her lips with his own.

She opened her eyes and stared into his. "Oh, Cord, it hurts," she said, then closed her eyes again.

Talley cleared his throat. "Can Lady Henrietta be moved?"

"We'll take her to Rathbourne House—it's closer. Bring Dr. Simons to the house." He lifted her in his arms and then commanded Talley to hold her until he mounted his horse.

She cried out when they shifted her between them. Pain stabbed in his chest with her distress. He cradled her close to his chest and cantered his horse to Rathbourne house.

CHAPTER TWENTY-SIX

Isabelle dug her heels into the mare's sides, urging her little mount into a brisk canter. Was the bastard actually aiming to shoot her? At the moment, she didn't care. Her harsh breathing reverberated inside her veil. Fear drove her deeper into the woods.

A branch ripped across her face, tearing her lace veil. "Merde." Her hand trembled when she tried to right the veil.

In the distance, she heard shouting. Soon the park would be filled with men searching. She didn't want to answer the barrage of questions about the gunshot.

Her horse stumbled in the underbrush. She barely avoided a fall, pulling hard on the horse's reins. She had been in worse situations.

Anxiety thrummed through her body and heightened her senses. She was aware of the dawning light, the first birdsong, and the pungent smell of damp moss. Her horse trampling the underbrush reverberated in her ears, sounding thunderous.

Was the shooter intending to kill her or Henrietta? A horse whinnied nearby, then the sound of hooves moved closer. She turned, trying to locate the sound.

She could see no one but could hear the steady movement of a horse's footfalls approaching. She scanned the area, searching for a place to hide. This was a city park. There were no hidden places or hidden caves.

The trees thinned ahead, light shone through the clearing. She was at the end of the woods, moving toward the fields of Hyde Park.

She weighed her options. Could her horse outrun her pursuer? The horse was small but sturdy. The similarity between herself and the fearless mare brought a hysterical laugh to her lips. She forced the rising panic down. No one would attempt an attack in the open fields. Frantically lashing at the horse, she charged toward the thinning trees.

She turned again to see her assailant. In the shadows of the trees, the hooded figure in a domino hurtled through the underbrush, gaining on her. His face was contorted with fury. How could he know her plans to obtain the book unless Lucien told him?

"No... Please. We can work something out."

The gunshot echoed.

She threw herself down and clung to the animal's back and kicked hard.

If she could get to the clearing, she could make it. She had time. He couldn't risk shooting her in a public place.

Another sound of a report and then the familiar heat, a numbing pain, then the warmth, the warmth of her blood flowing.

She gripped the reins. She could make it to the clearing. Darkness crept into the corners of her vision and sparks of bright light danced in front of her eyes. She couldn't seem to hold on to the reins, her hands had no feeling. Her mother's face wreathed in light beckoned to her. *"Maman"*

Lucien was too late. He spurred his horse through Hyde Park to Isabelle's meeting place when he heard the second gunshot. The discharge blasted the stillness of the woods. Birds flew from their perches. He pulled the reins and kicked his horse to a gallop.

In the clearing ahead, the bastard was bent over Isabelle who lay motionless on the ground, his hands frantically searched her body.

Lucien jumped off his horse and ran to Isabelle. Her black veil was torn away from her face, exposing her soft red lips—now pale. Her eyes were unfocused and staring. He bent to feel her pulse although he needn't. He recognized death. Her blood soaked into the knees of his breeches as he knelt beside her. He closed her eyes.

"The bitch didn't get the book." *Le Couteau* tried to roll Isabelle onto her stomach. "The bitch didn't get the book."

A red rage exploded behind Lucien's eyes. He pulled the bastard up by the neck and squeezed his throat. "You killed her, you deranged *secousse*. She would've given you the book."

Lucien tightened his hands around the cold, clammy throat. *Le Couteau's* erratic heartbeat throbbed. "I'm going to kill you."

The bastard was stupefied from the opium. He hung limp in Lucien's hands, unable or unwilling to fight back. It would be easy to kill him, to put an end to Fouché's manipulation. Lucien remembered his innocent sister and the revenge Fouché would extract if he killed his agent.

Lucien dropped him to the ground. *Le Couteau* lay on the ground, gasping for air. "She tried to kill me. She pointed her gun at me and shot."

"Why would Isabelle want to kill you?" Lucien wiped his hands on his breeches.

Le Couteau's eyes were red, sweat poured down his face. "She tried to kill me. The bitch tried to kill me. She never planned to give us the book," His voice grew louder, frenzied.

The bastard was in the grip of an opium mania. Nothing Lucien said would make any difference to his paranoid delusions. He had only told *Le Couteau* about Isabelle's plan to stop the fool's insane plan to abduct Henrietta Harcourt to obtain the codebook. The entire English army would've come after them if they had abducted Kendal's sister.

Lucien bent down and covered Isabelle's face with her veil. He brushed off the chilling prescience that his fate would be the same, alone on damp ground with a bullet in his back.

He kicked the crazed addict with his boot tip. "Get up. I hear horses coming this way. We've got to get away."

Until his sister was safe, he would play Fouché's game.

CHAPTER TWENTY-SEVEN

Henrietta whimpered when Cord gently placed her on his bed. The sound of her distress ripped through him.

At the Serpentine, she had said his name but now her only sound was a pitiful moan. She was pale, her breathing shallow. His hand shook when he felt for her pulse. Her heartbeat was rapid and faint.

He bellowed to the maid who stood nervously in the shadows of the dimly lit room. "Get me the damned doctor."

The maid shrank back into the dark. He heard the door close when she left the room.

Panic clawed at the edges of his mind in the dark silence of the room. He walked into the hallway to yell at someone. Where in the hell was the doctor?

Sloane and Dr. Simons walked toward him.

"You certainly took your damned time getting here," Cord said.

The grey-haired gentleman, unfazed by the antagonistic greeting, replied in a calm voice, "Lady Henrietta sustained a fall and has a possible head injury?"

The sound of Doctor Simons' voice echoed in his head as if he were in a vast chamber. There was an air of unreality, a sense of déjà vu, as if he was locked in his worst nightmare.

"A head injury may take a while to manifest," Doctor Simons said.

His stomach recoiled as if someone had sucker punched him. This couldn't be happening again. The doctors had diagnosed a brain hemorrhage after Gray's fall with no hope of recovery. Gray had lingered for days in terrible anguish.

Cord had begged God to take him instead, crying on his knees by his brother's bedside. Buried memories boiled up into his chest—the haunted look in his father's eyes when he desperately implored Gray not to give up, his mother's inconsolable weeping, heard though the night. He was reliving every painful moment.

"Lord Rathbourne, I'll need you to wait outside while I examine her ladyship." Dr. Simons bent over to feel Henrietta's pulse.

The doctor and Sloane looked at him expectantly.

"My lord, Doctor Simons has to examine Lady Henrietta," Sloane said.

Cord stared down at Henrietta. He couldn't leave.

"Would you like a drink in your study while you wait for Dr. Simons, my lord?" Sloane asked.

Something primitive kept him from leaving. "I'll wait just outside the door."

"I'll get you a chair." Sloane opened the door. "This way, Lord Rathbourne."

He sat in a chair outside the bedroom. He had mastered the unbearable memories before and he could do it again. He stood and began to pace. On his third or fourth round of the hallway, the door opened and Dr. Simons stepped out of the room.

"Lady Henrietta has several bruised ribs from her fall," the doctor said.

"Her head injury?" The words pulsed in his head, beat to the same rapid rhythm of his heart.

"I find no evidence of a head injury. The lady was awake for the exam. She fainted from the pain and the motion of moving her to Rathbourne house."

"She's alert?" The words hung in the air, suspended.

"Only briefly. I've given Lady Henrietta a generous dose of laudanum to relieve her pain. She'll sleep for hours. She isn't one to complain, but the pain from rib injuries can be excruciating."

"Does she have any other injuries?" He held his breath, unable to move air in and out.

"I've found none. She'll recover nicely."

Relief rolled through him like an enormous breaker at Brighton.

"I've bandaged the ribs tightly, and she'll need to keep to her bed for the next few days. She'll have intense pain with every movement she makes. I don't recommend she be moved to her own house."

"I hadn't considered moving her." His tone was filled with contempt for the doctor's preposterous idea.

"I'm sure you'll take good care of her ladyship." The doctor looked bemused. "It's the lady herself who wants to be returned to her own home. She's quite a strong-willed woman."

Cord detected the doctor's admiration for Henrietta.

"I had to convince her she would be no help to her family. She reconsidered when presented with the idea of causing them distress. You're a lucky man." Dr. Simons patted him on the back, a fatherly gesture from the man who had been with him through the death of his brother. "I'll visit her ladyship tomorrow. If she awakens, you can repeat the drops for pain. I think it's best if she eats lightly. I've given the maid all of the directions."

Only bruised ribs. He couldn't grasp that Henrietta wasn't seriously hurt. He needed to see, touch her to believe she hadn't died. "May I speak with Lady Henrietta?"

"She has undergone a painful ordeal with the wrapping of her ribs. The necessary movement caused severe discomfort. The sedative is beginning to take effect. It'd be best if you could wait until tomorrow to visit with her ladyship."

"Of course, I won't disturb her." The thought of Henrietta in pain, hurting, was distressing.

An involuntary mixture of terror and fury shuddered through him with the memory of Henrietta sailing through the air. He couldn't consider the possibility of losing her. Unwilling to examine his feelings of vulnerability, he'd needed to focus on solving the mystery of Henrietta's assignation.

He needed to go to Kendal House to examine Harcourt's papers and to have a very pointed discussion with Henrietta's uncle. Why had Lord Harcourt allowed his niece's participation in dangerous work? He and Harcourt were going to come to an agreement on curbing her involvement in intelligence work. She wasn't going to be pleased, but the lady's days of early morning trysts were over.

Cord went to his room to shed his muddied riding clothes. His aunt and Gwyneth could see to Henrietta while he was at Kendal House.

And hopefully Talley would soon have answers on the identity of the person that Henrietta met alone in the Serpentine. When he found the man who shot at Henrietta, he would make sure he was punished.

Henrietta listened to the voices outside the door. She didn't have a clear memory of events after she fell off Minotaur, but rather a recollection of sensations. The smell of leather mixed with Cord's lime and starch scent, the comfort of his arms wrapped around her and a sense of safety.

She snuggled down in the warmth of the heavy bedclothes. It'd be easy to stay under the covers and rest. She heard the deep rumble of Cord's voice causing heat to dance along her skin and her stomach to flutter in recognition. She lay still, trying to hear. The maid hovered nearby, straightening the covers at her feet.

She hoped Cord wouldn't try to talk with her now. She wasn't up for his questioning and was confused about his role. She wanted to trust him, but why would he have sent his mistress to obtain the codebook? Why had Isabelle aimed the pistol at her? Was she attempting to frighten or threaten her?

The medication must have been taking effect, because she was finding it difficult to concentrate. She needed to stay awake. The real and the fake codebooks were in her reticule. She needed to find the books and hide them. Whom should she trust? She would figure it out tomorrow when she felt better, but for now she wasn't going to trust anyone—not as long as Michael remained in danger.

CHAPTER TWENTY-EIGHT

Mrs. Brompton's revelations concerning Henrietta had driven Cord to his club for a drink. The first drink hadn't helped, nor the second or third. In fact, the alcohol had heightened his agitated state. Until meeting Henrietta Harcourt, he had always kept his feelings tightly in place. Now, he seemed to regularly be in the throes of extreme reactions. Such volatility was unheard of in a man who had gained his reputation for cold, composed control.

Cord inhaled deeply when he stepped out of his club. The night air was damp but fresh from the recent rain. The brisk walk home didn't alter his antagonistic mood. Henrietta had more twists than a Gordian knot and he planned to straighten every coil and convolution of the inscrutable woman.

Awaiting, Sloane opened the door. "Good evening, my lord."

He took the steps two at a time.

"Your aunt has asked if you would join her in the drawing room," the butler said.

"Aunt Euphemia is still awake?" This was exactly what he needed—a clear, logical discussion to restore his balance.

"Shall I bring brandy?"

"I seem to have missed dinner tonight. Can you remedy it?"

The revelations at Kendal House had left him completely distracted. He had spent the entire afternoon and part of the evening there. He couldn't recall eating anything since dinner last night.

During afternoon tea with Charles Harcourt, he'd been in shock. Later, when Mrs. Brompton had brought him supper, he'd been too focused on searching the study to even notice if he had consumed anything.

He was hungry, but his real hunger was for a battle with the woman who lay asleep upstairs. She had pushed him over the edge, the edge of restraint. Every muscle in his body clenched in aggravation and fear. Henrietta was up to her pretty little neck in code breaking.

And, as if that were not enough, he was now certain that she had the missing codebook. But, even as he seethed with feelings of frustration and betrayal, the thought of her lying injured aroused his most tender feelings.

He climbed the steps to his aunt's drawing room. "Aunt Euphemia. I'm glad to find you awake."

His aunt was decked out in an orange, toga-like gown with a matching turban with bright fuchsia feathers. "Gwyneth and I just returned from Lady Mandrake's ball. A dull enterprise, but your sister is making quite a splash in society."

"I apologize for not joining you. Did you receive the message that I was otherwise engaged?"

"Yes, Ash brought the message with alacrity and then deemed it necessary to dance with Gwyneth twice, all the while glaring at the young gentlemen who hovered around her. Quite entertaining."

His aunt implied that Ash was interested in Gwyneth. He'd needed to speak to Ash. Gwyneth was too young for his friend's kind of romantic intrigue.

"How is Hen...?" He stopped himself. "How is Lady Henrietta?"

"She has slept most of the day and the entire evening. The nurse has been with her. I've checked on her periodically, but she's been sleeping constantly."

It was futile to pretend mild interest under his aunt's scrutiny. "Has she had a lot of pain? Dr. Simons believed the bruised ribs would be very uncomfortable."

"The nurse has followed the doctor's instructions, dosing Henrietta regularly with the drops to keep her comfortable. I'm sure the laudanum is part of the reason she's still sleeping, but the poor child must be exhausted. It was only two days ago that her uncle was assaulted. And now she was shot at." *La Bataille* already knew that Henrietta's fall wasn't an accident.

"Have you been at your office all this time?" She asked.

"I was at Kendal House."

"How is Charles feeling today?"

"Still weakened, but mending slowly. I had afternoon tea with him."

His aunt slowly scrutinized his face. "You know about Charles Harcourt's state of mind?"

He remembered Henrietta's visit to his aunt with the deciphered communication. "When did you discover the changes in Charles Harcourt?"

"I visited Charles last week. It's a terrible loss." His aunt's energetic tone became subdued, her devilish sparkle vanished.

He hadn't considered that his aunt would be upset by the change in her friend. "I'm sorry."

"On making Henrietta's acquaintance at Lady Chadwick's soiree, I realized that I hadn't seen Charles in society. It wasn't that unusual since he always had been an intrepid scholar, choosing his work over the ton's entertainment, but my curiosity was aroused. Recognizing the connection between you and Henrietta, I was motivated to renew our friendship."

He chose to avoid comment about his connection with Henrietta.

"I didn't see any harm in letting the charade continue. Henrietta has been protecting her uncle for some time."

"No harm?" His voice went up a notch.

His aunt stared at some distant point in the room. "It must be heart-wrenching for Henrietta to watch her uncle decline, his brilliant mind deteriorating."

"But what possessed her to take over his job? You do realize the repercussions if her role were to be discovered? She's a woman."

"You've just come to the realization that she's a woman?" He was glad to see his aunt's somber mood improve but not at his expense.

He was very aware of Henrietta as a woman. He didn't seem to be able to forget her soft, womanly curves for a single moment.

"She isn't just a woman. She's an admirable woman, an English subject we should embrace. She has put her reputation in jeopardy to protect her uncle and continue to serve our country. After the loss of her mother, she ran the household and protected her uncle and her brothers, all the while continuing to work as a code breaker." His aunt's tone wasn't exactly strident, but it was clear she took issue with his hostile response.

He heard his aunt take a deep breath to continue when Sloane arrived with a footman carrying a silver tray laden with food and a bottle of brandy.

"Thank you, Sloane," he said.

Aunt Euphemia poured the brandy while he piled his plate with beef, cheese, and a crusty piece of bread. He slowed to arrange his plate, giving himself time to think. Aunt Euphemia wasn't one to give lectures, and her strong reaction gave him pause.

He hadn't seen Henrietta in the light of what her life had been. He could only think of the danger she risked by taking over her uncle's role. She would garner no sympathy from the French or Spanish if her identity were detected.

And unlike Aunt Euphemia, who held her in esteem, English society would also condemn her. Both men and women alike would see her as odd. He could protect her from the dangers of kidnapping or torture, but he couldn't stop the old biddies from tearing her reputation to shreds. He hadn't created the social strictures, but Henrietta was breaking all the rules of acceptable behavior.

His aunt leaned back against the pillow, her leg crossed over her knee. By her posture, she didn't hold to the rules of society. "You and she are very much alike, both responsible from a very young age."

His parents, too overwhelmed with the loss of Gray, forgot they had another son and a daughter. Their roles became reversed, with him trying to shelter his parents and take care of Gwyneth.

"You've both sacrificed your happiness for the benefit of family and country." His aunt stared down at her brandy.

Overcome with his own guilt at Grey's death, he had tried to make it better, mend his parents' broken hearts. When he couldn't fix the problem, he became lost. As any young man, he had acted out his helplessness with excessive living until his aunt and Sir Ramston had intervened.

He'd already spent too much time today dwelling on the past. He turned to his aunt. "I've received news today that Giscard Orly, Fouché's henchman, has arrived in England and is headed to London."

"I wonder what Fouché is up to?" His aunt leaned forward, her rheumy eyes sharpening.

"I'm wondering the same thing. The ongoing competition between Fouché and Talleyrand for Napoleon's attention might be related to the other message received from France today."

"We might be able to use their dog fight to our advantage." Aunt Euphemia was already calculating their next move. "What was the other message?"

"Our man heard shouting between Talleyrand and Le Chiffre," he said.

Aunt Euphemia slapped her bent knee. "I'd like to have been a mouse in the corner to witness Talleyrand and Le Chiffre, the epitome of savoir-faire, yelling at each other like fishwives."

He too would've liked to see the two formidable men caterwauling. "They argued about Le Chiffre misplacing the codebook."

She raised her eyebrows and waited.

"There may be a connection between the missing codebook and the arrival of Giscard Orly. Fouché wouldn't want to miss the opportunity of Le Chiffre's bungle to paint his arch enemy Talleyrand as an incompetent."

His aunt beamed at him, appreciating his deduction. "But why send Giscard Orly? His skill as an assassin won't be helpful in recovering a stolen book." She paused, rubbed her forehead back and forth until she had knocked her turban askew. "Unless you don't care how you recover the book—Fouché's usual violent solution."

He sighed, relieved that his aunt's concise conclusions were the same as his. It felt good to be able to process information with a rational and logical person, free of volatile emotions.

"Fouché has changed the game by sending an assassin." Aunt Euphemia sat up. "This means Henrietta is in incredible danger. We must keep her here."

He was grateful someone other than him understood the danger to the Harcourts.

"Henrietta asked Doctor Simons to be moved to Kendal house right after the accident. I don't think I can keep her here unless I bring her uncle and her brother." He didn't want to expose his raw feelings of vulnerability over Henrietta's safety. He needed to act as a head.

"It wouldn't be a good idea to move Charles to Rathbourne House with his recent injury."

Henrietta would refuse to stay at Rathbourne House while her uncle was at Kendal house. He didn't want to let her leave his house, but he couldn't hold her prisoner, although the idea had passed through his mind. He'd have to put more men at Kendal House once she returned there.

"Henrietta has the book?"

"I believe her brother sent her the book. Her uncle was assaulted when the men went to Kendal House to search for the book. When they didn't obtain it, they sent Henrietta a message to bring the book to the Serpentine." He reported his conclusions to his aunt, squashing his feelings of hurt and betrayal.

"But why did Kendal take the book? And where is he now?" she asked.

"I don't have any definite answers. I've considered the possibility that Kendal stole the book for money, but I've gone through the Harcourt's accounts and there is nothing leading me to believe they're in need of money."

"Their mother was French?" The traitorous implications were clear in his aunt's question.

Cord would be remiss in his job if he didn't consider the Harcourt's allegiance. "I see no benefit for the French to steal their own codebook. Unless Fouché had Kendal steal the book to embarrass Talleyrand? But what leverage would Fouché have over Kendal?"

"Then Henrietta has had the book for some time?" His aunt asked the question he had mulled over, chewed and re-chewed like a tough piece of mutton.

"We don't know when or how Kendal sent the damn thing."

Cord gulped the brandy.

"But why hasn't Henrietta given it to you?"

His aunt expected him to answer from his role as head of intelligence, not as a man whose betrayed feelings were burning in his gut like the brandy he gulped.

"I'm convinced Henrietta is protecting her brother. Kendal is being held for ransom and Henrietta was contacted to bring the book to the Serpentine today. It explains why she has been so concerned for her brother and her unwillingness to tell anyone what's going on. The assault on her uncle may have been a warning."

He wanted to give Henrietta the best possible reason for not giving him the book, not trusting him. His aunt understood his position. His reasoning, although logical, was defensive.

"Why kidnap Kendal? He isn't that important in the scheme of things." Aunt Euphemia asked.

"I've been asking myself the same question." And if they hadn't kidnapped Kendal, then there was no reason for Henrietta not to confide in him. He threw back the brandy.

If Kendal was kidnapped or in hiding, it still didn't explain why there had been no communication from Brinsley.

"You haven't been able to talk with Henrietta?"

"I'd planned to talk with her this morning but the doctor was adamantly against it." He poured himself another brandy.

"Does Talley have any leads on the person Henrietta met today at the Serpentine?"

"There were very few people about at that early hour. But Talley found two men who remember most explicitly a lone woman dressed in black with a veil covering her face. They were pretty clear that she was a Cyprian."

"Because she was alone in the park?"

"No, the lady's revealing décolletage was quite

impressive, according to the gentlemen's description. Not the usual lady's riding habit."

"Isabelle Villier?" His aunt asked.

"Exactly. Talley couldn't track her down today. Her maid said she was in the country, which I find suspect, so we've posted a man to watch her place. And Talley has men searching the grounds of Hyde Park.

"You've had a very eventful day. With much to be done tomorrow, you must get some rest." His aunt leaned forward with a serious look in her eyes that he remembered from his wild days. "Henrietta has been through a very frightening time. Try to understand that all of her actions have been out of loyalty and concern for her uncle and her brother."

He understood Henrietta's loyalty, but he couldn't reveal to his aunt how hurt, how deeply hurt he was that Henrietta didn't trust him. He couldn't share his jealousy of Henrietta's devotion to her uncle and brother. It seemed childish that he wanted her devotion and loyalty to be for him and only him. His need for her total affection made him feel like a greedy bastard.

"Consider carefully how you'll approach the lady. Like you, Henrietta is used to acting alone. She hasn't had the need for direction from anyone in quite a while." His aunt rose to make her way to bed. "I'm fagged and ready to retire."

He stood and came around to offer his arm.

"It isn't necessary to escort me. You finish your repast. I'll see you in the morning."

"Good night, Aunt Euphemia. And thank you." He bent and kissed her powdered skin, her familiar scent of roses filled him with comfort.

She swept toward the door, turned back, her face wreathed in a brilliant smile. "There will be fireworks tomorrow if I've taken the mettle of Henrietta correctly."

The type of fireworks he planned weren't the ones

his aunt expected. He took one last gulp of brandy.

Henrietta awoke, not clear on how long she had slept. The curtains remained closed. She scanned the darkened, ornate, maroon and gold room. It took her a moment to remember yesterday's events and why she was in a masculine bedroom. The candle beside the bed had burned down. She had fallen asleep without hiding the books.

She slowly stretched her legs then pressed her hand against the heavy bandage on the left side of her chest to splint the injury. She had to get out of bed and hide the books.

She braced herself and rolled to her side. A sharp pain pierced her chest. She gasped, making the strain even worse. Tears of pain and frustration flowed. She pushed herself to a sitting position.

Upright, the room spun, sparks of light shot before her eyes. She bit down on her lip, to stifle her cry. It hurt to breathe, to move. Her muscles tightened, her entire body clenched in anticipation of the excruciating pain when she stood. She waited for the room and her stomach to stop rolling then placed her feet on the ground. She knew better than to take a deep breath.

The blood rushed from her head when she stood. Woozy, she used the bedstead to steady herself. It hurt too much to stand upright. Bent over like an old woman, she took shallow breaths and made her way to the chair that held her clothes and reticule. Cold sweat dripped down her back, shivers raced up and down her body.

Hunched over to guard against more pain, she extracted the books from her pelisse and reticule. She'd have to hide them under the mattress since she couldn't walk any farther.

Grabbing hold of the bedside stand, she took tiny steps to the bed. To place the books between the mattresses, she had to stoop farther. A surge of nausea accompanied the deep knife jab when she lifted the mattress to conceal the books.

She'd have to repeat the whole torturous process to get back in bed. She couldn't do it, couldn't push herself upward and roll again. She'd lie back on the covers and then, after she rested, she would get back into bed. She eased herself back on the soft covering.

CHAPTER TWENTY-NINE

Dampening down his lusty thoughts about exploding fireworks, Cord headed toward Henrietta's room to check on her before retiring. Making his way by candlelight, he quietly opened the door and stepped into the darkened room. The nurse wasn't seated next to the bed, nor was Henrietta tucked under the covers. Henrietta lay across the bed as if she had collapsed.

What the hell was going on? Adrenaline charged through his brain and body, pushing him into high alert for possible danger. He scanned the room before he moved to the bed. Sleeping horizontally across the dark maroon cover, Henrietta's breathing was slow and easy.

Her mane of golden red hair fanned out in stark contrast to the dark fabric. He had never seen her hair down, the color of firelight. Gwyneth's white nightgown clung to all her curves and hid nothing, her voluptuous breasts jutted above the heavy bandage. His eyes roamed her body, enjoying its dips and curves. His groin hardened at the sight of the patch of fiery red between her legs.

He tried to control his body's reactions. He reminded himself that she was injured. Asleep, she looked young, vulnerable, and voluptuous. Lust and something more powerful—tenderness pumped through him.

"Henrietta?"

She didn't stir.

He spoke quietly as he put his arm under her shoulders. It was going to be painful to ease her to the top of the bed.

"Henrietta, I'm going to move you," he whispered into her hair.

She smelled of spring flowers, lilies, and honeysuckle. She groaned when he lifted her shoulders.

"I'm sorry, sweeting. I know it hurts." A rush of gentleness washed over him.

"Cord?" Her voice was low, sleepy.

He loved the way she said his name, the way she would say it when he pleasured her. His erection pushed against her leg. Hopefully, she wasn't too awake.

Bent over her, he murmured words of apology that he had to hurt her. He breathed in her sleepy, womanly scent. She was pale even in the dim light. He pressed a soft kiss to her cool lips, then rubbed gently back and forth to warm her.

Slowly she opened her eyes. She gazed into his eyes with surprise and gladness. "Cord." She ran her hand along his cheek, her eyes wide in disbelief.

"You need to rest." His voice was low, edgy as he felt.

"Cord, I must..."

"I know darling, I feel the same. But I'd be a brute to spend any time with you tonight."

"But Cord, I must speak with you." Her words came out in a rush of breathless.

"I've a lot to say to you too. But it can wait 'til tomorrow. You need your rest."

He was impressed with his ability to control the needs that drummed insistently through his body. He wanted to remove their clothes and lie naked next to her. He would never hurt her, but he wanted to stroke every one of those round curves and indentations. He wanted to put his mouth to her soft, womanly places and mark her as his. There would be no more secrets between them. "Let me lift you to the top of the bed. How did you get into such a position? And where is your nurse?"

"I'm not sure." She already sounded half asleep.

He slowly slid his arm underneath her knees. "This is going to hurt." He felt her flinch then take a sharp breath when he laid her straight. He tucked the heavy covers around her neck. "Do you want a sip of water? Is it time for another dose of laudanum?" How intimate this moment was, as if he had every right to care for her, comfort her.

"A sip of water." Her voice was muted, her eyes dilated with pain and the laudanum.

He slipped his arm behind her and lifted her head to the glass. She sipped. A sense of deep contentment eased into his body.

"You needn't worry. I'll take care of everything." He bent over and brushed his lips against hers. "Tomorrow we'll talk."

Henrietta floated through layers of unfocused images and dreams. She relived the sensation of Cord's warm lips, a wisp of his scent, his hot breath across her face. He cradled her in his arms and whispered words of love. Wrapped in a cocoon of tenderness, she fell back into sleep.

CHAPTER THIRTY

Henrietta sat by the fire, wrapped in a cashmere shawl with Gwyneth's white robe buttoned to her neck. She couldn't get warm or shake her melancholic feelings. The laudanum was probably contributing to her gloomy mood.

"Am I disturbing you?" Gwyneth stood in the doorway. "After all my chatting this afternoon, I hope you were able to nap." The young woman's smile sparkled like the diamonds on her neck and ears.

"I was glad of our time together. Recuperating by yourself is quite boring." Henrietta tilted her head and made an exaggerated perusal of the young woman. "You look exquisite."

Forsaking the usual bows and frills of a young girl, the cut of Gwyneth's ivory evening gown was simple, with a square, low neckline and cap sleeves. She turned full circle, the delicate material swirling and clinging in the most enticing way. With her dark hair cascading around her shoulders, Gwyneth looked like a beguiling Madonna.

Gwyneth had earlier confided that she planned to flaunt her womanhood to Cord's childhood friend Ash tonight. She more than exceeded her plan to look the part of a sophisticated woman, ready to entice the experienced gentleman.

Henrietta wished she could witness the supposedly

hardened man's response to this tantalizing woman. "Oh, poor Ash. He won't have a chance tonight. There will be a line of men begging to dance with you."

"I wish you could attend tonight's ball," Gwyneth gushed.

For all of her youthful eagerness, Gwyneth was mature for her years and remarkably insightful about her brother. The young man she described before the death of his brother wasn't what Henrietta had expected. Cord was a serious scholar, a gentle man with a great wit, not the reprobate that had cut a shocking swath throughout society with gambling, womanizing, and dueling. Gwyneth believed that Cord's wild behavior had been driven by pain.

"My brother is unable to attend tonight's ball. He also missed last night's ball. Neither Aunt Euphemia nor Cord feel that I should know about his dangerous work. They want to protect me as if I were a baby to be swaddled in bunting." She gestured with her hands and shook her head. "It's ridiculous to shelter me from the work my brother does."

Euphemia swept into the room in another loud costume. Henrietta was beginning to believe no one could have such bad taste. Euphemia wore her clothes almost as a badge of independence, or perhaps as a disguise.

Tonight's ensemble was a perfect contradiction to good taste. Her stout body was encased in a bright green dress with purple piping and topped with the most outrageous turban with a multi-colored, stuffed bird between the folds.

"What are you saying young lady about your brother's work?" Euphemia's lively presence crowded the spacious room.

"I was commenting on Cord's inability to attend tonight's ball because of his heavy workload."

"It's unusual circumstances that have delayed him. His message said he hopes to meet us at the ball. Your brother never shirks his responsibility to family."

Gwyneth's throat and face flushed with color. "Auntie Em, I wasn't criticizing Cord but rather your attempts to shelter me from the fact that he works for the intelligence office and today he's dealing with the murder of an agent."

Aunt Euphemia chortled and slapped her thigh. "What was I thinking? Of course you'd know. You're my niece."

Gwyneth did a small curtsy. "Thank you. I might be just eighteen, but I am a Rathbourne."

At that moment, Henrietta saw Gwyneth's resemblance to her brother, the same raised chin, confidence and arrogance in her bearing.

Gwyneth winked at Henrietta. "Good night. I'm sorry you can't join us."

"I'll look forward to hearing all the details of tonight's ball and a certain gentleman's reaction to you in that stunning dress," she said.

Euphemia, unlike Gwyneth, didn't mind if her dress would be crumpled before the ball. She threw herself in the seat next to Henrietta. "Were you able to rest this afternoon?"

"I'm not good at being a patient, but I did find myself dozing off. I'm ready to return to Kendal House and resume my responsibilities. Dr. Simons has given me permission to leave tomorrow."

"Have you spoken to Cord about your departure?"

"I've not seen him since the night of my accident."

"Cord visited your uncle yesterday and is aware of all of your duties, including the code breaking."

Henrietta gripped the arms of the chair. "He knows about Uncle Charles?" Anxiety thrummed in her stomach.

"Cord knows all your secrets." Euphemia's direct gaze didn't falter.

"Why hasn't he spoken to me?" Henrietta grasped her chest as if she could stop the fear running rampant.

"He didn't return until late last night, and now with the murder of our agent, I don't know when he'll be home."

"An agent was killed here in London?" Her heart hammered in uneven beats against her palm.

"And Cord feels responsible. He's been under a lot of pressure due to a missing codebook, and now with the death of an agent, he won't be in an understanding mood about your work or the risks you've been taking."

Henrietta straightened her shoulders, causing a sudden thrust of pain in her ribs. "I'm capable of taking care of myself."

"I'm sure you are, my dear, but my nephew is concerned for your safety and Rathbourne men can be very pig-headed. In fact, they become quite boring with their inability to believe women can take care of themselves." Euphemia shook her head, causing the bird on her turban to look as if it would take flight.

Henrietta sat up straighter, ignoring the pain in her side. "The mystery of the missing codebook will be solved today."

Euphemia threw her head back and laughed. The bird in her turban almost lost its perch. Henrietta didn't see any humor in the situation.

"You underestimated my nephew if you think it's going to be that easy." Euphemia reached across and took Henrietta's hand, her light-hearted demeanor growing serious. "I hope you'll have patience with my nephew. He's lost an agent and blames himself as he did with his brother's death. He'll be very hard on himself and everyone near him. He'll need a woman's comfort to deal with this newest loss and the devilish memories that haunt him."

Henrietta didn't know how to respond to Euphemia's request. His sister and aunt loved him, but both implied he remained hurt from his brother's death. "I don't think I'm the kind of woman that Cord will derive comfort from. He wants a woman he can bend to his will."

"Fiddlesticks. Cord would be bored in a minute by some whey-faced chit. He needs a woman with the strength to allow him to protect and care for her in his overbearing, autocratic way."

Happiness enveloped Henrietta as she considered the idea of Cord caring for her in his autocratic, tender way.

Euphemia continued, "You'd do anything in your power to protect your uncle and brothers?"

Euphemia didn't wait for a response. "It's the same for Cord. You're both good at taking care of everyone, but who takes care of you? Cord needs someone to take care of him, but he'll never admit it. You and he are alike."

Henrietta had never resented her family, but there were times when she wished she could have shared her burdens with someone who understood the pressures of running the estate, taking care of her uncle and her young brother. Could it be possible that Cord would understand her loyalty to her family and share her responsibilities?

"I won't insult you by pretending Cord is easily influenced. He's had years of building up defenses, and knowing my nephew, he won't adjust easily to the idea of your independence. You've many gifts in your arsenal to convince him to take a risk." Euphemia squeezed Henrietta's hand, tears pooling in her eyes. "I hope he can finally forgive himself and have the life he deserves."

Henrietta felt the ache of unshed tears behind her eyes as she shared with Euphemia. .

Euphemia stood. "I'm off to Matilde Bertram's ball. Can't wait to see Lord Ashworth drooling over Gwyneth. I've waited a long time to watch Cord and Ash, two heartbreakers, get their come-uppance. I hope you don't mind me giving you advice."

Henrietta leaned forward. She would've stood if she were capable. "Thank you, Euphemia. I'm glad we've had this conversation. You've given me a better understanding of Cord and his behavior when I first met him."

Euphemia bent over and kissed Henrietta on the cheek. "You're the answer to my prayers. I can't wait to watch my nephew bending to an independent woman. Oh, what fun for this old lady."

Henrietta eased herself back against the chair after Euphemia swept out of the room. She felt a kindred spirit with Euphemia. She had been alone without any woman's comfort since her mother's death. She would have an aunt and a sister. And for the first time since Michael had gone to France, she felt hopeful. The thought of sharing her worries with Cord brought a sense of liberation.

And she did have a lot of worries—her uncle, her brother, and the codebook. Edward would have no trouble adjusting to living with Cord. He already admired Cord after his kindness to Gus. And once Cord met Michael he would understand how easy it was for Michael to get into a McGregor. Cord would protect her uncle's reputation and she could continue to do the code breaking.

She wasn't going to take any laudanum tonight in hopes that Cord would visit her room. After last night's sensual dream in which Cord held and kissed her, she had a disturbing dream about Michael—a nightmare filled with frantic terror and dread. She ran down dark alleyways to find Michael, who was lost. The night grew darker and she grew desperate. She turned corner after corner with the expectation that Michael waited for her. And, as in dreams, suddenly everything shifted and a cruel man dressed in a black domino chased her into a dead end. She was trapped, with no escape.

CHAPTER THIRTY-ONE

Henrietta awoke to the sound of the door opening. The candle was out and the fire gave off a faint glow. A large figure moved in the shadows.

"Why in the hell are you sleeping in a chair?" Not the voice of the ardent Cord who had filled her dreams.

He loomed over her. Tension radiated off his rigid posture.

A prickle of danger skipped across her skin, up into her neck. "I must have dozed off after your aunt and Gwyneth left for the ball."

Cord lit a candle on the mantel then knelt to rebuild the fire, using the poker to arrange the logs. The fabric of his shirt stretched across his back when he bent over the fire, his breeches hugged his tight backside. He had come to her room without his coat or cravat.

He lit the candle next to her chair. His white shirt shone in the dim light. The candlelight glimmered across the angles of his face, but his eyes remained in the shadows.

After his aunt and Gwyneth's disclosures today, she felt a deep tenderness toward him and wanted to right all the wrongs he had suffered.

He seated himself across from her as his aunt had earlier.

She wanted to press her lips to the cleft where his shirt opened, revealing his dark chest hair, run her hand along the black stubble on his chin. She inhaled his masculine scent of lime, leather and brandy.

His eyes, the color of glacial ice, travelled over her face in detached assessment. "Has your pain subsided?" He didn't look or sound like the lover of her fantasies, who held her in his arms and kissed her.

"I'm feeling a lot better. I spent the day visiting with your sister and aunt. They're both delightful."

He held himself taut as if any minute his fury would burst forth. "This isn't your first acquaintance with my aunt. You and she have shared secrets before?"

She had expected his anger about her deception, but this was more than anger. There was an undercurrent of antagonism she couldn't understand. Ignoring her discomfort, she sat taller in the chair. "What secrets are you referring to?"

"You seem to have so many, perhaps you can't keep track of them?"

She leaned toward him in the chair, wanting to touch him. "You're upset that I didn't confide in you about my uncle, but you must understand my concern for his health and his reputation?"

His eyes narrowed. "Your concern for your uncle's reputation is commendable, but what about your own reputation?" His voice was even, too even.

"My reputation?"

"You'd be a pariah if anyone in society found out you were breaking codes. You and the family you've been obsessed with protecting would be ostracized."

He was angry out of concern for her. She checked her resentment over his high-handed tone and stretched her hand to touch him.

"Of course, your reputation won't matter if the French find out you're our code breaker, since they'll probably kill you or, at the least, torture you."

She had never worried about her safety. She lived in England. "My uncle has remained safe these years."

"You won't divert me tonight. I've underestimated your abilities to manipulate me."

She dropped her hand.

"You've prevented me from searching your desk after your uncle's assault and from questioning you after your fall at the Serpentine. Not tonight."

He bound out of his chair. "I could only think of protecting you, when the whole time you went behind my back, breaking codes, endangering yourself."

"You make it sound as if I purposely lied to you. I wanted to tell you, but you can be so..." Her voice trembled and that made her angrier. "...bloody obstinate."

He stood over her, trying to intimidate her. She wished she could jump up to confront him, but she would need his assistance.

"The pat on my head when I wanted news of my brother; you told me to go home and not worry my silly head. How could I know you would be sympathetic to my uncle or to Michael?"

"You've a low opinion of me." He shook his head. "You didn't believe I would be compassionate toward your uncle?" His tone lost its hard edge.

"I now know you're an honorable man, but I didn't know then. When I met you four years ago, you were notorious. Just weeks ago, you brought your mistress to Lady Wentworth's ball. Not exactly credentials for trustworthiness."

He stood still. His eyes and face were in the shadows, making it hard to gage his reactions.

"I was wrong, and I should've trusted you," she said.

"An agent was killed last night because of the codebook. You went alone to the Serpentine to meet with someone who planned to murder you."

She hugged her shawl around herself as the icy shivers darted up and down her spine.

He folded his long length into the chair. The dim

candlelight made the angles and planes of his face stark, his clenched lips unforgiving. "Who did you meet at the Serpentine?"

"Isabelle Villier."

He jumped up from the chair. "Isabelle? He towered over her. "What in the hell possessed you to meet her?"

A grown man would quake at an outraged Cord. Hoping her voice wouldn't wobble, she said, "I received an unsigned note, claiming to have news of my brother. I was to come alone or Michael's life would be in danger."

He walked to the side table and poured himself a glass of brandy. He took a large gulp, then a second gulp. "You didn't consider that I might be of assistance?" He shook his head, his voice filled with disdain. "Of course not. You've already said I wasn't trustworthy."

"Cord, I could only think of protecting my brother."

He paced in front of the fireplace, his heels pounding on the wood floor. "Did the note give any other instructions?"

When she had imagined this conversation with Cord, she hadn't considered how menacing he could be. "The note said to bring the codebook."

He turned to look at her. "Isabelle knew you had the book?"

"She implied you had sent her to get the codebook, since she was your mistress. I couldn't understand why you would send her instead of asking yourself." She wasn't able to hide the jealous hurt in her voice.

"Isabelle works for me." His tone was detached as if discussing the weather.

Well, of course she worked for him. He paid her to be his mistress.

"Yes, I know."

She must have betrayed her hurt feelings. Cord moved closer, as if he might touch her. "She was never my mistress. Isabelle worked for me in France and now in England." His voice wasn't warm but the antagonism had disappeared.

"Oh..." She looked up at him but his face and eyes hid any emotion.

He stepped away, his back to her. "What happened next?"

"I made a false codebook in case it was a hoax. I took both books with me."

He turned and tilted his head toward her. "You arrived at the Serpentine with two codebooks, one you've written and one your brother sent you?"

This wasn't the warm, caring man his aunt and sister described. He questioned her as if she was a suspect in a horrendous crime. She nodded.

"Go on."

"I was shocked to discover Isabelle."

"Did she say why she wanted the codebook?"

"She spoke in circles." She hesitated in explaining Isabelle's conjectures about their relationship.

"What did she say?"

"She said she worked for you, but as your mistress."

"She did?" His eyes couldn't hide his surprise. "She didn't ask for the codebook?"

"We never got that far."

"What?" Disbelief flashed across his face. "You didn't give her the codebook?"

"No." Heat rushed to her neck and face. "She acted like a scorned woman. She said I would never satisfy you the way she did."

"Isabelle sent you a note to come to the Serpentine with the codebook, but she never asked for the book because she was too busy talking about her relationship with me?"

It did sound incredulous when he recited her words in his cold, precise manner.

"All I wanted was news of my brother, to hear he was safe."

"What did she say about your brother?"

"She told me he was an idiot for taking the codebook and placing himself between Fouché and Talleyrand. She also warned me that it was dangerous to have the codebook in my possession."

"She knew that Fouché was after the book?"

"She said my brother was in great danger from both sides." She gulped down the despair, the hitch of hopelessness rising from her chest.

"What else did Isabelle say?"

"Nothing else."

"Then what happened?"

"Isabelle looked startled, as if she saw someone in the woods behind me. I turned to see what she was looking at and, when I turned back, she was pointing a gun at me."

"Did she demand the book with the pointed gun?"

"I didn't give her time. I hit the gun out of her hand with my riding crop."

He strode to the window. He spoke in a low, barely audible tone with his back turned. "You could've been killed."

"I believe Isabelle tried to protect me from whoever was in the woods."

He slammed his fist against the wall. "Damn it! Henrietta. Don't you realize how close you came to being shot? Isabelle saved you and your damn codebook."

She ignored his fury. "You didn't ask Isabelle to get the codebook from me?"

"No, I didn't send Isabelle. She was a double agent for France and England."

"Does Isabelle know that you are on to her and her demand for the codebook?"

"Isabelle is the agent who was killed last night."

"Isabelle is dead?" The woman who had tried to protect her was dead. She couldn't breathe. The room became stifling as if all the air was sucked out.

"She was found shot not far from the Serpentine."

"I can't believe it." She closed her eyes to stop the room from spinning.

Cord knelt on one knee and pressed a glass of brandy into her hand. "Drink this. It will help. I should've prepared you."

Her body and hands shook. She was unable to raise the glass. He wrapped his hands around hers to bring the brandy to her lips.

"Take a sip," he said.

She took a small sip, but Cord forced several more sips. Heat rushed into her stomach, warming her from the inside out. The shock of Isabelle's death slowly subsided. "But who would want to kill Isabelle if she was a French agent?"

"I don't know." She could hear his frustration.

"Please tell me you've heard from Michael." The high pitch in her voice didn't sound like her own. She couldn't believe anything bad could befall Michael without her sensing it.

His eyes darkened with an emotion she didn't recognize.

"Oh, Cord. I'm sorry to think only of my family. You cared about Isabelle." She squeezed his hands.

He rose, shaking off her hands. "She worked for me." He bent over the fire, slamming the poker against the logs.

"You can't blame yourself. You said Isabelle was a double agent."

"Isabelle was killed for the book." He dropped the poker and turned. "Don't you ever think of your own safety? Your brother put you at great risk when he sent you the codebook. I've no idea what possessed the young fool to take the book."

"Michael's intentions would never be to cause harm or put me in danger."

"You continue to defend your brother, knowing you might have been killed?"

"Wouldn't you risk everything to help your brother?"

"My brother is dead."

Euphemia's words echoed. He would be hard on himself and everyone around him. He needed understanding, a woman's comfort.

"Since my mother died, I've had only my brothers and Uncle Charles." Her voice wavered. "My mother never asked me, but when she was ill, I promised I'd take care of the men."

Cord took large swig of brandy and walked to the window.

"Michael and I've been inseparable since we were small children. I constantly followed him and his friends. He teased me relentlessly. I had to prove myself by besting him." She chuckled, trying to lighten the icy strain, the heavy silence between them.

"Michael and I've always competed. As Michael grew and became stronger, I had to adapt my strategies to beat him." Now wasn't the time to tell Cord she was the better code breaker.

"What was the age difference between you and your brother?"

Cord whipped his head around. "Your plan isn't going to work." His tone was cryptic and cynical. "Your womanly wiles will not soften my response to your wayward brother."

The odious man. She never had felt such a strong need to pummel a person before meeting Cord. She wanted to wrestle him to the ground and strike him repeatedly.

"Pardon me, my lord, but how could I soften a glacier?" She took a big gulp of the brandy. "How naïve of me to think that you could sympathize with my worries or have any understanding of a sibling bond."

"You already know the age difference between my brother and I and anything else my aunt and sister felt they needed to confide."

Her body trembled, not from exhaustion but from the frustration of trying to break through Cord's prickly pride and the walls of stone around his vulnerability. She wasn't up for sparring with the impossible man. "I'm tired and wish to retire."

CHAPTER THIRTY-TWO

Cord had lost track of how long he had been standing at the window until Henrietta said she wanted to retire. "Gray was eighteen months older." He stayed at the window but partially turned toward her. He couldn't see her face in the dim light, but heard her take a slight breath.

"Were you as competitive as Michael and I in your studies?"

He chuckled at the idea of Gray and him battling over their studies. "Gray had no interest in intellectual pursuits. Our contests were entirely physical." He realized tonight was the first time he had laughed about Gray and his antics in a very long time.

"Gray and I were always competing. We turned everything into a contest: who could get to the stables faster, who could eat the most tarts. Nothing was too trivial. As we got older, the contests became more sophisticated, but the drive to win never changed."

He wasn't going to share that when he and Gray got older, they competed for the favors of women.

"Gray was an incredible athlete. I was the studious one. He knew exactly how to goad me about my studies, how to get me to take part in his crazy schemes."

"Your library is obviously home to a scholar."

He could hear the admiration in her voice.

Henrietta loved books. She was an amazing conundrum of a woman. Young agents and spies were terrified by his wrath, but she had just stood up to his fury.

"Were you with him when he had his accident?" No wilting flower, his Henrietta. She wanted to help him exorcise his feelings about Gray's death. He sensed his aunt and sister's hand in Henrietta's probing.

"Gray was laughing, with his head turned toward me, gloating with his damn self-righteous smile, gloating that he had beaten me over the jump. He didn't see the shallow ravine."

God, how many times could he replay the moment, the moment he would do anything to change? A moment with a different ending, a moment of good judgment that would save Gray.

"Oh, Cord. I'm so sorry."

He sat down, crossed his ankles, feigning an air of relaxation, as if this night were routine for both of them. He didn't want to stir up the painful feelings swelling in his chest and gut.

"You must miss him terribly."

"He's just gone." He never admitted to missing Gray.

Henrietta's face was soft with a tender grace that warmed him. He never had been remotely interested to talk to anyone about Gray. Henrietta made him want to try. He had suffered, endured, but no one had made him feel as if they really understood.

"How terrible for your parents."

"My father seemed to shrink, to wither with the grief. My mother would burst into tears when she saw me. To her, I was a painful reminder of Gray."

Henrietta reached and took hold of his hands. Her small, soft hands squeezed his. "You lost your best friend and your parents."

"I always thought that with all our intense closeness that I would continue to feel a connection."

Henrietta tightened her hold on his hands.

"But there's nothing. Just emptiness...and a desire to tell him what I think of his stupid recklessness."

"You're still mad at him?"

"Mad at him?" Was anger the emotion he felt toward Gray? He didn't have only one feeling about Gray's death. "How can I be mad at him? He's the one who died."

"I was really angry at my father," Henrietta said. "How could he die and leave all of us heartbroken? It's rather shocking to be angry at a dead person."

He had never admitted his anger to anyone, not even himself. But how could Gray have left him, left him alone, left him to console his parents, who could never be consoled?

"My mother got ill a year after my father died." Tears formed in Henrietta's eyes. "She tried to fight the wasting disease, but her spirit was broken without my father."

He looked down on Henrietta's slight hands, covering his grip. He raised her hands to his lips. He brushed his lips against her softness. "I know you miss your mother." He recognized the sorrow of loss in her eyes.

She nodded. "I miss her every day."

"A day doesn't pass when I don't think of Gray."

She released his hands and touched his face, caressing his jaw with her delicate fingers. The simple act awakened a need deep inside him to be close to her, to share her pain. He wanted to take and offer joy to Henrietta, who had suffered as he had.

She leaned forward in her chair and ran her finger along his lower lip.

He was swept away in a hunger, a hunger he didn't know existed. It wasn't only passion, but a need to comfort her. He needed her to envelop his hard body and wounded feelings into her softness, into her sympathy. He rose on his knees to kiss her. His tongue searched the corners of her sweet lips. He savored the taste of Henrietta and the hitch in her breathing when he nibbled on her full, plump lower lip.

He lifted her onto his lap. She was buttoned up in her prim nightgown. His other hand massaged her leg.

She moved rhythmically on his lap.

He pressed his tongue into her mouth searching the warm, moistness.

Henrietta pressed her breasts against his chest and sucked on his tongue. He groaned. "We have to stop or I won't be able to."

"Oh, Cord, I don't want you to stop."

He laughed aloud. The joy in the sound surprised him. He felt free, as if he could finally breathe again after years of pain. "You enjoy living dangerously."

He began to unbutton her nightgown. "I want to touch you all over."

"I want to touch you too." Her voice had gotten husky with desire and caused his erection to throb.

She leaned back into his shoulder. He took advantage of her position to fondle her full luscious breasts. He plucked her nipples through the fabric, the buds tightened with his touch. His hand moved downward to cup her glorious softness. The bandage below her chest stopped him.

"My God, I had forgotten you're injured. What's wrong with me? Every time I touch you, I'm overwhelmed with wanting you."

"Cord, I'm fine. In fact, I've never felt better." She moved her hips against his bulging erection. His need to take her on a wild ride, right here in the chair drummed through his body.

She was an innocent and a virgin. She deserved a gentle, slow awakening.

"Too much has happened today. I don't know if I can be gentle tonight. Do you understand?"

Henrietta moved again.

He was ready to plunge into her. He needed to slow

down, to be gentle. Where had all his expertise, all his highly practiced skill as a lover gone?

She scattered kisses on his cheeks and neck, then turned toward him and pressed her breasts against his chest again, driving him close to the brink. "Cord, I want you as you are tonight. I don't need gentle. I need you." She kissed him passionately, thrust her tongue into his mouth. "I want to be loved by you. Don't deny me."

"Oh, darling. I want you, as you can feel, but I'm afraid of hurting you."

Her green eyes were ablaze with desire. "Cord, please."

His blood heated and pulsed with Henrietta's need for him. "I've waited a long time for you, Henrietta Harcourt, since Lady Chillington's ball."

He lifted her carefully and lowered her to the bed. Her hair fell across the counterpane, streaks of fire shining in the candlelight. Her face was flushed, but whatever she saw in his eyes made her smile widen in pleasure. She opened her arms. "Come, Cord."

He tore off his boots and shirt and tried to gain control of his rampant need to sink into her wet heat. Henrietta, waiting in a linen shift was more stimulating than any other woman in a silk negligee. "Do you know how many times I've imagined this, you just as you are now?" he asked.

He lay on his side next to her. He brushed her thick, glossy hair away from her neck. He sucked on the delicate whirl of her earlobe, gently twirling the pink, firm skin with his tongue. The idea of exploring Henrietta's firm, pink womanhood enflamed him. He thrust his tongue into her ear and fingered her nipple.

"Darling, you'll have to tell me if what I do hurts. I only want to bring you pleasure."

She was restless and breathless. "Cord, everything you're doing is pleasure."

"Will it hurt too much to take off this damned

nightgown?"

"It's difficult to raise my arms but if you help me slip the nightgown over my head, I'm sure we can manage." Her lips curved in a small smile. Henrietta was a natural temptress.

His hands shook like a callow youth when he tried to unbutton her nightgown. The dainty pearl buttons were difficult to pull through the embroidered buttonholes. Frustrated, he looked up at Henrietta watching him. Her eyes dilated with passion. He wrapped his hand around the nape of her neck and brought her close to thrust his tongue into her soft mouth.

She ran her hands through his hair.

He got the last button undone on the nightgown. "If you sit up, I'll slip the nightgown over your head without dislodging your bandage."

He circled her chest with his arms to lift her gently to a sitting position. He felt her wince from the pain, but she didn't complain.

"Are you sure this is a good idea?" He spoke tenderly, trying to be a gentleman, to pretend he was in control.

"I don't feel any pain."

A rush of exultation shot through him. He threw her nightgown on the floor. She had a muslin bandage wrapped around her pale chest. The bandage lifted her breasts. Her pink, ripe nipples jutted above the bandage. He bent and took one of the coral nipples into his mouth and sucked.

Henrietta gasped then squirmed, pushing her breast into his mouth.

"Let me help you lie down." Slowly he moved her lower on the bed and came down next to her. He trailed kisses along the bandage. "I don't want you to ever hurt again."

He suckled the nipples of each breast until Henrietta moaned and writhed, lifting her hips off the bed. He ran his hand down her smooth, soft abdomen and cupped her mound. His finger explored her opening, into her wetness. He inhaled her sweet, muskiness. "Oh, God. Hen, you're ready for me. He put his finger inside, gently expanding her tightness.

She was hot and wet and he was going to explode if he didn't enter her soon.

Henrietta whimpered his name and pushed against his hand. He put a second finger in her and slowly imitated the rhythm he would pleasure them both. He licked each breast while he maintained a slow languorous rhythm in Henrietta's hot body.

A panting Henrietta pleaded with him in a low, guttural voice. Close to the edge, she made mewing sounds that pushed him close to losing control.

"Darling, let yourself go. I'll catch you." He rubbed her nub with his thumb as he kept the rhythm of his two fingers.

"Cord, Oh, Cord." Her voice filled with wonder.

He could feel her spasm around his fingers when she found her release. Her whole body trembled against him. She was magnificent. She continued to shudder. He kissed her gently on the forehead and cheeks, trying to restrain himself from plunging into her warmth.

"Cord, I need you."

"Darling, let me take off my breeches." He jumped off the bed and quickly stripped off his pants.

Henrietta giggled. But when she looked down on his jutting erection, her eyes grew round. "Oh, my."

He couldn't help but be pleased by her astonishment. "I don't want to hurt you."

"I know you'll be gentle."

He lowered himself on top of her, holding all of his own weight with his arms. Nestled between her thighs, he slowly entered her. She was wet and tight and he was having difficulty moving carefully when he wanted to thrust and thrust until she screamed his name.

"You're perfect, Henrietta." He pushed forward until he felt the resistance. "I'm sorry, darling." He broke through the barrier.

Her hands tightened on his neck, her breathing hitched.

"Are you okay?" His voice was rough, but he was hanging on to his control by a thin, very thin thread.

"I'm fine, really."

Recovering from whatever discomfort she had initially experienced, she moved against him, against his slow, cautious pace. He kept a gentle rhythm until she wrapped her legs around him, pulling him into her passionate vortex. Her need drove them to a frenzied pace.

When he felt her spasm around him, he spilled his seed in one powerful plunge.

Breathless, they gazed into each other's eyes, both shocked by their intense lovemaking.

"I had no idea." Her hair was disheveled, her lips swollen, her eyes soft with passion from their lovemaking.

"Me either." He kissed her gently on the lips then her chin and neck. He worked his way toward her earlobe when he felt her body relaxing. "And what a delicious surprise you are."

"Oh, Cord, you were perfect, too," was the last thing she said before she fell asleep.

He shifted to his side on the bed next to her. Her breathing slowed as she snuggled deeper then turned on her side, her round bottom pressed against him. He wrapped his arm around her bandaged chest and pulled her closer. She was a perfect fit. He explored the smooth skin on the curve of her hip. He wanted to suck on the indentation of her soft, womanly curves.

She sighed and moved closer to him, against his hardening erection.

He couldn't believe his response to this woman. He

had just experienced an extraordinary orgasm and was ready again. He wouldn't act on his burning need, because she was tired and would be sore but these gentlemanly thoughts didn't lessen his bodily hunger. He stroked her hips, wanting her.

"I love you Henrietta Harcourt. Tomorrow I'm getting a special license and a ring. You can't escape me again."

Her response was a snuffle.

He didn't want to leave her yet, but he didn't want his aunt to find them. He wouldn't embarrass Henrietta or his aunt. He needed sleep. He hadn't slept for two nights. Hopefully, Ash had spread the rumors at Matilde Bertram's ball tonight that Isabelle's murder was the work of a crazed past lover.

He ran his hand down her smooth hip one last time and, unable to resist, cupped her soft buttocks. His probing finger sought the tempting fissure between the shapely globes, insinuated into the warm moist area. Henrietta moaned and moved against him in her sleep. He couldn't begin anything, but he was having difficulty resisting his need to be back in her welcoming body.

Henrietta was the only person in his entire life who had been able to distract him from his objective. He had come to her room to obtain the codebook or at least that was what he told himself. He had really come for a good fight with the code-breaking hellion.

Finally their fighting had ended in the way he had fantasized. Would Henrietta understand that their skirmishing and sparring had been the fire of their passion?

He should have gotten the codebook from her before she fell asleep. His future wife would bristle at the invasion if he took it out of her reticule while she slept. Not the way to begin their marriage. She and the codebook were safe in his house. She couldn't get into any trouble when he went to the offices at Abchurch.

He'd be back by the time she awoke.

He bent over to kiss her one last time. She slept soundly and didn't stir when he pulled the heavy covers over her. He would keep the new Countess of Rathbourne too busy in bed to have time for meeting spies in Hyde Park.

CHAPTER THIRTY-THREE

Henrietta longed to sustain the dream. Her body was relaxed, languorous, heat radiated between her legs. She reached for Cord, but he faded out of her embrace.

She stretched under the sheets, not wanting her dream to end. Memories from last night surged into her consciousness. Last night wasn't a dream. She and Cord had made love. Cord had been all she imagined as a passionate and tender lover. She rolled over to touch him, but found instead a cold, creased sheet.

On the periphery of her awareness someone pounded on the door.

Where was Cord? The knocking persisted. She pulled herself to a sitting position and winced at the tug of pain from her ribs.

"Lady Henrietta, I must speak with you." Brompton spoke through the door.

Her heart fluttered and her stomach clenched in fear. Brompton's unexpected appearance at Rathbourne House could only mean one thing. Uncle Charles was in trouble. Henrietta pulled the covers up to her neck, hiding her nakedness. "Come in, Brompton. What's happened?"

A flushed maid opened the door to the bedroom.

Brompton didn't enter the room but stood at the doorway. "Edward is missing."

Her brain went numb. How could Edward go missing? She struggled to understand. Edward was never alone. Gus and Mr. Marlow were his constant companions.

"How?" Her voice echoed in her head, as if she stood at the end of a long tunnel.

"He and Mr. Marlow went to the Serpentine to sail boats. Edward had run to retrieve his boat in the wooded area that skirts the lake. After a few minutes when Edward didn't return, Mr. Marlow went into the woods to look for him. He searched everywhere but Edward had disappeared without a trace."

Brompton stared at his feet after his speech, aware of her state of dishabille and this irregular circumstance. "Mr. Marlow took Gus back to the woods to see if he can lead him to Edward. And I've come straight here."

"I must get home." She pulled the counterpane around her and stood, oblivious to her shocking lack of propriety. Edward... She couldn't allow herself to think about her sweet, baby brother. She needed to do something.

"Brompton, go downstairs and find Lord Rathbourne. I must speak with him."

She dressed quickly and strode down the stairs. The pain in her ribs now a minor irritation. She and Cord would find Edward. Cord would know what to do with the codebook to end the threats to her family.

Brompton and Sloane were at the bottom of the stairs. They stood silent when she descended.

"Lady Henrietta." Brompton moved forward. "Lord Rathbourne isn't in residence. Sloane will send an urgent message to Hyde Park and his office."

"Is Lady Euphemia at home?" She asked.

"I'm sorry. Both ladies have gone on their social visits. I cannot say when they will return," Sloane said.

"Tell Lord Rathbourne to meet me immediately at

Kendal House. Tell him my brother has been kidnapped." Her voice choked around the words.

Brompton gently took her arm. "Come, Lady Henrietta, let's go home. With Tom and Mr. Marlow out searching for him, perhaps we'll have word by the time we get home."

Henrietta rode in silence to Kendal House. Her heart thumped, her mouth was dry, and she had an incredible burst of energy surging through her body. She needed to control the urge to panic or she be of no help to Edward.

She had to use her highly developed skills of deduction to find Edward's abductor. The men who killed Isabelle had taken Edward to obtain the codebook. There was no other reasonable conclusion. She would give them the damn codebook. She would give them anything to save her brother.

When she arrived at Kendal House, Mrs. Brompton rushed out, her arms open.

"Oh, my poor lamb. How could this happen?" She folded Henrietta in her beefy arms. "We'll find him. Don't worry."

Henrietta paused for a brief moment in the warm embrace, then summoned her strength to pull away. "Any word from Tom and Mr. Marlow? Any messages?"

"No messages and nothing from Tom or Mr. Marlow, but I expect them soon. Shall I get you tea?"

"What have you told Uncle Charles?"

"I've told him nothing. He's been in the study all morning. I thought it best for you to decide."

"I believe that without answers, it's best to not to tell him." Her voice got wobbly. She couldn't bear to think of Uncle Charles' reaction to Edward's disappearance. The boy and her uncle were inseparable.

She climbed the stairs. Her terror for her younger brother, alone and frightened, grew with each step.

Brompton spoke from the foyer, his voice excited.

"Lady Henrietta, a note has come for you. It was brought 'round to the servant's entrance by a street urchin."

She turned and descended quickly. Tearing at the seal, she read the note. In exchange for the codebook, Edward would be returned.

She didn't know if she could face this new threat alone. The remembrance of Cord's tender lovemaking bolstered her resolve. She wasn't alone. Cord would help her rescue Edward. "I must go immediately. Bring Minotaur around."

"Please let me go with you or at least wait until Tom can accompany you."

"No, Brompton, I must go alone. The note is very clear. And time is of the essence."

"Come alone, don't tell anyone..." Exactly like the message from Isabelle.

With a false bravado, she instructed Brompton as if she were in control, not seconds away from shattering. "When Lord Rathbourne arrives, give him the note. Tell him I've gone to the boathouse at the Serpentine."

Henrietta hurried to her room and retrieved her uncle's pistol.

Returning downstairs again, she mounted her horse and galloped toward Hyde Park. She nudged Minotaur between two wagons at a busy intersection, teeming with the daily business of keeping the great houses of Mayfair functioning.

She needed to stay focused on the task at hand, armed with the codebooks, a loaded pistol, and a very shaky plan to face a murderer. Her plan was simple: negotiate, give him the codebook, and pray until Cord arrived to deal with the murderer. If Cord didn't arrive in time, what would she do? There was no question in her mind that she would save Edward, no matter what the cost. She wasn't going to let anyone hurt her brother. She looked back at the busy crossroad, wondering if the enemy shadowed her.

CHAPTER THIRTY-FOUR

Henrietta entered the Curzon Gate, following the same route she had taken to meet Isabelle. Hyde Park was busy with the daily parade of fashionable people, here despite the gloomy skies of an approaching storm. How strange to have daily routines continue as her deadly drama unfolded.

She pointed Minotaur to the north side of the lake. Black angry clouds gathered portending a downpour. She shivered in the chilly air and in apprehension. The meeting was at the public boathouse in the middle of the day. Why hadn't anyone seen Edward's abduction?

She slowed her pace when she approached the decrepit wood cabin where the boats were stored. Birdsong lightened the heavy silence. She pulled Minotaur to the mounting block and dismounted. She patted the pistol again—she knew it was dangerous to have a loaded pistol tucked into her riding skirt, but so was this entire enterprise.

The place looked deserted—no boaters, no attendants. The door to the boathouse was ajar. She glanced behind her. She couldn't shake the feeling that someone followed, watching her every move. She pushed the heavy door farther open. It creaked when she put her weight to it. Fear surged through her like a brush fire.

"Come in, Henrietta. I've been waiting for you," The

Duke of Wycliffe said.

She couldn't believe a man of his position was a traitor or would kidnap her brother.

He remained obscured in the shadows. The room smelled of mustiness and the mold of wet cushions.

She stepped farther into the boathouse, her thundering heart the only sound in the small space. A cracked, dusty window gave scant light. She was shocked by the changes in him since the ball. He was dirty and disheveled. But more ominously, he was desperate and dangerous. She could smell his anxiety. His pupils were dilated as if he burned with a fever.

"Ah, I see you're surprised. I wondered if you or Rathbourne had guessed my role in this intrigue. I've overestimated both of you." His laugh echoed in the void. "Who could imagine your scholarly brother could create such a crisis? Did you bring the damn book?"

"Where is Edward? I won't give you the book until you release Edward."

He stepped closer to her in the dim light. The shadows contorted his agitation, his once handsome face now grotesque. "My darling Henrietta." He lifted her chin with one icy finger. "So fierce. I regret that I didn't seduce you when I had the chance."

She gasped and pulled away. "Where have you taken Edward? Give me my brother and I'll give you the book."

He grabbed her hand and pulled her against his clammy body. "You believe you can barter with me?" His putrid breath blew across her face. He cupped her breast tightly. "So sweet."

Outrage coursed through her body. "Stop it. Where is my brother?"

Beads of perspiration beat down his forehead. "Haven't you heard what happened to Isabelle? She failed me." He paused, letting his words take effect.

"I'll give you whatever you want, but let my brother go." She spoke calmly, not wanting to further bait him.

"The day grows more interesting," His tone became menacing. "Give me the book, and I'll consider your fate and that of your brother."

"I have it right here." She reached slowly into her reticule. "Yes, right here," she mumbled, trying to delay him.

He grabbed the purse out of her hands. "What plan are you concocting in that clever brain?" He opened the bag and took out the book. He threw the empty reticule back at her.

"What will you do with the book?" she asked.

"Not decipher secret messages, if that's what you think." His laugh was harsh.

He pulled out his pistol and waved it at her. "Enough idle chatter. It's time."

"Edward! Where is he?" Primal fear blasted through body.

"Did you notice the boat? You're going to be joining your brother."

She froze in panic, her knees locked. Had he drowned Edward? She mustn't give in to the fear if there was a chance to save Edward.

He pressed the gun to her back. "No tricks or you'll never see your brother."

Henrietta moved slowly, weighing her options as her heart beat a frenzied tattoo. She knew she must play along until she found Edward then she would use the gun in her pocket.

He thrust the gun into her back. "Keep going."

She moved outside, surveying the bushes. Where was Cord?

A ferocious sound pierced the silent woods, then a blur of yellow fur catapulted through the air. The impact of the four-stone dog aiming straight at his chest, knocked the Duke of Wycliffe to the ground. He dropped his gun.

Henrietta seized the pistol and pointed it at the prone man.

Gus had his paws on the duke's chest, his sharp canines bared. She was grateful for Gus' growl and intimidating posture. "Good boy, Gus."

"Henrietta?" Cord ran down the path toward the bathhouse. "Thank God."

She wanted to run into Cord's arms but kept her position over the duke. Her nervousness caused her to chatter. "He killed Isabelle. He has Edward hidden. I was to go with him by boat."

Cord took the pistol out of her hand, kicked Wycliffe with the toe of his boot. "Get up."

Wycliffe stood, brushing the dirt from his breeches.

Gus sat next to Henrietta and began a slow, insistent whine. She patted the broad head of the dog. "It's okay. We'll find Edward."

Wycliffe sneered. "Rathbourne, I'm sorry you had to discover our little tête-à-tête. But let me assure you, Henrietta was pleased with me."

Cord lashed out and smashed the duke in the face. There was a cracking sound of breaking bones.

Wycliffe fell sideways and reached down to pull a knife from his boot. "I'm going to kill you." He plunged the dagger at Cord.

Henrietta pulled her pistol out of her pocket and tried to take aim. She couldn't get a clean shot off without possibly hitting Cord.

Parrying the duke's thrust, Cord dodged the knife. Wycliffe lunged forward, the knife pointed at Cord's heart. Gus lowered himself to the ground ready to attack Wycliffe. She grabbed him by the collar to prevent him from getting caught in the fight. She kept her gun aimed on the fighting men with one hand while her other hand held Gus in place.

Cord leaned backward, barely avoiding the knife aimed at his chest. He twisted his torso, kicking the knife out of Wycliffe's hand with a swift jerk. He pulled the hammer back on the duke's pistol and aimed at Wycliffe's chest.

"Cord, don't kill him. He has Edward."

Cord barked. "Get away from here, Henrietta."

There was a rustle of noise from the bushes. "I'm sorry to interrupt the fun."

"Lucien?" Henrietta stared at the pistol the comte held in his hand.

Henrietta stepped forward with her pistol aimed back at the comte. "Are you part of this—kidnapping my brother?"

Lucien didn't appear fazed by her or Cord's pistol. He walked calmly into the clearing. "I'm not part of the kidnapping, but I know where he took your brother."

"You bastard." Wycliffe sneered.

"Please, Lucien. Tell me," she begged.

"Damn it, Henrietta, get behind me." Cord kept his gun pointed at Wycliffe and grabbed her by the arm to push her behind him.

"I need to find my brother. Lucien, please tell me where my brother is."

"Give me the book." Lucien kept his gun pointed at her.

"You fool. Fouché will never release your sister." Wycliffe gave a chilling chortle. "He's probably killed her already."

Lucien stepped closer and pointed his gun at Wycliffe's heart. "Unlike Rathbourne, you're no use to me alive."

"Go ahead. If you don't kill me, Fouché will. Fouché will kill us both," Wycliffe said.

"Henrietta, keep your gun on the duke." Cord turned his pistol on Lucien. "Drop the gun."

Lucien fired at Wycliffe's chest.

The duke fell backward, blood immediately covering his shirt. His face contorted in agony. "You bastard."

Wycliffe fell to the ground with his eyes open. His chest rattled with one last motion.

Lucien stared at the duke. "It's all been for nothing. Fouché will never release my sister and I'm a dead man." A report echoed from the woods into the quiet space. Lucien suddenly fell forward onto the dead duke, a gaping hole in his back from an unknown attacker.

Cord tackled Henrietta to the ground. Her breath was knocked clear out of her, her face pressed into the dust. Cord's weight on top of her didn't allow any movement or any breath. She panted.

"Stay down. Someone fired from the bushes." Cord lifted himself off of her and crawled on his stomach toward the lake. Gus followed Cord.

"Cord, be careful," she cried.

"Stay down until I signal it's safe." With his pistol in his hand, he proceeded toward the sound of the shot.

She couldn't get the air to move into her lungs. Panic skittered up and down her spine. The dead bodies of both men lay a few feet from her. Her heart pumped frantically. She wanted to scream, to run. Instead, she rolled to her side and searched for her gun. She waited on her side with her gun pointed at the woods.

Cord returned from the bushes with Gus close behind. "The shooter has fled through the undergrowth. The recent rain has made it easy to see his footprints."

"I've got to find Edward."

Cord reached down and took her hands. "We'll find him." He pulled her into his arms and held her tight. She hugged him around his waist, breathing his clean smell and leaning into his warm strength.

"What is that sound?" Cord asked.

Gus stood next to the boat in the water and whined in a pitiful way. "It's Gus. He'll lead us to Edward!"

She took hold of Cord's hand. She needed to stay connected to him.

Cord squeezed back, his heat seeping into her cold hand.

"Gus, find Edward," she said.

Gus ran back and forth between the lake and the boathouse, his nose to the ground, howling an unsettling cry.

"Edward must be close," he said.

"You don't think Wycliffe harmed Edward?" Her voice, like her entire body, shook.

"There would be no reason for Wycliffe to kill Edward. I'm sure we'll find Edward none the worse for his adventure." He pulled her close against him. His confidence and soothing voice calmed the panic whispering along her skin.

Gus ran ahead, nose to the path, howling an eerie lament, for the lost Edward.

Behind Gus, they hurried through the bushes on the overgrown path that skirted the lake. She clung to Cord's hand, although the brush became so thick they had to proceed single file.

Gus ran through the bushes then started to bark frantically.

"Gus must have found Edward."

Cord turned and put his fingers to her lips to warn her to be quiet. He whispered. "Let me go first to make sure there is no one guarding Edward."

"I can help you distract whoever is guarding Edward."

Gus continued to bark.

The undergrowth cleared when they moved deeper into the woods.

"Stay here. If Edward is guarded, I'll signal to you. Shoot your pistol into the air. With the distraction, I'll take the man unaware. For no reason are you to come forward until I give you the signal."

He took her by the shoulders. His eyes focused on her. "Henrietta, promise me."

"I'll do as you say, but..."

"Let me focus on finding Edward. I need to know that you'll be safe."

He asked for her trust. She looked into his eyes, his

feelings were hidden. He waited. She nodded an affirmative.

"I'll wait for your signal. But don't take too long," she said.

He kissed her quickly. "Thank you. I know how difficult that was."

Henrietta checked the powder in her pistol despite her shaking hands. It was dry and ready. She silently prayed they'd find Edward unharmed.

The song of a wood thrush was the only sound except for Gus' excited barking. Her hope mounted, assured that if anything was wrong, Gus would've been distressed.

Cord shouted, "Edward is here and safe."

She ran with her pistol in her hand through the low bushes and emerged into a small clearing of trees. Cord was bent, cutting ropes away from Edward's legs.

Edward had been gagged and tied to a tree. Her stomach lurched as if she might vomit.

Gus circled and barked at his best friend.

"Gus, I knew you would find me." Edward's voice was tinny, as if he was ready to cry.

The dog jumped up to lick Edward's pale face.

Henrietta ran to her brother, tears falling from her eyes. "Edward, are you all right?" Edward's face contorted as he tried not to cry, but the tears dripped down his cheeks.

Gus yipped and ran between Henrietta and Edward, jumping on both.

"He said he was going to kill us. He kept me here for hours." His voice cracked.

"He will never harm you again. He's dead," Cord said.

Sensing Edward's near collapse, she brushed the hair from his face. "He could never have hurt a Harcourt. What do you think of your brave dog?"

When Cord cut the final rope, Edward slid down the tree to the dirt.

Henrietta gasped. "Edward."

She reached for him, but Cord was quicker. He grabbed Edward and held him upright, his arm around Edward's shoulder. "Do you want me to carry you? Do you need to rest?"

"I want to go home," Edward pleaded in a voice that she hadn't heard in years. Edward threw himself into her arms.

She squeezed him tight against her. He wrapped his arms around her.

Her voice sounded strained with the pent-up emotion. "Let's go home. Mrs. Brompton has promised you anything you want for dinner tonight."

"I'm starved. I missed tea," Edward complained, already recovering.

Henrietta couldn't tell who required more support. She held onto Edward, planning to never let him go. Cord wrapped his arm around Henrietta and Edward. A triumphant Gus led them out of the woods.

CHAPTER THIRTY-FIVE

What was taking Henrietta so long? Cord stood and began to pace in the Kendal library. She had taken Edward upstairs to get him settled while he stayed to entertain Uncle Charles, who was oblivious to the day's terrors. Charles had finally retired after a lengthy discussion about mummification. And Henrietta still hadn't appeared.

He understood her need to hover over Edward. He had the same need to hover over her. He wanted her by his side, to touch and hold.

He took the Rathbourne betrothal ring out of his pocket and examined it again. The shimmering emerald matched the bright color of her eyes when she was in a temper or in the throes of passion. Remembering Henrietta's response to his love-making last night had kept him in an aroused state since he left her that morning. Was it really just hours ago?

How could events have gone so awry? When he left her earlier, he had planned to return to obtain the codebook and to propose to her. Instead, Edward had been abducted and Henrietta had embarked alone again into danger.

He had failed to calculate that the eleven-year-old needed protection. He had Talley guarding Uncle Charles. He had underestimated the desperation of the enemy. What had happened to the rational, analytical spy? Love.

He had been so blinded by his overwhelming need to protect Henrietta that he had failed to consider her brother. He had guards in place at Kendal house, but he hadn't thought Wycliffe would be desperate enough to risk an abduction in a public park.

He fingered the ring again. He wouldn't leave Kendal house tonight without her promise. He was about to resume his pacing when Henrietta entered the dimly lit library. Cord felt the shock to his system. He could barely breathe with the sight of Henrietta dressed in her simple nightclothes.

"Cord, I'm so sorry to have kept you waiting. Edward was distraught. He had to recount his experience several times."

He couldn't focus on what she was saying. The soft, white material clung to all of his favorite curves. She took a step toward him, then another, and molded herself into his arms.

"You were wonderful with Edward. You're going to make a great father."

He couldn't speak, enveloped in her smell of lilacs, her warm softness pressed against his body. Although new to love-making, Henrietta was progressing masterfully in the art of seduction. He was in a tortured state of physical and emotional arousal. His failure not to anticipate the abduction and to protect Henrietta had him tied into crazy knots.

She fussed with his coat lapels. "You do want children, don't you, not just an heir?"

His brain failed to grasp what she was talking about. He couldn't think. His body had superseded his brain. "What's wrong, Cord? You seem tense?"

He had to suppress the need to laugh out loud. Tense didn't come close to what he was feeling. His hunger for Henrietta, mixed with his guilt, swirled into a reckless potion.

"I failed to protect your brother, and, because of me, your life was in danger."

"Oh, darling, you're not responsible. Wycliffe and Lucien were the villains." She rewarded him with a slow, sultry kiss.

"I promise to do a better job of protecting you." He was having trouble delivering his thoughtful speech when Henrietta used her tongue most effectively to cause his blood to pump in an incessant beat through him.

"Cord, you've done a splendid job protecting all the Harcourts." She traced his jaw with her tongue to his ear.

He was breathing like a draft horse. He pulled her tight against his hardness. "I never thought it could be like this—all consuming, the need to be with you, to protect you." He needed to make her understand. He took her by the shoulders. "I was angry at your meeting with Isabelle because..." His voice choked. "I didn't want to lose you like Gray. When I got the message today that you had gone to meet a murderer... I'm never afraid."

She stepped back to look into his eyes. "Because of you, all the Harcourts are safe... well almost all the Harcourts. I wish I knew that Michael was on his way home." She said the last words against his chest.

"We finally received a message from Brinsley. Michael escaped Paris."

"Oh, thank God!" Henrietta sobbed.

Cord held her, kissed her hair. "I'm sorry I didn't tell you sooner. With all that has happened today, there wasn't time."

"He's on his way home? But why haven't I heard from him?"

"The French must have been intercepting the messages from Brinsley. It's the only thing that makes sense. I'm not sure if it was Talleyrand or Fouché's men who were intercepting the messages."

"I don't think Michael had any idea when he took the codebook that he would initiate the dangerous intrigue between the two Frenchmen.

"Fouché's assassin was seen down at the docks leaving London. I'm sure he killed De Valmont at the Serpentine to prevent any connection between him and Fouché from surfacing. Fouché doesn't want Napoleon to suspect his nefarious plots."

Henrietta stared at him as if trying to understand. "Three people killed over a codebook." She shook her head in disbelief.

"Don't think about them, they weren't innocent." He kissed her on the forehead, on the cheeks.

"When will Michael be home?"

"The message was brief. Michael and his bodyguard, Denby, left Paris with a child."

"A child?" Henrietta laughed. "Sounds like Michael got himself into another McGregor?"

Cord hadn't found any humor in Kendal's latest imbroglio. Kendal needed a firm hand to guide him and Cord was just the man to do it. But tonight wasn't the time to reveal his plans for her wayward brother.

"Cord, why didn't you tell me that Michael was being guarded by two of your men when I came to your office?"

"At that point, I wasn't sure what was going on. And then, you were so damned skeptical that I wouldn't be able to protect your brother. Of course, after today's debacle with your younger brother, maybe you were right not to believe in me."

"Cord, you did protect me and my brothers. Caring for people is a risky business. How could any of us believe Edward would be a target? But you and Gus found us and saved us. You did the best any person could possibly do."

She took his hands and started to kiss his palms. Slowly, reverently, she looked into his eyes. "I've regretted the day in your office. I didn't know what a trustworthy man you were. I was in shock by Sir Ramston's retirement and seeing you. I didn't understand that my fierce reaction to you was my own fear. I never wanted to need anyone until I met you. I was trying hard to fight my attraction to a rake." With this comment, she started to run her hands over his chest. She looked back into his eyes. "I'm finding loving a rake quite pleasurable." Her voice got lower, husky with the age-old invitation.

They had both been afraid to need another person, to trust their feelings, the intense and frightening feeling of needing another person. Recalling the force of his emotions when he saw her walk out of the boathouse at gunpoint, his voice deepened. "Don't ever try anything like what you did today. I damn near died when I saw Wycliffe forcing you out of the boathouse with a gun pressed against your back. I don't think I can live through another experience like that again."

She looped her arms around his neck. "Darling, I knew you would rescue me. I was just waiting for you. I think I've been waiting for you my whole life."

"Henrietta, I've been thinking of our lovemaking all day. I hardly accomplished anything in my office. My every thought was to rush home and make love to you again."

His words and his caresses were having an effect. Her face was flushed, her breath was coming in little puffs.

"It's the same for me. After today, when Wycliffe had that knife pointed at your chest, I kept remembering that I hadn't told you how much I love you. I never want to go a day without our love-making. And I will tell you over and over again, I love you."

She was kissing the side of his neck and at the same time pulling off his coat. He quickly abandoned his plan of telling her how he was going to keep her and her family safe.

He peeled her robe from her shoulders, running his hands down her arms. He felt her shudder. "What am I going to do with you?" He slid her nightgown down, nipping at her neck. .

She melted against him. "You don't know what to do with me? With all your years of love-making?"

He growled and picked her up to carry her to the settee. "I've never made "love" to anyone. It was never love before you. You are going to be my wife." His words came out as a command.

He looked down at his Henrietta, sprawled naked on the settee, total trust in her eyes. He knelt down beside her and took her slight hand into his. "Henrietta, will you be my wife?"

"I was wondering when you would get the hint about our children. I shall never let you go." She grabbed him around the neck, pulling him down. He began to feast on her full pink nipples. He could hear the hitch in her breathing. He needed to be next to her. He stripped out of the rest of his clothes, his eyes never leaving hers.

It was a fierce loving, the yearning of two bodies to reach beyond desire, to meld their futures together.

Cord didn't want to move but his weight was crushing Henrietta. He kissed her reddened face lightly and rolled to his side. Seeing her sated, sleepy, he knew he wasn't going to spend any more nights without her. "How about tomorrow for our wedding?"

She sat up.

"We're marrying as soon as possible. I don't want to spend another night apart. I sent Ash for a special license this morning before all the chaos erupted."

"Tomorrow? I don't want to be apart, but I can't marry you until Michael returns home."

Naked, he towered over her. "Henrietta, let me be clear. I admire your fierce loyalty to the Harcourt men, and I'm willing to embrace them as my own family. We'll take good care of them, but I'll not wait on your errant brother. It may be weeks before he returns. I can't wait weeks."

His voice grew huskier when he looked at her. God,

he wanted her again. "When Michael returns, we'll have a wedding ball at Rathbourne house to announce our marriage and to welcome Michael home."

"A wedding ball, what a splendid idea." She began to cover herself with the shift lying on the floor next to the settee.

"We can share the joys of the wedding with your family, but I won't wait to share the joys of the wedding bed every night." He moved toward her, his erection jutting out.

"But Cord, what about Uncle Charles and Edward?"

He took a deep breath. It should've been obvious to Henrietta that he was done talking about her family.

"Your uncle and brother will live with us. We should try to keep everything as familiar for your uncle as possible, so the Bromptons and most likely Robert and Thomas will have to move to our household." He watched her consider how he had already organized their lives to become intertwined.

"What of your family? Will they mind the intrusion of all the Harcourts?"

"My Aunt Euphemia will be a tonic for your uncle. And if what my aunt tells me is true, Gwyneth will not be residing much longer at Rathbourne House.

"I just couldn't imagine leaving my uncle or Edward."

"I'd never want you to have to decide between me and the intrepid Harcourt men."

"Thank you." She stretched her arms out to him, beckoning him.

Their second lovemaking was as slow and tender as their newly expressed love for each other. Afterward, he held her tight against his chest, grateful for the future they would share.

He ran his finger down her spine, caressing her soft skin. "I assume you're planning on continuing as England's code breaker?"

"You don't object?"

"Object? I'm the head, how could I object to having the best?" He watched her face to see if she appreciated his double entendre. He moved his hand up her leg, stroking behind her knee.

"Are our daughters and sons going to be learning codes at their mother's knee?"

"Of course, but our children will learn the most important code of all."

"What code is that?"

"The code of love."

CHAPTER THIRTY-SIX

Charles Talleyrand, Foreign Minister of France, sauntered in silence with his archenemy, Joseph Fouché, down the long, gilded corridor. Anyone observing them, one fierce in a severe black uniform with gold buttons, the other nonchalant in dark velvet and lace, wouldn't believe the casual amble between two sworn enemies.

Afternoon light shone through the windows lining the ornate ministry hallway, squares of sunlight illuminated the path the two men walked.

Fouché's boots struck a cadence on the parquet floors. "How did you get the codebook back?" Talleyrand was amazed. Fouché was acknowledging his plot to attain the codebook.

"I never did recover the stolen codebook. Kendal escaped Paris and had already sent the codebook to England," Talleyrand said.

Fouché, usually a dour man, chuckled. "Of course, my idiots let them pass too."

"As did my man. Who would've guessed?"

There was a silence as both men paused to reassess. Neither man had risen to his position of power by trusting an enemy easily.

"How will you hide the fact that the English have obtained the codebook?" Fouché asked.

He pondered whether he should divulge the truth.

Fouché couldn't possibly use the information against him. The Emperor had confided in him this morning that Fouché's reign was drawing to an end. "Chiffre and his staff are developing a new code."

"What about the codebook the English have? Will it help them?"

"Le Chiffre doesn't believe it will make a large difference to our efforts in battle communications."

"All the intrigue around the codebook was for naught?" Fouché asked.

Talleyrand didn't see any reason to point out that the entire debacle was caused by the man at his side. Fouché had killed De Valmont, one of Talleyrand's best spies. Fouché had ruined his plans for political chaos around the English election.

This was the problem with political work—one could never clearly predict the outcome of one's manipulations.

"What about the murder of the Duke of Wycliffe by your man?" Fouché asked.

"I've heard the murder has been hushed up at the highest level."

Fouché guffawed. "Of course they had to hush it up. Why would the English acknowledge that one of their dukes was a traitor?"

"All swept away by Rathbourne," he said.

"If I were in Rathbourne's position, there would be strong repercussions for young Kendal, who started the whole intrigue," Fouché said.

Talleyrand looked at Fouché's coarse features. He knew what Fouché consider strong repercussions. Fouché didn't realize there were going to be consequences for his latest violent scheme. If he were to believe Napoleon's promises this morning, the police minister had gone his extent in French history.

"I don't think Kendal will suffer too much. Rathbourne just married Kendal's sister."

EPILOGUE

Michael Harcourt lay on his stomach on the settee in the drawing room. Waiting wasn't his strong suit, nor was enduring pain. At home, Hen would entertain him, making illness or injury more tolerable. He missed his sister, his family, and England.

How did this jaunt to Paris become so muddled? His curiosity had gotten him into sticky situations before, but this was his most awkward ever. He hoped the new head of Abchurch was tolerant of inquisitive individuals. Hen would soften the old man when she gave him the codebook.

Denby entered the library, his posture ramrod, reflecting his years of military discipline. "We're surrounded. I was followed by at least three different agents, including Le Chiffre's footman and two I've never seen before. Fouché's officers are watching our house."

Michael's whole body tightened, causing pain to shoot into his ass. "Fouché's secret police?" What had gone so wrong? The brutality of the minister of police's men was legendary.

"Yes, their stark, black uniforms are quite distinguishable."

Michael gulped his brandy. "How did you escape?"

"I took them all on a merry chase through the streets of Saint Germaine, down the Rue du Bac, over the Pont Neuf and into Notre Dame."

Denby got to outwit the French police as he fretted, unable to do anything but lie on his stomach. "Were you able to lose them?"

"I entered Notre Dame and blended with the devout, attending Matins. I hid in a side altar dedicated to Saint Genevieve, crouched behind the statue of Our Lady for what felt like hours."

"Pour yourself a brandy. You deserve it. And while you're at it, please top me up—most of my brandy is on my dressing gown."

Denby took the glass off the floor and proceeded to the side table filled with glass decanters. He poured generous amounts for both of them.

"It's been most interminable to be immobile. How many followed you into Notre Dame?"

"Three agents. Fouché's men remained watching the house. The agents passed from altar to altar, pretending to pray. After waiting them out, I came from behind the statue, only to be discovered by Sister Marie Therese."

"Sister Marie Therese?"

Voices were heard coming from the front hall.

"My God, they're already here." Denby jumped off his chair.

Michael's heart thumped painfully against his chest. Had the footman admitted Fouché's men into the house? He tried not to betray his fear but his voice trembled. "Fouché's men?"

"Someone is watching over us." Denby looked upward toward heaven. "I've already been saved twice today by St. Genevieve, the Patron Saint of Paris."

Michael looked down into his brandy glass. He must have drunk more than he thought. Denby, a hardened solider, believed in heavenly intervention?

The footman opened the door to the drawing room and announced Sister Marie Therese and Sister Genevieve. The sisters were encased in black except for large wimples that looked like upside-down croissants. The white head covering smashed their faces as if they were wedged in a vise.

Michael attempted to stand. He was quite adroit at avoiding any pressure or pain in this maneuver. Using his arms to push himself off the settee, he planted one leg at a time, twisting forward, preventing any backside contact.

Hurrying to greet the approaching guests and to secure his dressing gown from revealing any part of him, he twisted a bit too quickly and fell backward on his wound. The pain on impact was excruciating. "Son of a bitch." He knocked over his brandy in the fall, spilling the liquid into his boots. "Double son of a bitch."

Denby greeted the two nuns. The older nun held a young boy's hand; a round, smiling nun carried a large portmanteau. Denby turned back at the commotion. He signaled with his thumb for Michael to get off the floor.

Without any help from Denby, Michael was left to stand.

"Sister Marie Therese, Sister Genevieve. You found your way with no difficulty. This must be Pierre," Denby said.

Hampered by his dressing gown, Michael struggled on all fours to obtain an upright position.

His eyes wide, the boy giggled at Michael's gymnastics. He whispered to the older nun whose severe lines softened when she leaned down to answer the youth.

Sister Marie Therese's penetrating gaze left Michael feeling fully exposed.

"Monsieur Denby, I'm not sure this is the man for the job." The sister shook her head. "No, this will not do."

Now upright, Michael walked toward the nun. He tried to move forward with decorum, his hands holding his dressing gown together. He glanced at Denby, whose face was red. Could a stalwart of the cavalry be embarrassed by the woman's censure?

"Please, Sister Marie Therese. You've caught Lord Kendal at an inopportune time. He's all I promised."

Michael walked toward the group. "Please, Sister Marie Therese..." he stumbled, unsure of how to address the sister. He could feel three sets of eyes inspecting him.

"Sister Marie Therese and Sister Genevieve, may I present Lord Michael Harcourt, the Earl of Kendal." Denby said.

With the correct amount of aristocratic poise for greeting the nuns, who had just witnessed his disgraceful fall, Michael bowed. He ignored the pain that shot down his backside. "A pleasure, I'm sure. May I ring for tea?"

The round Sister Genevieve smiled. It was obvious that she had an amiable personality, unlike her superior.

"Thank you. I don't believe there is time. Please only a snack for Pierre. He's a growing boy," Sister Marie Therese said.

"How do you do, Pierre?" Avoiding further pain, Michael nodded instead of bowing to the youth.

The boy whispered almost inaudibly, "Monsieur." He kept his eyes down. A hat covered his hair.

"We should make the switch quickly. The men watching your home will be suspicious of your entertainment of the Sisters of the Visitation." Sister Marie Therese's voice was brisk, her manner fixed.

Denby escorted the sisters to the settee and chairs. He kicked Michael's brandy glass under the settee. "I haven't had time to explain our plan to Lord Kendal."

"We'll give him the details during the dressing." Sister Marie Therese pointed toward her companions. "Sister Genevieve and Pierre, unpack the portmanteau on the settee his lordship was resting on."

What the hell was Denby thinking? Michael wasn't

going to let a nun dress his wound. And by appearances she planned to do it in front of Sister Genevieve and the young boy.

Sister Marie Therese turned toward Michael.

"Lord Kendal, you'll need to remove your dressing gown."

He turned to Denby for an explanation, but Denby was looking at the ground, his face bright crimson. The seasoned solider was acting like a chaste debutante.

"I'll not remove my dressing gown."

"Lord Kendal." Sister Marie Therese stepped closer to him. Her voice was impatient and the look in her eyes was one she might give to Pierre and other wayward children. "You and Mr. Denby will leave Paris disguised as Sisters of Visitation."

AUTHOR BIO

Descended from a long line of storytellers, Jacki spins adventures filled with mystery, healing and romance.

Jacki's love affair with the arts began at a young age and inspired her to train as a jazz singer and dancer. She has performed many acting roles with Seattle Opera Company and Pacific Northwest Ballet.

Her travels to London and Paris ignited a deep-seated passion to write her romantic, regency mystery *A Code of Love*. Jacki is certain she spent at least one lifetime dancing in the Moulin Rouge.

Although writing now fills much of her day, she continues to volunteer for Seattle's Ballet and Opera Companies and leads children's tours of Pike Street Market. Her volunteer work with Seattle's homeless shelters influenced one of her main characters in *An Inner Fire*.

Jacki's two Golden Labs, Gus and Talley, are her constant companions. Their years of devotion and intuition inspired her to write both dogs as heroes in *A Code of Love*.

A geek at heart, Jacki loves superhero movies--a hero's battle against insurmountable odds. But her heroines don't have to wear a unitard to fight injustice and battle for the underdog.

To learn more about Jacki and her books and to be the first to hear about giveaways join her newsletter found on her website: www.jackidelecki.com. Follow her on FB—Jacki Delecki; Twitter @jackidelecki.

Printed in Great Britain
by Amazon